EQUINOX

EQUINOX

DAVID TOWSEY

An Ad Astra Book

First published in the UK in 2022 by Head of Zeus Ltd,
part of Bloomsbury Publishing Plc

9 7 5 3 1 2 4 6 8

A catalogue record for this book is available from
the British Library.

ISBN (HB): 9781801101646
ISBN (XTPB): 9781801101653
ISBN (E): 9781801101677

Typeset by Divaddict Publishing Solutions Ltd

Printed and bound in Great Britain by
CPI Group (UK) Ltd, Croydon CR0 4YY

MIX
Paper from
responsible sources
FSC
www.fsc.org
FSC® C171272

Head of Zeus Ltd
First Floor East
5–8 Hardwick Street
London EC1R 4RG

WWW.HEADOFZEUS.COM

For Ray

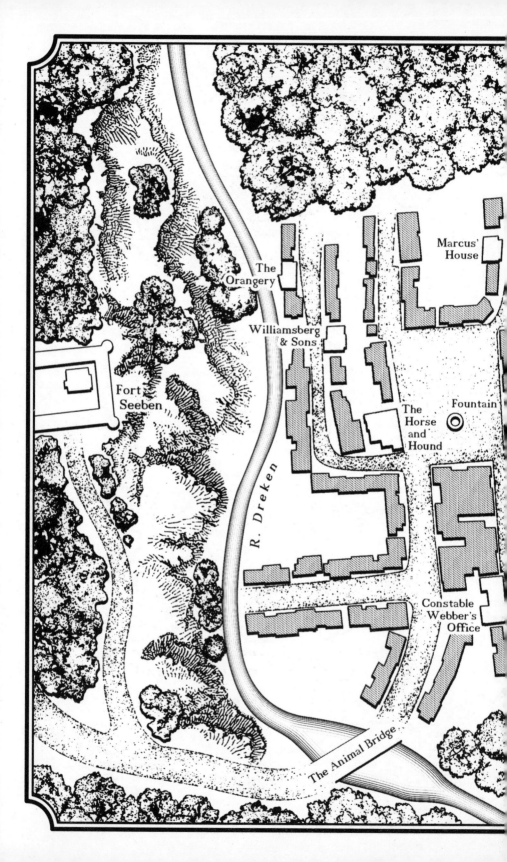

Marcus' House

The Orangery

Williamsberg & Sons

Fort Seeben

The Horse and Hound

Fountain

R. Dreken

Constable Webber's Office

The Animal Bridge

Church Lane

Graveyard

Church

The
Eder
House

Mayor
Eder's
Office

Magistrate
Channock's
Home

Smithy
Baerson

A map
of the town of
DREKENFORD
in the Kingdom of Reikova
in the year
1721

CHRISTOPHOR

13th October 1721

I have seen the sun, despite what my day-brother might say.

The night of the summons I was watching the sunset. The orange sky turned to red behind the tiled roofs and cracked chimneys of Esteberg. I wondered what the warmth of a midday sun would be like on my face, on the back of my neck, on my hands. Then the stars blinked into existence and, in child-like imitation, so did the street lamps.

When the knock came at my door, I turned and crossed our room. The room I shared with my day-brother.

I opened the door to find a messenger – one in the King's livery no less. The short boy had one hand against the wall as he caught his breath. The other hand he raised to forestall me. I gave him a moment.

My day-brother, Alexsander, and I rented the top of a boarding house, and in all fairness the steps *were* steep. Our position also benefitted from the heat and stench and endless noise of those below; all of which would have been lessened if everyone lived alone, as my day-brother and I. But there were many married couples living on the floors beneath us. In those first few minutes of the night, at least, there was quiet as people woke to the familiar disappointment lying next to them.

When the boy had quite recovered, he straightened his coat and asked, 'Special Inspector Christophor Morden?'

'The same,' I said.

'At the King's pleasure,' he said. With great care he produced a sealed letter, the paper pristine despite the boy's own rumpled appearance.

'We live to serve,' I said. Something in the boy's eyes echoed my feelings on *that* particular matter. At least I was nearing the end of my service; he had a lifetime at the King's pleasure. One more small charge complete, he braved the descent back to the streets of Esteberg.

My own charge rested heavily in my hand. I closed the door and placed the letter on my writing desk. Doing so, I passed my day-brother's modest collection of instruments which, after all our years together, he had finally agreed to keep tidily. As much as they frustrated me, with their strange echoing and phantom notes that would sound as I went about my business, I understood they were not the easiest items to keep in order. It was as if they actively resisted it. Those bulbous stringed ones, and the flutes and trumpets with more cranks and knobs and moving parts than a water mill. Our low, sloping eaves didn't allow him to hang them. Hang them all, I said, but of course he was deaf to my poor pun.

I broke the King's seal and read the summons. It was as functional and bereft of detail as they typically were: I was to present myself to the warden of St Leonars prison at my earliest convenience. There was nothing convenient about St Leonars, not least it being at the other end of the city.

Before I left, I remembered to water and mist our small ettiene plant. Alexsander had forgotten to do so for as long as I could remember. Or perhaps he simply remembered that it was part of my nightly ritual: one more little, vital excuse to avoid the city. The ettiene's leaves immediately rose, its summer flowers doing their best to add some colour to the room. I mostly saw them by candlelight.

There was such a plant in every room, in every house all across the Kingdom of Reikova – and likely beyond. It was not entirely understood why, but chewing ettiene aided the transition from day to night, and from night to day, for every man, woman, and child.

Ettiene was not the cause of the change. Just an aid.

The transition was inescapable for everyone. But it could be disorientating, uncomfortable, a fracturing rather than a smooth slide from night-brother to day.

There were children, fools, and worse who tested the change – those that tried to forgo sleep. But who could escape such a thing as sleep? And no one can escape themselves. Those that did try found their way, one way or another, to places like St Leonars prison more often than not.

I gathered my hat and cloak, mindful of the gathering clouds to the south. My notebook and pencil were already in my pocket, to which I added the summons. I closed the window and spared a glance at the mirror before fleeing the old man that looked back.

On my way down the steep stairs I heard the opening salvos of an argument. A young clerk and his wife lived there by night and, from what I could remember from my day-brother, the same marriage held during the day. That was increasingly uncommon in Esteberg, and likely the whole of the Kingdom of Reikova; there were even rumours of the King's daylight dalliances. I hurried on my way.

Blank faces looked up from their meals as I strode past the dining room and out of the boarding house. The evening air had lost the day's heat, instead holding a taut anticipation of a clearing storm. I pulled up my collar as much for the small anonymity it provided as its protection against the first sputters of rain. Felden Street and those nearby were starting to fill with the night's workmen and women, many mirroring my own sense of weary purpose. Stalls and shops were slowly opening for the night; the same stalls and shops that opened during the day, perhaps run by night-brothers and night-sisters but perhaps not. Like my day-brother and I, others did not necessarily share the same occupation both night and day, both sides of the ettiene. Not all were suited to honest labour. I passed hawkers setting out their trays in the street. They looked up at me, bleary-eyed, yet to find the wherewithal to call out their wares – some consolation for an early summons.

Though St Leonars prison was inconveniently placed on the other side of the city, I was called there so regularly I knew the way well enough. I had, on occasion, paid for a carriage during the winter months but that had necessitated collection of certain other revenues; a Special Inspector's salary was not as generous as most people assumed.

Incorrect assumptions were a fairly common occurrence with regards to the King's Special Inspectors. We were just one small branch of the constabulary, not many in number, and not so visible as our uniformed colleagues. A branch formed nearly a hundred years ago, not long after Reikova was formally ratified as a state. The Special Inspectorate was, at the time, considered a more *modern* response to certain questions raised by the arcane and the unknown. Before, such things were dealt with in a more ad hoc, individual, and, dare I say, chaotic way.

Special Inspectors were assigned cases, and we completed them to the best of our ability. But to many citizens we were still a delicious mystery. *Witch hunter*, they whispered, *demonologist, inquisitor*, and more such words they didn't really understand. Every Special Inspector was different – specialising as many in the constabulary did. Though throughout my years I had arrested and hanged a number of men and women guilty of witchcraft, I had also arrested and hanged men and women guilty of murder, of arson, of treason; all of the mundane variety. Citizens were quick to forget this when *Special Inspector* was uttered, assuming I was only interested in the arcane. Something I found advantageous at times.

The cobbled, mercantile Felden Street was soon behind me and I entered the slums. The street lamps were sporadic here, many glass cases broken or simply stolen. I was in no hurry for a better look along the squalid alleyways; I would be no help to the mange-ridden cats and hollow-cheeked children that loitered there. Both would flee from me even had I wanted to help them. I told myself it was an inspector's duty to be seen *in*, if not to see *into*, the darker parts of the city. But I knew this to be flimsy at best, vanity at worst. There was no way to St Leonars that didn't cross paths with the politely ignored underbelly of the King's city.

Entering a square, I happened upon a crowd in its early stages of formation and, like others, became part of its invisible pull. I drew no one's attention, my cloak and hat working to hide my badge and any hint of my office: just another early riser seeking distraction on an otherwise routine night. Given what I saw at the front of the crowd, this was just as well.

A rope separated us from a low, shabbily-curtained stage. The curtain twitched with a clumsy flash of fingers and an enormous, watery eye took in the crowd. A child at the front squawked and backed away but I knew the effect to be an artless use of thick glass. The adults and older children tittered, unwilling to take their cue from one so young but otherwise unsure of what to make of it. Old Tanter must have been working the northern part of the city these last months.

The squat trickster sprang out from behind the curtain, his flourish of a worn velvet cape an attempt to hide a wobble in his knees.

'Laugh if you must,' Tanter called to one and all. 'But is there anything more pure, more sincere than a child's fear? Anything at all, in this Esteberg, this forsaken city?' For emphasis, the stage lamps – pilfered street lamps – were put out by an assistant.

Tanter had misjudged this crowd, who didn't take kindly to the sudden darkness. For myself, I put a hand on my coin purse just as the afeared child himself brushed past me, his fingers probing my cloak. I caught his arm and, meeting his now wide eyes, shook my head.

'But...' he whispered.

'But nothing. No purses tonight.'

A flash lit the stage, followed by a plume of green smoke. Tanter did his best not to cough. We were both too old for this dance. I waited through his laughably short routine, noting when he sawed his assistant in half that he had finally taken my advice and put shoes on the fake legs. A blind drunkard could see fake feet, especially fake toes, from thirty paces. I also noted his flagrant use of pig's blood and fester-root. But, for Tanter's sake at least, he did not use even a modicum of *actual* magic. He was finally seeing sense in his later years.

When the show was over and the departing crowd had been pressed for a few undeserved copper kreers, I stepped beyond the curtain. I found Tanter shaking down the boy, who was hurriedly trying to explain.

'What do you mean, someone stopped you?' Tanter hissed.

'Exactly that,' I said.

'And who— Hello, Inspector.'

'Put the boy down.'

'Yes, yes, of course.' He brushed at the boy's ill-fitting coat. 'You didn't happen to see the show?'

'The fester-root. Now.' I held out my hand.

'Would you believe—'

'No, I wouldn't.'

Tanter's ingratiating smile turned to a more sincere grimace. 'How am I supposed to do justice to the dread queen's memory without the root? Nothing smokes so strong, so despicably coloured, so true to her character. You're denying people their history, Inspector.'

'I'm on my way to St Leonars. I could deny *you* more than history.'

The showman hopped to, rummaging among crates I had neither the time nor the inclination to search. He eventually produced a leather pouch tied tighter than my own coin purse. As I looked inside at the sickly green shavings, Tanter fidgeted.

'Is this all of it?' I said.

'Yes.' He nodded emphatically. He was a poor liar and a poor magician. Ultimately, he was just poor. 'You… you wouldn't make a King's matter of me having that, would you?'

I paused long enough for Tanter to picture the gallows. 'No,' I said, and he all but collapsed. 'Pay the boy, even though he didn't lift a purse.'

I continued on through the slums towards St Leonars, the pouch of fester-root secure in my increasingly burdened pocket. When burned, fester-root created a harmless, though acrid, green smoke. When ground and put in food, a pinch could kill a man *and* the horse he rode. What that same ground powder did to metal, when a little water was added, was a sight one couldn't un-see. It was a good thing a man like Tanter wasn't important enough to have real enemies.

St Leonars prison was an appropriately imposing building. It rose out of the surrounding shacks and huts, solid stone with a singular, unified purpose – one building in the centre of a scattered jigsaw. The walls were easily twenty feet high, and gave the impression they were twenty feet deep. Guard towers stood at each corner of St Leonars' great square, with mounted muskets pointing both inwards and outwards.

At the entrance, night-releases were still coming out. They looked tired, beaten, and those that met my eye recognised the same when they saw it. They knew what I was.

In its way, despite the walls and guards and muskets, St Leonars prison was entirely escapable. The night-brothers and sisters of those incarcerated were, before my very eyes, walking out of prison. There were those relatively rare people who were convicted criminals day and night, both sides of the ettiene. But the rest were released at either sunrise or sunset when the change occurred. They willingly returned just the same because the King's Justice *wasn't* escapable: the King couldn't hang just one brother or sister. Hanged at night was still dead come sunrise, and vice versa.

I presented the summons at the gates, where it was read. And read again.

'Bad business,' one guard muttered, showing the utterly functional script to his partner.

'Excuse me?' I said.

'The warden's in her office, Inspector.' He waved me through the main gates. He smelled of cooked cabbage and pipe smoke.

I knew the way well enough, through long straight corridors with bars every twenty paces. My summons garnered unfathomable looks of sympathy, at the last of which I snatched the envelope back and demanded the man hurry up. He just shook his head and let me through. All these gateways and checks seemed unnecessary for an administrative wing, but I supposed the warden knew what she was about. She had been there long enough, day and night.

She didn't look up as I entered her office. I waited as she squinted at letters an inch tall, in a room with more candles than a cathedral. Stacks of papers took up every available surface, including the floor, where there was an obvious path that made me feel like a soaring bird looking down on a mountain road.

'Special Inspector Morden,' she said. She carefully signed whatever she was reading, then sat back and took my measure. I shifted, as cattle shift under the butcher's gaze. 'How's Alexsander?'

I shrugged. 'Busy, I think.'

'That's good.'

'Are you going to tell me why I'm here?' I said, trying to keep my voice even.

'You're here for the same reason I'm here: because you were told to be.'

'And tonight?'

'That's not so good,' she said softly. She stood, her aches and pains as evident and heavy as the keys around her neck.

I followed her down and down again, deeper into St Leonars than I had ever been before. Despite the warden's presence, the guards at each gate made no effort to hide their pity.

A narrow staircase led us finally down to a damp, dark corridor. The walls and floor were formed of large, sweating stones, and the ceiling was low enough to force me to hunch uncomfortably. This felt like an older part of St Leonars – a building I'd always assumed had sprung into existence all at once, at the beginning of time when God created man, woman, and prison. There was an unexpected quiet as we passed door after door. Just as I was beginning to think the cells were empty, the warden stopped.

She started to speak, but caught herself. She came to some kind of decision, wincing at her own noise as she whispered, 'See it first. Then I'll explain what I can.'

I glanced at the iron-studded door. The boards had warped considerably and beads of water ran down their uneven surface.

'What—'

The warden took a key from around her neck and, with a rhythm of clunks that sounded like the tolling of a mourning bell, unlocked the cell door.

The room was utterly black. I took a step back.

'We removed the candle. It only seemed fair,' the warden said.

I waited a moment, and my eyes adjusted enough to make out a figure huddled in the far corner.

I said something to the prisoner. Words that must have been comforting in both their sound and their meaning, but I wasn't really aware of either. He started to sob, which silenced me. I felt a gap between us, then, yawning up like a chasm. This boy, no more than sixteen years old with a life yet to be lived, and I... a man with little left. But what separated us was more than simple time, the chasm was a depth of suffering. The boy had suffered more than I ever could. I nearly turned and fled.

Instead, I felt compelled to step further into the room. The light from the corridor gave the young man shape: short hair, cut back like most prisoners; a thin, prominent nose; and holes where there should have been eyes.

He trembled violently.

Crouching, I cleared my throat and said, 'Hello?'

He flinched and tried to bury himself further into the corner of the room, but St Leonars' stone offered only resistance.

'He's become mute,' the warden said.

I glanced back to see her haloed in candlelight.

'Tongue's still there, mind.'

In another situation I may have been shocked by her casual delivery, but I had little shock left. I turned back to the boy, who wore a rough-looking smock but no shoes. He smelled faintly of lavender. 'Can you hear me? Do you understand?'

He continued his struggle to put a distance between us. I waited for him to calm himself, but eventually it became obvious I would only be a continuous source of agitation. I stood to leave.

'Inside the sockets,' the warden said. 'You need to... You should see.'

I could tell nothing from the warden's expression, except

that there was no room for argument. Tentatively, I stepped towards the boy as I would a dangerous animal; I felt shame at that thought, but it was there nonetheless. He was shaking his head with such force, his scalp ground against the stone wall and filled the cell with the smell of blood.

There was something else where there should have been eyes, just as the warden had said. A white pip lurking in each of those pools of darkness. Drawing closer, I took them to be bone – perhaps the boy had shattered a bone in his face and that had ruined his eyes. With such poor light it was hard to be certain and I found myself inexplicably reaching out a finger. My hand, my whole arm shook. As if sensing my intent and giving what permission he could, the boy stilled.

I touched the hard white pip, feeling a slight serrated edge. I withdrew quickly, hurried out of the room, and slammed the cell door shut.

'Teeth?' I said, incredulous, but the warden was nodding before I even finished.

'Likely the cause of it; the pain becoming too much.'

'I'm sorry?' I said.

'The teeth. That's why he tore his own eyes out.'

We returned to the warden's office in silence. I tried and failed, over and over again, to imagine how it would feel to have teeth growing behind one's eyes. To imagine your own body turned against you in such a manner, and the pain that would produce. So much, it evidently drove the boy to pull out his own eyes just to be rid of it. As a King's Special Inspector, I had witnessed many terrible acts. But rarely had I seen anything like that.

The warden cleared me a seat, moving a stack of papers with a candle perched perilously on top.

'What is his name?' I said before I sat.

'His name?' she echoed, sounding momentarily surprised by the simple question. 'Yes, his name. Gregory Harsson. His day-brother is Jan.'

'Which of them did it?'

The warden looked uncomfortable for the first time. 'Jan. Before Gregory stopped speaking, he kept asking why we were keeping him in the dark.'

I held my hands in my lap; there was dirt under my fingernails. 'Tell me.'

The warden painted a patchy picture. Jan was brought to St Leonars from a small town, or large village, far to the south. The warden paused to look up its name: Drekenford. I had never heard of it, but then I hadn't travelled the southern borderlands. Their large skies and endless forests held little appeal; even less so with the increasingly frequent reports of trouble with the tribes that still claimed that land as their own. Why send the boy so far, I asked.

'Why does anything happen? Because someone important wanted it that way.'

When Jan first arrived, the warden continued, he was kept with all the other day-men, night-releases. Convicted of theft of the dull, domestic variety, he appeared to warrant little attention. He was given a rough welcome from the other prisoners, easily singled out as being from far away, though nothing serious. Gregory was managing to find work in a strange new city. But then, a month or so later, they both started complaining to anyone who would listen. Headaches, pain behind their eyes, not being able to find rest. A prison doctor examined Jan and found only a rotten tooth, which he took out. When later questioned, the doctor confirmed there was nothing extraordinary about the procedure, though admitted Jan did scream throughout. Even with the opiates. Then, as he recovered, Jan attacked one of the nurses so he was moved.

'What about at night?' I said.

'Gregory wouldn't leave after that.'

I frowned, struggling to believe anyone would *choose* to stay in such a place. 'But he was a night-release. Were the brothers that close?'

'Evidently. Inspector, ninety-nine in every hundred prisoners here are at war with themselves. No amount of ettiene chewing can ease our prisoners' struggles with their siblings. But when that previously secure one-in-a-hundred is shaken somehow, or breaks down, well...' The warden shook her head. 'A day later, we heard his screams. The whole prison heard the screams. We found Jan surrounded by his own blood. And the eyes. He held them up, like this.'

I looked away. 'Gregory, he didn't know what had happened?'

'Said he couldn't remember. Kept asking about the dark, but eventually I think he realised, perhaps pieced it together – that's when he stopped talking.'

'Find someone else.' I got up.

'I hadn't even— Look, no one is sure how this happened. Strange things can happen to a person, to the body, all on their own.'

'You don't believe that, and neither do I.'

'Christophor, you think I have any say in this?' She had the good grace to look apologetic, even if she wasn't actually apologising.

'You said Jan – the day-brother – took out their eyes. Have one of the daylighters look into it.'

'They want *you*. The kind of "they" that get what they want. The King's seal, Christophor.'

'And what do they suggest I do?' I said.

'Just what you're paid to do. Find out who did this to Jan, who made his body turn against him, and by what dark arts.'

'No.' I stepped out into the corridor, glad the walls were bone-dry.

'Whatever this is, it isn't some petty street-magician, Inspector.'

'Exactly.'

'This kind of witchcraft – that's why they want to send you,' the warden said. 'They know you're... cold. You don't get attached. They know you're experienced.'

'And that's why the answer is no.'

14th October 1721

Alexsander knew I had been upset, I could tell that much. But he didn't let that affect his day. It was, as it always was, something he felt as an itch at the back of his mind – one that was beyond scratching.

He was slow to leave the boarding house. He washed thoroughly with a bucket of clean, cold water, with extra attention to underneath his fingernails. They were important to him, our fingers. No matter what instrument he played, no matter where he played it, they would be involved somehow.

Sometimes I remembered that; I took care of them when I could.

It was perhaps mid-morning when Alexsander sat in a coffee house somewhere in the city. The pastry was tasteless, greasy, but he knew that when he ordered. He watched the street from a window-table with the same intense concentration an artist bestows on their model. Was he waiting for someone? Hoping to see someone? A woman, probably, and one of poor reputation.

He wasted an hour, perhaps two, in a small, scrubby park. The fountain he perched on didn't work and the sun was rare between the clouds. He seemed to play the same piece again and again, until even the pigeons could take no more.

He smiled at something; I don't know what.

The ale house was half-full, entirely uninterested. He played to backs of heads and lazy applause that he accepted graciously. A fight broke out and a man's nose was broken. Alexsander was fascinated.

This was all I recalled of Alexsander's day. The memory was much like a dream; some parts of the day were only available as snatches and snippets, whereas others felt vividly real to me. There seemed little rhyme or reason as to what was the former and what the latter. In the end I had no control of my day-brother's actions, nor my recollection of them.

For every man, woman, and child of this world it was our blessing, and our curse.

I woke with a headache and moonlight on my face. For a dizzying, terrible moment I pictured teeth crowning behind my eyes, becoming fangs that pierced my skull. I blinked furiously to rid myself of the image and the dry feeling it conjured.

Having said no to the warden of St Leonars the previous night, I had no pressing official duties. I had refused the warden's case for this very reason – my career was well into the final, darkest hours of its night. For years my role as Special Inspector had me travelling the length and breadth of the kingdom, ever since I joined as a young man. I came to the force with no predisposition for seeking out the darker arts, just simply an open mind and a readiness to pursue leads wherever they took me. The visions came later. In truth, I joined because I felt – and still feel – that between my day-brother and I, one of us should have a respectable profession.

At this point in my career my duties were few, but there was some pride in knowing I spent my considerable years ensuring the safety of the citizens of Reikova. I was content to keep doing so for those living in Esteberg, but far off southern villages could tend to themselves. The King and his advisors would find someone else. Someone younger, hungrier, with more to offer the world beyond their own doorstep.

What happened to the boy in the prison cell was not the beginning of a quick, simple investigation. I was not too proud to admit such a case may have been within my abilities, but was not within my means.

Telling myself this again and again, I tried to find distractions. I took little joy in slowly drinking my coffee, though it did clear the distant drums of my headache. With no sunset to watch, I turned instead to the alley beneath my window, which was the rear of Felden Street. Rarely did I find more than tomcats disputing territory, but tonight a baker's assistant – I knew him to be so from his apron and ghostly covering of flour – was being reprimanded by the baker. She was also the boy's mother, I hoped, given the personal nature of her insults. I closed my window on the slurs against the boy's father, who had evidently run away to the army. It seemed likely the boy would soon follow.

I allowed myself a thin spread of jam on my bread, hoping to dislodge some of the bitter taste too much sleep had left me. It was, of course, Alexsander's fault: he took so little care with his chewing of the ettiene leaves. There were some days he forgot to chew them altogether, and I woke from the transition with much worse than a headache. He could also have been drinking – I couldn't remember one way or the other. The blood from the ale house brawl loomed large, but I pushed this and other similar thoughts away. I managed not to look at yesterday's summons for the entire morning as I fussed with this and that. When a cloud obscured the almost full moon, I took the seal to be throbbing with some kind of frustrated royal light, forgetting I had lit a new candle only moments before. It crackled and sputtered and I cursed myself for a fool. I had to get out of the house.

A fog had rolled up river from the coast, carrying with it distant smells of ash and the sound of running water that I found sinister. The night-children of Felden Street felt differently: some spread their arms like gulls and flew off into the lamp-lit fog. Others played hide-and-seek. One girl snatched at a wisp, as if she might catch and keep and study this thing she did not understand. I strode past them, head and hat lowered against the smoky tide, trying to ignore the damp heat of the night.

The fog had muted the city, once I was beyond the streets deemed suitable for children, and I enjoyed a quiet, uninterrupted journey.

I entered Larn & Gale's Curiosities, and both Gloria Larn and Wendeline Gale looked up from their large, cluttered counter. The bell above my head waggled silently, the clapper removed long ago; that they had kept the bell despite this went some way to describe the women, and how they conducted their business.

'Do you have them?' I said, our business relationship being beyond the need for pleasantries.

'Indeed. He returned early this week.' Gloria – the broader of the couple – withdrew a wide drawer from beneath the counter. 'We haven't yet unpacked it all.' She set the drawer down carefully. My breath caught and I tried to look everywhere at once, taking all the blown eggs in, the next more exciting than the last.

'So many,' I said.

'And yet, still birds in the sky.' Wendeline gestured to the stuffed peregrines and falcons mounted above her.

I put on a soft felt glove and, with appropriate reverence, picked up a bespeckled guillemot egg. The deep, lustrous grey was veined and dotted in a dazzlingly complex manner. The single blow-hole was immaculate and unobtrusive, as were the two marks on the bottom – the functional LG of the seller and the more ornate C of the nester.

'He returned this week?' I said, still staring at the egg. 'Why wasn't I sent for?'

'Did you not see our smoke signal, Inspector?'

The couple chuckled at their gentle joking, but in truth I was lucky not to find Mr Coller's hoard plundered to the same extent as the nests he himself pursued. I replaced the grey guillemot, glancing over its whiter brethren; these interested me less, though I couldn't say why. Many collectors preferred the stark white, but I found it jarring. I had discussed as much with Wendeline, on occasion, and she claimed it was a common divide between night and day collectors, but Gloria struggled to support such a simple generalisation.

'And when will Mr Coller be leaving again?' I said, picking up a molten-looking avocet.

Gloria shrugged. 'Soon, I shouldn't doubt. He'll want to make the most of the season, as will we all.'

The rest of the avocet clutch were not quite as vivid, but I had been waiting for just the right set to add to my collection. I counted once, then counted again to be sure.

'Five?' I said, gesturing along the row.

Wendeline could not contain her grin. 'Nothing gets past you, Inspector. Mr Coller was most pleased, most pleased. Perhaps the find of his season, though with that man who can say?'

'Yes,' I said, not really listening. A clutch of five, with such colour – granted there was a queen among the maidens, but still. I made the rough calculations, determined not to be surprised one way or another when they named the price. 'Interesting,' I said. I made a good show of examining the rest of the drawer and inquired as to how much was left 'unpacked', as Gloria put it. 'Very well. How m—'

The shop door opened. I staggered, as if under cannon fire. I rounded, ready to chase off whatever dandy browser or collector sought to interrupt.

'Morden,' the chief inspector said, as he stepped into Larn & Gale's with undisguised curiosity.

'Sir,' I said. 'I did not realise you were also a customer of this establishment.'

'I'm not.'

I wished Gloria had the tact to return the drawer, but perhaps she thought I might lose sight of my purchase.

'Eggs, Morden?' the chief said, leaning over the drawer.

'Yes, sir.'

'Are they... expensive?'

Wendeline barely stifled her laughter, pretending to cough until she didn't have to pretend and appeared to almost choke. The chief watched the woman with his soft, half-hooded blue eyes until he seemed certain the shopkeeper wasn't in any mortal danger.

'Not very,' I managed, then nodded to Gloria. 'The avocets. On my account.'

The chief raised an eyebrow at that but allowed me to move our conversation out into the street.

The fog had lifted, only to be replaced by a light drizzle – a type of rain that would leave an unsuspecting man drenched. The chief was not unsuspecting. He guided us a few doors down and into a sunken doorway: a coffee house I had not frequented and, as far as I could remember, neither had Alexsander.

We took a table near the back of a long room. The fresh-faced enthusiasm of the waiter took both the chief and I by surprise. I stuttered through a simple order of black coffee, no sugar, and the chief ordered a pot of chamomile tea.

'A letter arrived this evening,' the chief said. 'From the warden of St Leonars. I imagine there will be another letter soon, bearing the King's seal.'

'Did the warden explain the situation? The southern boy?'

The chief stared at me, letting a hypnotic silence grow between us. His half-open eyes, his thin waves of hair that seemed oblivious of the notion of fashion, his dry lips. I couldn't outlast him.

'I can't go,' I said. 'It's too far, and I'm too old.'

'Go where?' the chief said.

I checked for any sign of mischief, but he was as sleepily straight-faced as ever. 'The boy's village, Drekenford.'

'And why would you go there? Small town, farmers and the like, not much to recommend it. A long way away, isn't it?'

'Yes,' I said guardedly.

'And the boy took out his own eyes here, at St Leonars, a month after coming to the city.'

Our drinks arrived and the chief fussed with his small tea pot. I stirred my coffee needlessly.

'What he did,' I said, 'what was done to him: that didn't come from the city.'

'You sound certain.'

'I *am* certain. Compulsion to self-harm, the teeth... there might have been people capable of that kind of witchcraft, once. But you've seen them all hang. And I put enough of them in the noose myself.'

'Good,' the chief said, 'then you and the King agree. Tomorrow's letter won't just have the King's seal, but his signature too. Do I need to explain the significance of the King's personal signature, Morden?'

'No, sir.' I sipped my coffee, finding it stronger than I would have liked. 'But surely there's someone else? Someone posted that far south?'

'Sadly, no. From what I hear, the town counts itself lucky

to have a constable of the regular kind,' he said. 'Of course, there are others I would've chosen: Pitchler is younger; Mayr has your experience and grew up in the south; and Ebna, well, she is just better than you.'

I wouldn't be baited in so obvious a manner.

'But like you,' the chief said, 'I wasn't *asked*.'

I thought back to St Leonars, the warden's own claim of powerlessness, and the eyeless boy huddled in the dank cell. 'The King's personal signature?'

'I know a good framer, if you'd like? It's quite an attractive signature, really.'

'Tomorrow,' I said.

'You leave as soon as it arrives.'

'There is no alternative, no escape from this, is there?' I knew the answer, but I wanted to hear him say it.

'No. The King rarely takes this kind of interest in a case,' he said. 'Do you want my opinion?'

I didn't say yes, but I didn't say no.

The chief lowered his voice. 'I know you are not a man of the court, Morden, so I will speak as plainly as is possible with such things. His majesty has been distracted of late. Not himself for some time, maybe even years.'

'The King?' I said.

He hushed me, looking about the coffee house. 'If I were to *quietly* use words like paranoia, or obsession, or even madness, you'd understand these were just said between two old friends in a very public place.'

'I see.'

'Perhaps such words always waft along the corridors of power?'

'I wouldn't know, sir.'

'No, of course not,' he said. 'Let us be even clearer, then. The King's attention rests firmly on the south. You are to end this dark business in Drekenford *before* that attention takes a very physical, very martial form.'

'War.'

'Your word, not mine. But we both know what trouble it causes in an investigation.' The chief sipped his tea. 'The King chose you personally for this case, Morden, over all others. You look surprised? So did I.'

'Then why me?'

'Because you have a reputation of being made of stone. "Determinedly unflappable" I believe was the phrase used. You won't be swayed by what you find in Drekenford.'

'I supposed I should be flattered.'

'But you're not, and that's the point.' The chief paused, and then appeared to reach some kind of decision. 'There was something else. A suggestion, little more than a hint, that the King himself was aware of a certain... talent of yours. Any idea what that might be?'

I sat very still under his gaze. 'No, sir, no more than you.'

'Well then, there's a horse waiting for you at the station; cheerless old thing, I'm sure you'll get on.' The chief placed a heavy purse on the table. 'For eggs, and such.'

15th *October 1721*

Alexsander found my note, blocking out the dawn sun as it was. He read the scant details and then swore many times so I would remember. What I also remembered was the resignation in his tone, which was already moving towards pragmatic acceptance.

That was the way of our relationship. The way of the vast majority of brotherly and sisterly relationships that crossed sunrise and sunset in the Kingdom of Reikova. We had some power to make our night- or day-brothers aware of something specific; a power often exercised through saying a thing repeatedly, perhaps with the aid of a mirror, or the written word – as I had chosen that day. But total certainty was impossible. An obstinate day-brother could do their utmost to ignore the night before, or see a note and choose not to read it. In that sense there was some degree of control – or the illusion of control – in what we remembered of each other. It was possible, for instance, to be the prying sort. I might know much of what my day-brother did with his sunlit hours. Instead, I had long ago decided his doings were tedious at best, distasteful at worst. I preferred to ignore them as best I could. I imagined he felt the same way of my nightly endeavours. But as with all Reikovan citizens who made something of their lives, who avoided the clutches of St Leonars prison and the like, we lived in a peaceful enough accord with each other. An accord that, on occasion, relied on wilful ignorance.

To that end, by the time the day began proper Alexsander was already making plans for our departure.

He visited a number of drinking establishments. A drink, a conversation, a handshake in each, and his month's plans were undone. The innkeepers looked unnervingly similar, smiling with red cheeks and understanding. He crossed the city in a haphazard way, stopping finally at a well-to-do house where he had lunch with a small group I took to be his friends by the way they laughed easily with each other.

There he spent the afternoon. If I was mentioned, or the reason for his leaving, it was too brief to be noteworthy. Instead, the name Clarissa was often invoked and brought forth a mix of embarrassment and pride in him, even as it immediately set him to shaking his head. Unconscious gestures were typically the most pronounced when I recalled his days. No, he would miss Clarissa, whoever the harlot was. He could not hide it from me or his friends, with their gibes and jests. At least he didn't blame me.

He returned to the boarding house, swaying slightly as he climbed the stairs. Behind one door a couple were arguing, another making love; both done loudly and both making Alexsander pause. He spent his remaining few hours taking care of his instruments: oiling, dusting, polishing in a kind of mindless rhythm. The rhythm I could understand, even if the intricacies of his care were lost.

When the time came, he chewed the right amount of dried ettiene leaves to ease our transition and fell asleep.

Arriving at the station I was told the chief had been called away. I pressed the desk clerk for more, which was apparently the only encouragement he needed. He leaned over his high desk, so only an inch from my nose, and whispered, 'The palace.' He glanced left and right conspiratorially. 'All day and, so far, all night.'

I shared some of the clerk's surprise at that, though I did know the chief held his office on both sides of the ettiene.

'I'm expecting a letter,' I said.

'Letter, Inspector? Letter, letter, yes,' the clerk said, finding it eventually.

I started for the back of the station.

'Aren't you going to open it?' the clerk said. I was, but not before such a gossip as he.

I made for the station's stables, pushing through the heavy wooden doors and into the labyrinthine corridors of the station. There, I met no fellow officers of the law, and the cold stone floor left me to my correspondence. In truth I opened it reluctantly; more than a wish for privacy, I did not want my assignment to be made real, irrefutable. And what could be more binding than the signature of the King?

I read the letter twice, seeking some hidden meaning or instruction in the mundane orders. I was to travel south to Drekenford with the King's Dragoon Guards, as a civilian attaché. The regiment was mustering outside the city and would not wait for me should I delay. Once in Drekenford I was to 'investigate the interference to Jan and Gregory Harsson'.

Interference. As empty and as telling as my own title of Special Inspector: to many there were things in the Kingdom of Reikova best left unnamed.

I briefly entertained the idea of refusing to travel with an army regiment but, though the company would be odious, I was not taking a summer night's ride across the capital. The roads to the south were reputedly so dangerous they were the favourite setting for Esteberg's more bloody tragedies. I hadn't seen many such plays myself, but I recalled red-spattered highways and the roaring applause they produced from Alexsander and his drunken friends. One ignored the theatre's lessons at one's own peril.

Despite the danger of such a journey, I had packed as lightly as possible. I expected the weather in the south to be as changeable as the region's fortunes and as unwelcoming as its people. One of the bags slung over my shoulder held warm layers and extra woollen breeches. I had no way of knowing what would be required of me or my equipment during this investigation, no idea of the length or extent of what lay before me, so I carried nothing more specialist than a pistol, a long knife, and my simple wooden crucifix worn around my neck. I had to hope Drekenford would provide.

When I emerged from the station's corridors into the stables, a sturdy brown mare was one of two horses in the many stalls. The other held a princely white horse being saddled by a young man. He tied an expensive-looking bow of white wood behind the saddle and wore a quiver across his back. I watched him for some time before he noticed me.

'Inspector,' he said by way of greeting; evidently he knew me, though I was at a loss as to who he was.

'Long ride ahead?' I said.

'Could be.'

'I'm travelling south.'

The man grunted and went about checking his saddle straps.

'Do you own that horse?' I said.

He looked over the saddle at me, his head and shoulders cast like a bust of an ancient conqueror. 'I don't come from here,' he said, 'but our countries share much. And then there is much for the taking.' He flicked a coin, which I only just caught. A heavy gold crown pressed with a likeness on one side, a tower-like building on the other. I recognised neither.

'What is this for?'

But he turned back to readying his horse and I felt as dismissed as if I were boring the King himself. I hefted the crown in my palm as I wandered to the mare I assumed was for me. The mare made the same assumption, standing inert as I secured my bags to the old saddle. She remained docile even as I tried to lead her out of the stall. Docile and immovable. I pulled and yanked, clicked and cajoled, and soon was reduced to cursing.

A sharp whistle sounded and the mare stepped forward, almost sending me tumbling. Righting myself, I saw the young man silhouetted in moonlight, now mounted at the open end of the stables. I thanked him and he turned away and was lost to the city. I felt a sadness I could not explain, except that I knew worse nights were to come.

The mare responded calmly to my every command, as if the whistle had awoken this princess from a spell. Riding through the city was a disconcerting experience, so rarely had I been at such a height: the cobbled streets and low pavements were transformed, alleys were elongated in their darkness, and I found myself shying away from even familiar routes like a scared child. I couldn't help but stare down into the dimly lit rooms I passed, seeing more of people and their lives than I had any business to.

I had one stop to make before I left the city. A ritual of mine was to begin each investigation by visiting Esteberg's cathedral. Or, more specifically, the library beneath it. I often found the information it held helpful, and on occasion crucial, to the hunt.

The cathedral was just as imposing as St Leonars prison, though the two could not be more different in their architecture. The cathedral was blessed with a multitude of high, thin windows. Beside them were similarly shaped recesses full of saints worked in stone. Saints stacked one on top the other from the ground all the way to the heavens – or so it seemed as I looked upwards from the hitching post. The mare took to this latest station with a respectful bow of her head. I told her I would not be long.

I entered through the main doors, removed my hat, then crossed myself and offered a prayer to the Holy Mother. I pulled my cross from beneath my shirt and kissed the simple wood. The cross was a gift from the Archbishop, but it was not his guidance I sought that evening. The high vaulted ceiling created a vast space of still air – an aspect of the cathedral that never failed to inspire a kind of peace in me. Nor did it fail to remind me how small I was in the presence of our Lord.

I made for a side aisle, not wishing to disturb those at prayer on the pews. Some wore the robes of the clergy, but many more were regular citizens seeking solace from the dark streets of Esteberg; the cathedral was awash with the light of hundreds, if not thousands, of candles. The way to the crypt and the library was gated and locked at all times – the simple ironwork gate one of the few unadorned items in the entire cathedral. There was no desire to draw attention to what was held below. My station as a King's Special Inspector provided me a key, as well as the impetus, to enter such a place. I opened the gate as quietly as I could and was sure to lock it behind me. The descent was well-lit, though I held the rail regardless.

Cooler air wafted up from below, which carried the dusty smell of books. As many books as the cathedral had candles.

At the main desk I was fortunate enough to find the very man I sought. Custodian Ignatius was deep in conversation with another custodian – evidently regarding a matter of categorisation of a particular text. Was it a codex, an incunable, or a manuscript?

'Good evening, brothers,' I said, not entirely certain which address to use with the cathedral's librarians. 'I'm afraid I must interrupt, and ask for your assistance.'

'Special Inspector Morden, it has been too long,' Ignatius said, adjusting his plain brown robe. The other custodian took this interruption as an opportunity to retreat to the stacks.

'Too long?' I said. 'Given the dark troubles I bring with me, I imagine the reprieve was somewhat welcome.'

'You do God's work, Inspector. That is not always as painless or as godly as we might hope.' Despite being many years my senior, Ignatius had lost none of his fervour. He had, however, lost all of his hair and much of his sight – he wore thick spectacles to compensate. 'Now, how might I be of service?'

'Your library has helped me identify sorcerous acts before a hunt,' I said. 'I need your help again, Ignatius.'

For the second time in as many nights I recounted the tale of the Harsson boy and his sufferings in the cell of St Leonars. Ignatius was attentive and nodded often. He was not shocked. Between the stories I had brought him over the years and the endless accounts of what befell saints and sinners shelved in his own library, he had heard it all before. That was why I sought him out: his knowledge of unusual suffering was second to none.

He wasted no time once I had finished. He turned and led us among the rows of shelves, deep into the crypt. We passed many tomes and codices whose spines were barely legible, and many robed custodians who pored over illuminated manuscripts on large tables. They did not look up from their work. Eventually, we came to the restricted archives. These were gated in a similar fashion to the crypt, but my title did not allow me unsupervised entrance here.

The blasphemous works held here were reserved for only the holiest of souls – only they could resist their sorcerous influence. Many dark incantations, rituals, and hexes were trapped on these shelves. Page upon page too dangerous to be freed, and too dangerous to be destroyed.

As Ignatius fumbled with his extensive set of keys I was reminded once more of St Leonars: the gate here ran from floor to ceiling, much like those in the warden's block. Bars that kept the dangerous within, and the unsuitable or unsuspecting without. Ignatius ushered me through and locked the gate behind us. So secured, he asked his questions in a hushed voice. 'Teeth, you said. You're quite sure? It wasn't bone?'

'Teeth. They were unmistakable.'

Ignatius pushed his spectacles higher on his nose. 'Northern Kettoman shamans were once recorded as eating the eyes of their mentors to gain their insights. This would have been, oh, six hundred years ago, before the Kingdom of Reikova was formally founded. Poul was the scholar, I believe.' Then abruptly he was off, and it was no small effort to keep pace with the custodian. That gave me little chance to be distracted by the bent and twisted-looking inhabitants of these restricted shelves, whose leather bindings spoke of the unspeakable.

'But he did not eat his eyes,' I said to Ignatius' back, aware of how simply I stated such a thing.

'No? But the teeth.' He turned a corner, then stopped. With great care he lifted a lantern from its sconce. 'We rarely light these shelves. Some believe the codices here prefer the darkness. That they are... restless in the light. I remind you not to touch anything, Inspector.'

The darkness all but swallowed us and our small lantern. The stacks were monstrously tall here, and the texts packed tightly. Who could believe so many unholy words had been committed to the page? I did my utmost not to let my gaze wander, but even over the shoulder of Ignatius I saw texts ahead of us that seemed to wriggle and squirm in the lantern light. One such spine was adorned by a serpent, as were many, but this particular embossed creature was eating its own tail. Its scales flashed as emeralds might, but softly, softly, and so it called, softly, softly. If I were just to—

'Inspector!' Ignatius slapped my hand; I had not realised I'd raised it towards the shelf. He looked to the text in question. 'Bartrey's *History of the Baalimine*? Possibly, Inspector, possibly. Was the boy from Drekenford a heathen?'

'We did not discuss his faith,' I said. 'He was in no state to discuss anything.'

'There is a line in Bartrey's, I believe, that refers to the "unfaithful". Though there is some debate on the exact translation. Still, Poul would be a stronger start. This way—'

'Show me, Ignatius.'

He studied me for a moment, before he relented. He took the text from the shelf as if the serpent on the spine were only in slumber. He would not let me see any of the pages as he found his way in the text. Instead, I was left to gaze at the cover: seven crowns that appeared burned onto the front. Seven crowns that would not sit still, but swirled as if caught in a maelstrom. I blinked rapidly, thinking it an effect of the poor light, of the close air, but the crowns did not stop. Instead, I closed my eyes, determined to resist such an unknowable force.

'Here it is,' Ignatius said. 'My memory was correct. You may read it for yourself, Inspector. Inspector?'

I opened my eyes. His thick finger indicated a line scrawled in faded ink. It read:

The unfaithful lose sight of themselves

'The Ritual of Berith, from the lesser known demonologies. But not without adherents over the centuries.'

'What of the lines below?' I said.

Ignatius brought the book close to his face. 'Like many such rituals, Berith demands certain conditions be met. Typically these are quite abstract, to allow the misguided hope of equally misguided individuals. Here, see for yourself.'

'The sword—'

'Careful, Inspector. Even here, in the Lord's house, to say such words aloud is unwise.'

I read the ritual's list silently.

The sword shrivels to flakes of snow
The law devours its history
The stone moves on water
The broken heart bleeds gold

'I don't understand,' I said.

'Be glad you do not.' Ignatius closed the book before I

could read any further. 'The mention of sight is intriguing, but I believe we would fare better with Poul. And, of course, there's Hendrick's work on bestial teeth. Are you quite sure they were *human* teeth, Inspector?'

'Quite sure,' I said, and followed him once more among the infernal stacks.

I struggled to concentrate in the hour or so that followed. Ignatius led me to many other texts. Poul did indeed recount his time among the eye-eating shamans of Northern Ketts. Hendrick had much to say on the powers of animal teeth. Lisherwood fleetingly mentioned curses placed on those already incarcerated. Gibson wrote extensively on the many manners an eye might be extracted. And so it went, on and on, but I kept being drawn back to the Bartrey text with the serpent and the crowns. Eventually, I was exhausted – and long before Ignatius' knowledge, or his appetite for sharing it. I could take no more of the baleful influence of such texts. I asked him to lead me back to the surface, back to air free of books, back to the living city.

As he closed the gate to the restricted archives I kissed my cross and gave thanks to the Holy Mother.

'Will you have further need of the archives?' Ignatius said.

'I may. Though I leave for Drekenford tonight.'

'I see.'

'Should I request a tome, would it be sent?'

The custodian looked quite suddenly uncomfortable. 'We all serve under the King and the Archbishop, Inspector. But... so far?' He glanced back at his precious, restricted texts. 'Villages such as Drekenford are a long way from godfearing civilisation. They're full of heathens, idolaters, and book-burners!'

'Anything requested—'

'Low-minded peasants, unable to read the word of—'

'—would be looked after,' I said, putting my hand on Ignatius' shoulder. 'You have my word on that.'

'I see. Of course, forgive me. And God's speed in your hunt for the witch, Christophor.'

I left the cathedral well after midnight. Though it was slow going, neither the mare nor I were in any hurry to be away from the city. Who knew what lay beyond? But that was where we were bound.

The imposing South Gate was busy, or so it appeared to me. The duty guards were only checking the carts and travellers entering the city; the lines looking to leave were moving swiftly under the double portcullis. Despite telling myself not to, I watched those dagger-tipped lattices with every step the mare took, feeling as if they hung over me the whole way.

But my relief at passing through the gate was fleeting, and replaced by an awful foreboding. The stone bridge in front of me stretched across the Esterly river which, in a moment of unnatural stillness, took on the character of an oil painting of a castle moat. Those crossing into the city were frozen in their suffering; dead-eyed and weighed low by their total worldly goods. Behind them blazed great fires of a country burning, their fields and homes set to flame, the smoke destroying the stars.

The whole world burned in front of me.

I had the sense the displaced fleeing the flames were just delaying the inevitable. There was no escaping such an apocalyptic vision.

I might have stayed there, paralysed by the terrible tableau, were it not for the press behind me and the mare's stolid, less fanciful sensibilities. She drove us towards those flames, as if they were nothing more than campfires. To my relief she was, of course, correct.

A burning world with half-dead refugees streaming into the city – this was not the first vision I had experienced in my duties, but certainly the most vivid. I wondered just what those apparitions were fleeing, exactly? The most obvious answer being war, except there was more to the vision than that – a greater sense of darkness, of a hellish nature not entirely under the command of men at arms. Perhaps that was why the King was taking a personal interest in my bringing the Drekenford witch to justice; perhaps the vision was a warning against my failure.

I resolved to put aside my doubts, my reluctance to accept such an investigation, and press on.

A woman hailed me as I neared the end of the bridge, waving her scabbarded sword high above her head. Her dark navy uniform and cocked hat were almost lost to the night, but not so her horse which was such a fiery brown as to almost be red. The horse's flesh and muscle appeared to dance and ripple, even as it stood still as only a warhorse can.

'Inspector Morden!' the woman called, once again waving her sword. I was only a few yards from her. 'Come, sir. I'm s'pose to take you to the colonel.'

Drawing closer, I realised I had been wrong to think this soldier was approximately my age; she appeared young enough to remember the inside of a classroom in some detail. Her skin was smooth about the eyes and brow, and her curling black hair was heavily oiled. She introduced herself as one Cornet Pitzmun and, as she already knew my rank, I offered her my first name alongside my hand. This produced a huge grin characterised by well-kept teeth.

She wheeled her great red warhorse alongside my utterly unfazed mare, and led me towards the regimental camp fires that had created such an infernal impression upon me. They were actually a good distance from the city gates. I could not help but look back at Esteberg and wonder which, the city or myself, would be more changed when I saw it again. The words of the warden of St Leonars came to me: there was no way of truly knowing who or what waited in Drekenford, but they were no street-magician, of that there could be no doubt.

'We're breaking camp at dawn,' Pitzmun said.

I grimaced, wondering what my day-brother would make of that. 'Are all you soldiers both-siders?'

'Almost all. Those that ain't have other duties – cooks and stablemen and the like. Don't fret, Inspector, we ain't so different. We get along like most.'

I supposed I knew that already, to some degree; how else could the King keep fighting his wars? The expansion in the south was one more folly in a long line of Reikova's martial follies; another bid for recognition, glory, and a little wealth from a small nation with an overly large mouth.

'Is this your first posting, Cornet?'

'Oh, no, sir. Baby-faced maybe, but I was at Pottersdrum, and Hayden Field, and—'

'The Kettoman Succession?' I said, not believing she could have fought in the northern lands over ten years previous.

'That's right. Good job we won that one, or we'd all be speaking Ketts!'

My maternal great grandmother had been Kettoman. On her death bed she refuted the statehood of Reikova, spat on the name of the King, and told my mother to use less soap when she washed her linen.

We were waved into the camp, which was made up of perhaps a hundred tents. A pall of smoke and sweat was heavy in the air. Men and women were sitting at their leisure, many cooking or dicing. Others oiled rifles with the kind of absent attention that I recognised from Alexsander's care of his instruments. I had packed his favoured fiddle, our typical compromise – he could certainly fill an ale house or aid a family celebration with it, and I could manage its case as part of my travel luggage. None of the soldiers looked up at our passing, which went some way to lessen my self-consciousness at my lack of uniform and the size of my horse.

The colonel's tent was no different to any other from the outside, though I wondered if there was some differentiating mechanism that only a soldier would understand. Cornet Pitzmun dismounted and I waved away her offer of assistance.

'Wrinkle-faced maybe, but I wasn't at the siege of Esteberg, nor the Christ's Day Revolution.'

Pitzmun appeared to take great joy in our shared joke, her laughter worryingly enthusiastic. I resolved that when I exited the colonel's tent, whenever that may be, I would not find myself in Pitzmun's company for too much longer. There was something off about the young woman.

She held open the tent flap and then announced me as if I were a minor royal.

The colonel held up a finger to forestall my greeting. He was sitting in a handsome wingback chair, reading under ample candlelight. He wore a tightly curled wig and had a moustache that could have been the envy of every fashionable man in the King's court. His ruddy complexion suggested the life of a soldiering officer agreed with him. With a nod of satisfaction he closed the book, though he kept a finger there to mark his place.

'Tabitha should have seen off that scoundrel, Mr Wolff, a long time ago,' the colonel said.

'Excuse me, sir?' I said, glancing towards Pitzmun, but she was already taking her leave of the tent.

'Romances, Special Inspector, I cannot get enough of them. There's not a one printed this year I have not read.'

'I see.'

'I only hope, one day, we will produce as many books as we do rifles.' He sounded wistful.

Perhaps it was this, alongside his apparent taking of me into his confidence, that made me reply casually, 'Would that be good or bad for Reikova?'

He regarded me for an intense moment and then said, 'I will give that some thought.'

'I—'

'Now, Inspector, you are to be billeted in your own tent. The King was very clear on that. Very clear you should be made comfortable and safe for the journey. Your tent is a bit smaller than our usual fare,' he said, gesturing to the ceiling of his own accommodation, 'but then you won't be sharing with four others now, will you?'

From his pause, I realised the question wasn't meant to be rhetorical. 'No, sir,' I said.

'Very good. Three days to Drekenford – the town for you, the nearby Fort Seeben for my men and I. What do you know of the place, hmm?'

'Not a great deal,' I admitted. 'Only it is not so big, and a long way from the capital in more senses than just the geographical.'

'Quite so. But, if I may offer some advice, Inspector. Do not be so quick to dismiss the town. It is small, yes, but it is old – older than this fair country of ours. Its traditions and roots stretch deep and wide. It may surprise you, for better or worse.' He cleared his throat. 'Well, three days riding, as I said. Though, with any luck we may manage more riding hours with the late sun. How is your day-man set, hmm?'

'He understands.'

'Inspector too, is he?'

'Musician, sir.'

'Quite right. Mine's a poet, blasted ingrate. Wish he'd write a good Romance. But then there's no telling them, is there.'

'No, sir.'

He looked startled at my answering what was apparently *not* a question. 'Get yourself settled in, there's a good man.'

I was shown to my modest tent by a trooper. He seemed a dutiful young man, and I was grateful when he insisted on seeing to the care of the mare. He went to commend her on her good behaviour, but stopped short and looked at me expectantly. I realised I had no idea what the horse was called. There was no indication about her person, no name tag or label on the saddle. I saw no alternative but to re-christen her. For a dark moment I considered calling her Jan, to remind me of my duty, but that would have been utterly selfish and in poor taste.

'Tabitha,' I said to both horse and trooper. The mare flicked her tail against a horde of flies, and it was settled.

I ate a small supper of bread, cheese, and a handful of dried fruit. The smell of cooking meat was pervasive in the camp, but I had neither the strength nor the inclination to eat among others. As the sky began to lighten, I chewed a sensible amount of ettiene and slept soundly, hoping to ease Alexsander's travels.

16th October 1721

He rode all day in the rain.

I woke stiff and aching. When I tried to stand, my legs buckled and I fell awkwardly against the side of the tent. Muscles I did not realise I even had were complaining the loudest, and were only quietened after a good deal of stretching. With difficulty I made my way out of the tent.

Someone other than Alexsander had taken care of the horse. I left her at rest and went in search of breakfast. Though the night before I disdained the soldier's spits, now I had a hunger great enough to tear the very leg from a pig and eat it raw. Fortunately, the covered mess area required the less visceral but no less heroic feat of queuing in a line of similarly afflicted men and women.

I caught snippets of their muttered conversations, mostly concerning the weather – both of that night and the nights to come as the regiment moved south. Few were looking forward to a winter posting.

'I wouldn't worry,' a woman ahead of me said to her companion, 'we'll be plenty warm. The King'll stir the hornet's nest and we'll march so far south we'll be fighting in nothing but our britches!'

None of the King's soldiers shared his interest in the lands of the southern tribes, with its hot swamps and thick jungle. His sanity was called into question in numerous and colourful ways, some of which included descriptions of His Majesty's imaginary friends, his desire to own every copy in existence of his favourite play, and his roaming the palace halls naked. Another popular suggestion was that the King's interest in the tribes was purely to sate his personal desire for young, fair-haired boys. But then the talk descended into a broader, directionless sort of bawdiness.

Somewhat embarrassed by their open conversation, I looked about the camp. I had no recollection of where we were, how we got there, or what the surrounding area might be like. All I could remember of Alexsander's day was the hard riding and hard rain. To the west, where the sun was about to be lost, I saw a low patchwork of hills and fields. A forest lay a good distance to the south and east, but I recognised the trees as those native to the north of Reikova; they lacked the sense of immensity that I knew was the character of our destination. I wondered if Esteberg could still be seen to the north, but struggled to see beyond the tents. Such a sight would have done me little good.

When my turn came I was passed a plate.

A broad-shouldered man looked at me expectantly. 'You must be the attached-ey?'

I blinked, then understood. 'Yes.'

'Come to me for some brekkie have you?'

'Please.'

The man walked to the back of his stall and patted the flank of an enormous black packhorse. 'Well, then, gots some porridge.' He reached into the horse's bags. 'One quarts wheat, three quarts barley I makes it. To you, that's two silver kreers.'

'Two silver?' I stuttered, looking about to see if the soldiers either side me were similarly shocked. I wondered if they earned so much in a month.

'You see, they pays much more than that.' The man gazed out at the eating soldiers. 'They pay with their lives, don't they?'

Rather than back away I paid the man and ate every thin mouthful until I was no longer ravenous. I found that to be the case with most of my interaction with the King's prized Dragoon Guards: everything was dealt with to my satisfaction, but that satisfaction was as shallow as the puddles left from the day's rain. The large man waved to me from beside his black horse as I left the mess area.

It was a short night, between the extra hours in the saddle and my bodily exhaustion. I spent some time wandering the camp, exchanging soft words with wary soldiers. My general impression was of a less than enthusiastic fighting force. They seemed surly, with a distrust not just of me – a stranger, a civilian – but of everything and everyone. This was no regiment marching gloriously off to war, singing songs and waving hats as they did so. They had many a muttered opinion regarding their orders, their posting, and their divine monarch. Many of which I found myself agreeing with, not that they would find that much comfort.

I saw Cornet Pitzmun inspecting a supply wagon, and

ducked behind a tent to avoid the young woman. I was in no mood for her unusual enthusiasm.

Eventually, I returned to my tent and fell asleep wondering if Alexsander and I would become more accustomed to life as a soldier in the few short days to Drekenford; like the colonel's books-against-rifles, I wasn't sure how I felt about that proposition.

17th *October 1721*

He lacked the spirit and strength to be angry.

Alexsander too had developed a fondness of the mare, also calling her Tabitha, and mounted the horse whispering apologies.

The land changed as he rode, growing bigger in every sense. The trees became monstrous. The horizon lengthened somehow, as if the road from Esteberg were really a kind of funnel. It could not continue in such a manner – the world would swallow creatures so small and insignificant as man and horse. Cresting a hill was a vertiginous experience. The rivers were like hurrying lakes. It made him lonely.

He played the fiddle from horseback. Mournful songs the soldiers knew, though he played bawdy tunes at their request. An officer – he didn't know her rank – dropped back along the column to listen. She stayed for the better part of an hour without comment. Then she said, 'You'll be popular in the town, at the inn.'

'"*The* inn?"' he said.

She laughed. 'Don't worry, they like a drink in the south as much as anywhere.'

When Alexsander readied himself for sleep, he told me I should have packed his flute.

I woke to find the camp in turmoil. Soldiers ran back and forth in front of my tent, their jackets removed and red cloths tied over their faces. I stared, dumbfounded, wondering just what feverish or maddening influence had overtaken the dragoons. I was not so far from the truth, I found, when I hailed a trooper.

'Pox, sir.'

'Pox? Here?' I said uselessly.

'Best stay to your tent, sir,' the trooper said. 'That is, unless you are running a fever? Vomiting? Any pustules?'

I assured her I was fine, and rolled up my own shirt sleeves as a kind of evidence. I had some experience of pox and the like during previous investigations, though always in a civilian setting. I hoped the military would be more organised in the face of such crisis.

'I would like to help,' I said.

'Help, sir?'

'I have survived the pox, trooper. At the very least I can attend the suffering. Take me there, now.'

'Right you are. This way.'

I hurriedly donned one of Alexsander's burgundy shirts and tied a red-spotted handkerchief over my face, as the troopers had done. The demon pox did not like the colour.

I joined the stream of red-clad men and women, all heading towards the far side of the camp. There, tents that were roped closed – using ropes dyed red, of course – held those afflicted. The sound of retching rang up and down the line of tents like a peal of bells. The slap of vomit on metal buckets added yet another layer to the horrible chorus of the pox. Determined to be useful, I entered the nearest tent.

I found four low-frame beds occupied by four squirming soldiers. Another trooper was struggling to attend them. His mouth-covering had slipped. He looked just as exhausted as those he helped.

'The sun has set, trooper,' I said.

He glanced from me to the tent door, as if he did not quite believe me.

'Go, chew your ettiene, and ease your night-brother into his turn.'

He thanked me and left, not even thinking to question who I was to give such soft, welcome orders.

There was a bucket of water in the corner of the tent. I began by refreshing the cloths pressed against each soldier's head. Of the two men and two women, all but one were gripped by fever and vomiting. The fourth had developed the pox's rash, which would in time change to the viscously filled pustules that scarred so in their falling.

As difficult and tiring as the duties of the night proved to be, it was those first moments that were the hardest. I had not realised, but like me, the night-siblings were then waking to the pox for the first time. Waking to their pox, bodies already ravaged from a day's suffering.

I cradled one trooper as he wept and cursed his day-brother. Between emptying buckets of thin, blood-flecked bile,

I shushed delirious blasphemy and the like. The demon of pox was invoked and insulted regularly. In their more lucid moments, some of them spoke of their surprise at succumbing to plague while still on Reikovan soil – something they were all but expecting to face in the jungles of the southern tribes. I told the soldiers to save their strength. This was a test sent from the Lord, and they would not be found wanting. They were the King's Dragoons, were they not? Strength, duty, honour. That was met with more bile. It was painful to see proud young men and women reduced to such a state.

Once, during the night, a crate of weak beer was brought to the tent by a bare-chested trooper. He stayed for an hour, perhaps longer, and helped me administer what draughts the suffering could take. It was a slow, frustrating task but we schooled each other to patience. What was our frustration in the face of the pox?

And so the night progressed by the rhythm of the moving of fluids.

It was still too soon for fatalities. But I couldn't help wonder how many in this tent would survive the coming days.

18th October 1721

The row of tents was left behind. Alexsander stared from the road not entirely understanding, not entirely remembering, its significance. He was lucky in that, though he thought it strange that none of the soldiers looked at the tents, which were bold and incongruous in the empty, churned field. In the pale light of dawn he shivered and would not play his fiddle when asked.

He spent the day's ride wondering about the tents. A sense of sickness was there, the sharp smell of a stomach's contents was clearest to him. He tried so hard to remember what he thought I must have known. But there was no asking the soldiers, that much he *did* understand, so instead he worried at the thing, even catching himself biting his nails – something we did rarely. Soon there were more pressing concerns. For both of us.

He ate well. Though he would not have called them friends, he had an easy manner with the staff of the mess. His silver was no good to them.

Squinting against the setting sun, Alexsander saw Drekenford seep into view at the far end of a huge, forested valley. Black and lifeless it looked to him. Had he not been surrounded he might have turned Tabitha around.

He followed the dragoons, and left our arrival to me.

At Fort Seeben I was granted a final audience with the colonel. The fort was barely worthy of its own title, being a single wooden structure surrounded by walls. It sat, squat and ugly, in a cleared patch of forest atop one side of the valley. To say it looked down on the town would be too grandiose, would convey a sense of successful purpose. The troopers' barracks huddled against the inside of the fort's walls as if bracing against a constant storm. I was keen to be away.

I was surprised to find the main building had two storeys

– it did not look tall enough. Cornet Pitzmun joined me at the entrance. As she shook my hand it appeared nothing could dampen the young woman's enthusiasm. We climbed the narrow stairs to a room that was arranged exactly like the colonel's tent. And again I had to wait as the colonel finished reading.

'Inspector. I trust you had a comfortable journey?' the colonel said.

'Compared to my day-brother, I would say so. But what of the pox, Colonel?'

'Damnedest thing, that,' he said. 'Lost ten good troopers. Could be more.'

'I wish I could have been more help,' I said.

'Are you a doctor as well as an inspector, hmm?'

I judged this to be one of the colonel's rhetorical questions.

'Well, I don't doubt your business down in the village will keep you busy enough,' he said.

'I believe it will,' I said.

'You'd do well not to forget that we are here, this garrison, this King's fort.'

'Yes, Colonel.'

'This is not a stable region, Inspector. There are forces at work here that go well beyond you or I. Some of those forces you may think you have some understanding of, some experience in handling. I can tell you now,' the colonel said, meeting my eye, 'you do not.'

'I'm not sure I follow your meaning,' I said, quite truthfully.

'We all serve at the King's discretion. We will be watching.' Despite the colonel's even tone there was obvious threat in what he said. The air in the room grew close and I became more aware of the Cornet beside me, armed as she was.

I nodded. The scant camaraderie Alexsander and I had established with the King's Dragoon Guards was obliterated in that quiet room, under the steady gaze of their wigged officer.

He appeared satisfied, and his taking up his book was a welcome dismissal.

I led Tabitha away from the fort and down a winding track towards Drekenford. I didn't doubt her, but the moon was new in the clear sky and I carried a lamp to light our way. The air was heavy with pine; I tasted it on my breath, felt it on my skin, and could think of little else. Thick shadows moved like molasses between their great trunks as we passed and I had to school myself against looking too closely. I knew how easy it was to conjure my own demons out of the darkness. Instead, I focused on taking one step after the other, on navigating the uneven, rock-strewn track, and on the simple regular sounds of Tabitha beside me.

The decline of the track was not particularly steep, but its persistence was wearing. The backs of my legs began to ache and the fall of my own feet jarred: I was already out of rhythm with this place. I stopped to unbutton my cloak, not quite ready to take it off completely – my one piece of armour. As I did so, I heard a faint sound far ahead on the track. A grinding, creaking sound.

I held up the lamp and peered beyond its ineffectual glow. Tabitha became unusually agitated. She pawed at the ground and whickered, though my firm hand on her reins stopped any thoughts of flight. The grinding was worse now. It echoed along the treeline as if the pines were the walls of a cathedral and the noise a terrible choir. I hurriedly put down the lamp and drew my pistol from beneath my cloak. My hand trembled as I loaded the powder. When I finally raised the pistol the long, pale head of a horse appeared from the darkness.

Somehow, even from such a distance, I could make out its teeth, which were uncommonly sharp. Grinning so, the horse came fully from the dark and I saw it pulled a cart. Just as the horse, the cart was pale like bone under the new moon. Its wheels were the source of the grinding and it approached under that constant sound. I could not clear the track completely, unwilling to step into the forest or subject Tabitha to what I would not do myself, but I led the mare as close to the trees as I dared.

I was glad to find the cart had a driver of the ordinary kind, though even in the poor light I could see how age weighed heavily on her shoulders. The woman brought the cart to a halt on the track and turned to face me with difficulty. She was terribly thin, her cheekbones like drawn daggers, and her eyes were aflame in the light of my lamp.

I began a stuttering question as to her purpose, but she interrupted me with a voice as deep and black as the forest.

'Come,' she said, then took a shuddering breath, 'from the village.'

'Supplies?' I said weakly.

'I don't bring, I take.' Her cart was empty. 'Pox up there.'

On instinct I glanced back along the track but saw nothing of the fort. Perhaps it wasn't there at all, or never had been. This far south anything was possible. 'I didn't realise more had caught it.'

'Quarter will go, before all's told,' the woman said without a hint of sorrow or pity.

'And you're to help?'

'So you say.'

There was a pause between us then that I felt was awkward, though she gave no sign of discomfort.

'The village, is it far?' I said.

Without a sign from the woman, her horse set off. The grinding started again and I couldn't move until it grew faint and then was lost to the ragged sound of my own breath. It was an unsettling first encounter with someone from Drekenford. I hoped I would find more of a welcome in the town itself; I would no doubt need local assistance in the coming investigation.

After half an hour or so ignoring shadows and avoiding loose rocks, the track wound down to join the road at the bottom of the valley. There was a strange marker at the crossroads: a kind of tiny house made of stone. It had a definite roof – there was a clear impression of tiles carved in its top – but instead of walls there were four tall columns at each corner. Only one sign gave any direction, along the road to Drekenford.

The road was more open than the track, though trees still lurked on either side. I picked up my pace when the lights of the village became clear in the distance. Rarely before had the thought of a soft bed and a warm meal so spurred me onwards. I had been spoiled by my years in Esteberg – as a younger investigator I had travelled, understood and withstood its demands. Three nights and I was longing for old comforts.

As I drew nearer the village, the road rose to form a bridge over what I presumed was the eponymous ford. I glanced behind me, noting that the Dreken river oddly did not meet the road again as far as I could see. Instead it was lost, like so many things, among the trees.

I imagined I could walk away from the road, the village, and into the trees myself, never to be seen again. Here, so far from the chief inspector's reach and the King's seal, no one would stop me and no one would particularly care. Perhaps such a course would be preferable to Alexsander. He of all people might prefer the great unknown to the slow death of a provincial village. But I could still feel the ghost of the boy's teeth on my fingertips, and still see the burning vision at the gates of Esteberg. The resolution I made there, to pursue the King's Justice in this case, held firm.

I checked my pistol, still loaded from the strange encounter on the track to the fort. I decided it was best kept so until I had a better sense of the place. Pulling my cloak tighter about my shoulders, I walked on with Tabitha.

The bridge was long and lit at intervals by ensconced lamps, above which were animals carved in stone. A large cat, a bird I took to be a raven, a fish, and many more exotic animals, their likenesses very good. I gently brushed the broken fang of the cat; some of the animals had weathered better than others. The lamps gave a number of them a sinister character.

'They come alive on All Hallows' Eve,' someone said.

I flinched at the sound. There was no one on the road. I peered into the shadows between the lamps and found one shadow more solid than the others: a boy.

'The animals come alive?' I asked, glancing at their well-defined stone muscles and claws.

'Don't look so scared,' the boy said. 'The adults use marionettes for the festivities, that's all. Anyone can see the strings.'

The boy turned his back to me and leaned over the wall of the bridge. I approached cautiously, trying to be clear I intended him no harm, but he was now occupied with whatever was in the river. I had the feeling it was something he had put there himself.

I joined him in staring at the darkly churning waters. He held a line of string, as if fishing. His shirt and breeches were both near-black, as was his short, straight hair. It was little wonder I'd failed to see him, so clandestinely dressed.

'What are—'

'Sshh!' the boy said. His concentration was absolute. 'There!'

A flash of red shot under the bridge. My first thought was that the boy had thrown the corpse of some poor animal into the river and now revelled in the speed with which it passed below. But then he thrust an expensive-looking pocket watch at me and said, 'Do you make it twenty-two minutes past one?'

Bewildered, I could do nothing more than confirm that I did.

'You are sure?' he said.

'Twenty-two minutes past.'

'I was right!' He leapt into the air and then shook me by the hand. 'Julia won't be able to deny me this time, not with you as witness. No chores for a week!' He started to wind the string around his hand.

'Just what have I witnessed?' I said.

'Why, an experiment of course.' He shook his head at my ignorance, at the ignorance of all those over the age of eleven. The flash of red turned out to be a large handkerchief attached to the string, now both dirty and sopping wet from its journey under the bridge. With practised care the boy cleaned off the worst of the muck and wrung it out. 'Are you lost?' he said.

'No.'

'Most people who come here are lost. Are you a soldier?'

'No,' I said. I was unused to being questioned by a child.

'Then just what are you?'

'A man ready for his bed.'

'Inn's that way,' he said, waving vaguely towards the village. 'If you see my sister, Julia, tell her the time. Of the experiment.'

'And what does she look like?' I said.

'She looks like me.'

I gave the little scientist my word, as a man ready for his bed, that I would do as he asked. I led the ever-patient Tabitha onwards across the bridge and down into the village.

Before I made it beyond the first set of houses a girl came hurtling towards me. I hailed her by name, which made her skid to an abrupt halt. The sleeves of her dress were rolled up beyond her elbow and some kind of grease stained her cheek.

'What?' she demanded of me, a stranger.

'Your brother,' I said, quite taken aback. I had expected southern bluntness from the men and women of Drekenford. I had not anticipated it in its children.

'Yes?'

'Twenty-two minutes past the hour,' I said.

'Blast!' And off she ran once again.

I decided to follow the road from the bridge, assuming that would form the main street through the village. The houses I passed were unsurprisingly but pleasantly parochial, with long thatched roofs that almost reached the ground. The distinct flicker of candlelight could be seen in most windows, suggesting few could afford oil for lamps. I snuffed my own, trying to limit just how greatly I stood apart from the people of Drekenford, though their young sentry had already taken the measure of me.

I came to understand the warden of St Leonars' difficulty in categorising Drekenford as either town or village. By northern standards it was indeed small, but as I came to a wide, well-appointed square I had the altogether unexpected impression of neat prosperity. The cobbles were free of weeds or moss, and boxes of late-summer flowers still had some bloom left in them. These were not just in the street but up the walls and in the windows of the taller buildings too. A fountain stood a few feet from me, a girl reading that made for a kind of monument, but most of its lettering worn away.

A busy little market was at the far end of the square and accounted for the crowds of people gathered under awnings, sitting on benches, and ambling between stalls and shops. It also accounted for the overwhelming smell of salted bread and spiced apple. I briefly considered buying a loaf for Alexsander, by way of a small reconciliation, but there was more than enough time for that. Instead I made for a large, slate-roofed building that spilled both light and laughter into the street in the manner of inns and ale houses the world over. The Horse and Hound, though the hound was curiously absent from the sign's picture. An alley led to the stables at the rear.

'Put her in there,' said a woman before I could even introduce myself. She wiped her brow and went back to mucking out the stalls.

'I would like a room,' I said.

'Not out here you wouldn't. Mrs Lehner inside will see you right.'

With Tabitha stabled, I climbed the short stairs and entered the inn from the rear. Dark wood panelled the walls of a corridor, adorned by a line of horse brasses. These were of the typical kind and design, though I noted a striking number of royal sigils among their number. I had not expected a great deal of love for the King from the people of Drekenford. A short, balding man pushed past me either on his way to the stables or, judging by the manner in which he carried himself, to the privy.

The common room was full, every table occupied and many small groups standing at its edges. Spurts of laughter were the only thing to break the loud, constant conversation. The large hearth was empty, though the room was plenty warm and lit well enough – candles, I noticed. The horse brasses continued and were joined by other brass items I could only assume had some farming or logging function. I had to duck under one such funnelled object as I entered; I didn't count myself as a tall man, but perhaps this far south I was unusually so.

I came to a well-polished bar, edged, to no surprise, in brass; copper mines must have featured heavily in the area. I stood between a man and woman who glanced at me regularly, though they tried to hide it, until I realised I had come unknowingly between them. I stepped away, to their obvious relief, and ignored the woman's giggling. Silently I wished them well, whatever stage their courtship was in.

When my turn came, the woman behind the bar, who I took to be Mrs Lehner, gave me a broad smile and asked, 'What'll it be, love?'

I was briefly disarmed, and the young woman from before

set to giggling again. 'A room,' I managed, forgetting my manners completely.

'That'll explain them bags,' Mrs Lehner said. 'Day, too?'

'Please.'

'My day-sister's husband has the run of the place then, but that should be no bother. A meal before you go up?'

Tired as I was, I was considerably hungrier. I could have requested the meal sent to the room, but there was no better way to judge the mood of a village and its people than a full common room. Mrs Lehner disappeared momentarily to the kitchen, and then came to lead me upstairs. She was not a small woman and took the steps one at a time.

'I am relieved to find a room available; you seem to be very busy,' I said, simply to say something.

'Oh, those are just my regulars. We don't get too many travellers this way, not once summer's over.' As she made the top of the stairs, she set her apron right and dabbed her hairline, though I couldn't see that she had a single hair out of place.

'And the soldiers at the fort?'

'Same really – come in for a drink when they can, but rarely go so far as to need a room. Here we are then,' she said, opening a door that I had to duck through.

The room was large enough for my simple needs, with a writing desk, mirror and wash basin, and a wardrobe. Mrs Lehner named her rates, which were more than reasonable, and said the same would be the case for my day-brother. She asked how long we would be staying.

'Hard to say. I have some business in the village.'

'Well, wash up and such, and your plate'll be ready when you come down.'

I made to thank her, but she was already closing the door. I hung my cloak on the back of the door and, rolling up my sleeves, washed my face and neck in the basin. The towels smelled faintly floral and though I couldn't say which flower, it certainly wasn't the ettiene that was in the window. This ettiene had lost its flowers, possibly from too much direct light, but its leaves were healthy enough. I plucked a few of them, assuming the plant was for the use of guests; my own supplies were not inexhaustible.

At the mirror I tried to make myself presentable, carefully brushing what hair I had left. The time would come when I could avoid a wig no longer and I would spend my remaining days scratching myself.

Shutting the door behind me, I noticed there was a key in the lock. As it turned it made a reassuringly heavy sound, and I focused on that reassurance rather than memories of prisons, damp cells, and destitute men.

Mercifully, the inn had emptied a little and I found a table without any trouble. A plate of cold meat and hot vegetables was placed in front of me by an apathetic-looking serving girl.

'Drink?' she said, without intonation.

'Wine. Not too expensive.'

She gave a small sigh and left me. The food was reasonable and cooked well, which was unexpected. That I had underestimated Drekenford in many respects was clear, even if I found the south's reputed bluntness justified. And perhaps, over the course of my investigation, I would come to consider that plain manner of speaking a virtue rather than a characteristic worthy of northern derision.

I had almost finished my meal when the two children from

EQUINOX

the bridge sat down at my table. They both wore expressions of utmost seriousness. I did my best not to smile.

'Hello, sir,' the boy said. He introduced himself as Victor, and his sister Julia.

When he looked expectantly at me, I told him my name was Christophor.

'My sister believes I coerced you—'

'With a bribe,' she interrupted.

'—into telling a false time.'

'I see.'

'Don't you deny it?' Julia said.

I judged her to be the elder of the two, but perhaps by only a year. They both shared the same straight black hair, and looked so alike in features as to be almost twins.

'Monetary gains aside, there seems little reason for me to fabricate the results of an experiment that I know nothing about,' I said. 'And I can assure you, your brother has not given me anything.'

'You might be lying,' she said.

I spread my hands in an open gesture. 'I appreciate a week of chores is no trifling matter, but you'll just have to trust the honesty of a stranger.'

She slumped back in her chair. Her brother was magnanimous in victory and did not gloat.

'What was the experiment?' I said, removing my napkin from around my neck.

'You're not going to eat that meat?' Victor said.

'A trade, then. Your answers for what's left of my dinner.' I pushed the plate towards them. They took to the food with ferocious efficiency.

'Measuring the speed of the river,' Victor said between mouthfuls.

'Whatever for?'

He shrugged as if to say, 'What else would I do in Drekenford?' I thought on the matter for a moment.

'Are you taking into account the phases of the moon?' I said.

'Of course. We have separate measurements for each phase.'

'And conditions further upriver?'

'I'm only eleven,' he said, flatly. This was clearly a contentious issue.

'Well, then, what are your findings so far?'

'It's getting faster, so Victor says.' Julia's tone made clear her thoughts on the matter, and that this was the element the two children wagered on. 'But *I* think it's too early to be sure.'

'Too early?' I said, finding myself strangely intrigued by their scientific foray. 'How long have you been doing this?'

'Five years, two months,' Victor said.

I looked at them both, seeking any sign they were jesting with me but found them utterly sincere. 'Impressive,' I said.

Victor waved a hand dismissively. 'It's only *one* of our experiments.'

'There's one special—'

'Julia!' Victor silenced his sister.

I decided not to press the matter, but made a mental note of their secret, special experiment. Victor's raised voice also appeared to summon their father from across the common room. A large man, finely clothed and immaculately groomed, put a hand on each of his children.

'Come now, I think you've bothered this good man long enough,' he said. That he'd waited until the children had cleared my plate was fairly obvious. With mumbled goodbyes, the children left with their father.

After, I found the atmosphere of the common room changed. Suddenly those at nearby tables were purposefully looking anywhere *but* at me, and those further away stared in open curiosity. I should have sent the children away the moment they joined me. Tired though I was, the night still had many hours to it and the thought of pacing my room in useless agitation did not appeal, so I gathered my cloak and left the inn.

It was a mild night and I wandered among the market stalls, browsing the local wares under amber candlelight. The crowd wasn't so thick as to make my passage difficult, and those people that did stand beside me to examine cheeses, breads, and crafted goods were all of a jovial disposition. Of the cheeses there appeared to be a great number of goat's milk varieties, and the goods were largely carved from pine. Candles were also popular and made from the wax of local hives. Perhaps the only part of the whole market to come from farther afield was the coinage that paid for it all; kreers passed from hand-to-hand with customary disregard for the King's likeness pressed into the copper and silver.

I stopped at one stall and allowed myself to be talked into the purchase of some spiced cider. A small cup, little more than a taste, which was heavy but pleasant. I raised the cup in a kind of greeting to those I saw who had made a similar choice, and my earlier feelings in the common room now seemed like unfounded paranoia. I moved easily among the smiling, chattering people.

Beyond, in the square proper, the older citizens of Drekenford sat on the benches and took turns to play and sing songs I didn't recognise. Clearly they were village favourites and everyone knew the words, even if they lacked the confidence to sing along. A battered old accordion was passed around, though the lone fiddle never left the capable hands of one particular woman. One or two of the men enjoyed the opportunity of performance, dancing and clapping in a very measured manner that I assumed was a custom here. I stayed to listen for a good while, applauding each song and mouthing along the more repetitive refrains. I caught a glimpse of the children, Victor and Julia, hurrying off to some experiment, no doubt.

Eventually I returned to my room. Mrs Lehner waved from behind the bar, where she polished glasses and tankards. I imagined her role as innkeeper to be quite demanding, and though she appeared to hide her fatigue well I could see the strain was there. I hoped my staying would not be too much of a burden, and so I carried my own fresh water up to bed with me.

19th October 1721

Alexsander woke in a strange room, but the bed was soft. He lay there appreciating the warmth and comfort and the knowledge the day wasn't to be spent in the saddle. After some time he decided he would make the best of the situation, of Drekenford. He wasn't angry with me – hadn't seriously been angry with me at all – and now the light, airy room was dispelling the remnants of his frustration.

He remembered the two drawers where I had unpacked his belongings, though he was unimpressed by my folding of his shirts. He dressed in a coat of a fashionable kind, clean breeches, and boots that were comfortable for walking.

The common room was empty except for the landlord, Mr Hennig, who was polishing the tables. Alexsander introduced himself, ordered breakfast, and sat at a table that shone with his reflection. Like me, he could not look for long.

'Where do the days go?' he mused aloud.

Mr Hennig had no answer. Breakfast was filling. Alexsander ate too much and pretended to be content.

The square was lively with the comings and goings of a small town. The benches were rarely empty for long and he entered amiably into conversation: yes, the weather was cooling, though it was still mild; no, he hadn't realised the crocuses were already coming out; that's right, he was just visiting on some business. The people sitting next to him changed, the conversations did not. By the time Alexsander left, he had the impression of a friendly community who lacked the healthy distrust of strangers I found so essential at home.

He spent a while admiring the fountain. This one was unusual. A girl who looked to the horizon, rather than the book open in her lap. He considered himself quite the expert in regarding fountains, seeking them out with unnerving ease and practising his arts beside them. Sometimes he placed a cup at his feet and, at the right kind of fountains, raced the water to the first penny. He lost more than he won but then he didn't grant wishes, only brief entertainment. At dinner parties he joked the two were one and the same, and the diners would laugh though few understood. That he already missed his friends was something he tried hard not to dwell upon.

Walking through the streets he had no plan, so he turned whenever possible to keep the sunlight on his face. Tilting his head skyward, a small smile on his lips, he wandered the winding backstreets and alleyways with just as much relish as the main thoroughfares. There he was wished good morning by scullery maids and craftsmen and even a painter, standing in front of a sizable easel on his balcony.

Alexsander hailed the man and asked what he was painting.

'Whole town and valley,' the man said, 'as much as I can see from here. I paint one every year.'

This piqued Alexsander's interest, and he was always bold. 'I'd very much like to see them,' he said.

The painter, a man by the name of Marcus, indulged him gladly; this was not an artistically minded town. The painter sold his work farther north. Reikova? No, not that far. Not since his formative years had he travelled that far. The painter lived above a little framer's shop – a happy, brotherly coincidence – that was rarely open. His lodgings were modest but tastefully furnished. One room was given over to what the painter called his studio, but was clearly more of a storeroom: canvas after canvas were stacked against the walls and on the shelves. Few were fully visible, giving the room a kaleidoscopic character. Those that Alexsander could see he judged to be good, though he was by no means an expert. He commented on the sheer amount of work in the room.

'I paint faster than I sell,' Marcus said. 'And I don't paint all that fast.'

'Perhaps I will buy a piece before I return north,' Alexsander said.

'Would you like to see the valley?'

They moved into another back room, which was empty except for what hung from the walls. Every inch was covered by what appeared to be the same painting, replicated over and over but with different frames. It was dizzying. To steady himself, Alexsander focused on the closest painting. A small brass plaque on the bottom of the frame read 1693. The view depicted was obviously that from Marcus' balcony: the town stretching out below, the hills beyond, and the sky soft and autumnal.

The paintings moved through the years, and he began to see changes and even small sequences or progressions. A broken chimney that became a roof under repair. Trees pared back, then chopped down. One street grew from obscurity to bustling commerce. And in the distance Fort Seeben suddenly scarred the landscape.

'These are astonishing,' Alexsander said.

'My memory goes, but they remind me of so much.'

'And your night-brother, does he paint too?'

'No, but we do share a love of wine,' Marcus said.

Alexsander excused himself, not wanting to keep Marcus from his work. He was glad to be out in the open air once more and away from the heady smell of oils. He strode to the edge of town in order to walk out among the trees but, despite Marcus' detailed depictions, he had forgotten the river. So, saving the forest for another morning, he walked upstream until he grew hungry, then walked back to the inn. There, he spent the afternoon gossiping with anyone who was likewise unencumbered by significant employment.

My first task was to introduce myself to the local constable and determine some of the background details pertinent to my investigation. Mrs Lehner was kind enough to provide me with directions and I set off into an unpleasantly wet evening. The streets of Drekenford were all but deserted in the downpour, and of a far more subdued character than that of the market the night before. With no moon to speak of and so few streets blessed with lamps I was forced to navigate by my own hand lamp, which was poor in such weather. I soon found myself lost in the maze of unfamiliar streets.

At first I grew frustrated but, with no appointed time for my unannounced visit to the constable's office, I began to view my lack of direction differently. Like the common room before, I was simply gaining a sense of the place and its people. I made my way down prosperous streets where the houses boasted well-kept front gardens, edged paths, and an air of privacy to their curtained windows and smoking chimneys. But only a street away there were no curtains, no smoke, and in places no glass in the windows at all. These homes radiated a sadness from their very brickwork.

I was struck by the proximity and seemingly random distribution of such different natured homes. In Esteberg there was a definite system, areas clear to see on any map that had borders as secure and as guarded as any country. Such a map of Drekenford would be a mess of lines and no use to anyone.

Eventually I came to my destination: a thick door, ajar, and under the light of a lamp. I closed the door behind me as I entered, and paused in the small stone-floored hallway for the worst of my own dripping to subside. Ahead was a desk, behind which was a man a good few years older than I. He was busily scribbling in a ledger of some kind, leaning so close to the page that he didn't notice my approach. In the weak glow of his single candle I could make out two holding cells behind, which I took to be empty, but couldn't be sure.

I gave a small cough, startling the man.

'I would like to see the constable,' I said.

'Done something wrong?' he said, peering at me through heavy spectacles.

'No, I—'

'Seen someone doin' something wrong?'

'In a manner of speaking.'

'And what manner would that be?' he said.

'That's for the constable to hear,' I said, beginning to lose my patience.

'Well, you can tell me. Or you can ride a day in most directions and find someone else to tell.'

I looked down at the thin man, dressed plainly but smartly and with no trace of ink on his fingers. 'You're the constable.'

'And town historian,' he said.

'Is there much overlap between the two?'

'Of course!' he said, surprised at my question. 'What could be more important to the history of a town than its misdemeanours?'

'Is everyone in Drekenford recording something?' I muttered.

'Excuse me?'

'You oversaw the arrest and transfer of Jan and Gregory Harsson.'

The constable leaned back in his chair, it now being *his* turn to take the measure of *me*. 'You have me at a disadvantage,' he said. 'Perhaps it's time you told me who you are, sir.'

By way of answer I put my badge down on the desk, pleased at the heavy *thud* and its echoes. But this was not a man easily cowed. He picked up the badge as a bird might a twig, turning it this way and that as if deciding whether it was worthy of a place in its nest.

'Well, Special Inspector Morden, aren't you a long way from home.'

'By request of the King.'

The constable raised an eyebrow at that. 'Jan and Gregory Harsson.'

'That's right.'

'Theft. Silverware mostly, if I recall. Surely the King doesn't send out inspectors every time some knives and forks go missing?'

'Not every time, no. Whose knives and forks went missing, Constable...?'

'Webber. And it was Mr and Mrs Eder's silverware that Jan took. He worked for them, up at the manor.'

'What reason did the boy give?' I said.

Again the constable regarded me for a moment. 'You didn't speak to him,' he said. 'Before coming all this way, you didn't speak to him. Now why's that?'

'He was in no state to be interviewed.'

'Dead?'

'Worse,' I said.

Webber stared at the candle's flame. 'Claimed he was innocent,' he said eventually. 'Like they all do.'

'You didn't believe him?'

'Found the silver at his lodgings. His night-brother, Gregory, he lived somewhere else in town. Wasn't much more to it.'

'You never wondered why he stole the silver?' I said.

'No mystery to it, Inspector. He was greedy and he wasn't very clever.'

'And why was he sent so far north to serve his sentence?'

'The Eder family thought it would be better, for everyone, that way. *Mayor* Eder was keen Mrs Harsson be spared the shame.'

'Mrs Harsson,' I said.

'Lives on Church Lane. Now, you want to tell me what this is all about?'

'Someone... interfered with Jan Harsson. While he was in a locked cell.'

The constable considered this. I was beginning to see he was a thoughtful, deliberate man who, I would guess, was rarely to be rushed. My travels as a young inspector had led me to expect a very different kind of officer to be sitting behind that desk. My time as an older inspector in Esteberg led me to be wary of capable men.

'I suppose that explains the *Special*, then,' Webber said. 'Can't say I know much of anything in that regard, we don't have any *Special* Inspectors in these parts. But I'll help any way I can.'

'For now, I require discretion. And any details you have regarding Jan Harsson's arrest.'

'Take a seat, Inspector, I'll copy you out what I have.' He began hefting pages in his large ledger and looking down the tight columns, his nose less than an inch from the yellowed paper.

I sat on a hard seat in the hallway until my backside could

take no more, then I stood and paced. The constable was fully absorbed in his task with what I perceived to be some relish. I wandered to the cells, which comprised of barred walls sunk into floor and ceiling, and which were surprisingly well-furnished. Two cells, one bed in each. Their comfort and cleanliness told me much of Drekenford's history of misdemeanours.

I wondered which had held Jan Harsson. How had the boy spent those last hours in his own town? Did he rage and spit and curse the constable, his employer, his fate? For some reason I couldn't picture him there, in the relative comfort of a dry cell complete with bed and blanket. Instead, he huddled in the corner until he noticed me. Until he *heard* me. And then he was struggling to be away, pressing himself against the unyielding walls, confused and afraid – but not of me. Afraid of someone much farther away. Of someone—

'Here we are then, Inspector.'

Constable Webber was beside me, holding a file inside which were papers covered in neat handwriting. Dates, times, dry descriptions. Exactly what I needed to begin my investigation.

As I took my leave, Webber once again offered his assistance. I assured him we would speak again.

I made my way to the residence of Mrs Harsson, who was apparently Jan and Gregory's only living next of kin. I hoped she would be more forthcoming regarding her sons' characters than Constable Webber had been. Church Lane – the address provided by the constable – was not particularly difficult to find; the church spire was visible from almost every street in Drekenford. The hourly bells echoed throughout the valley so clearly I had no doubt Fort Seeben set its sentries by them. When I arrived at the house there was no reply to my knocking. The curtains of the small house were drawn, with no hint of movement or light behind. I knocked once more, louder this time, and then made sure I was alone on the street.

I tried the door handle. I would not have done so in Esteberg, but if there was anywhere in Reikova that people did not lock their doors it would be in a small town such as this, on the same street as a church. Mrs Harsson, however, had locked her home.

I wandered down to the church. It was sizable and ornately decorated with gargoyles and animals, which reminded me of the stone creatures on the bridge. The walled grounds held rough rows of gravestones in varying states, with many generations buried together in family plots. As interesting as these were, I was more taken with the stones that had worn away so much that no dates or names were visible. These blank slates were sombre, of course, but at one such grave someone had left a modest bouquet. I knelt and tried to trace what could have been a name with my finger.

I flinched: just as I touched the hard, grey stone there came singing from inside the church. I wondered if it were an angelic chorus, but soon found the voices too poor for that.

I entered quietly and took a seat near the back. Pews of dark wood, stained glass windows, and too few candles made for a gloomy atmosphere. The choir stood in front of a priest, and I felt sure Mrs Harsson was among them; many of the first row were of the right age. They were struggling valiantly through a requiem I recognised from my childhood. There was a rolling beauty to it, to the swells of baritone and the punctuation of the sopranos. It ebbed and flowed like the sea, which was so far from this town that the comparison felt awkward. My breathing slowed and, before I could stop myself, I had closed my eyes.

From the darkness, like the coming of a remembered dawn, a fire grew. I could not move from the pew though the heat, the heat, the heat was like a pounding hammer against my forehead. From that sun came four riders. I knew them, one and all: the foreigner with his white bow; Cornet Pitzmun atop her fiery warhorse; the dragoon quartermaster; and the pale cart driver. And I knew my scripture. They stood before me, the four horsemen, and I felt the end of all that was, is, and would be – felt it happen to our body as skin and flesh were flayed from me, leaving only bleached bone and ash. They watched, impassive, as I screamed. As I screamed, and—

'Sir? Sir? Are you all right?'

I woke with the priest leaning over me, his hand on my shoulder. I stared up at him and found my own terror mirrored in his young face, if only briefly.

'My... apologies,' I said, blinking against the memory of four figures, four riders, and the end of everything. 'A vision.'

'Pardon me?'

'I was dreaming, Father.'

'You gave Mrs Tomas quite the fright on her way out.'

The choir was gone. Most of the candles had been snuffed and the Father was wearing a cloak. 'I'm sorry,' I said. 'I didn't mean to fall asleep.'

'It happens more often than you'd think,' he said with a smile. 'I don't normally wake people, but I have to lock the door.'

'Lock the door...'

'Are you sure you are all right?' the Father said, sitting beside me. His blue eyes were startlingly bright, even in the dim church.

'You aren't from here, are you?' I said, then winced at my own tactlessness.

He waved away my apology. 'My grandparents travelled north to Drekenford when my mother was a babe-in-arms. Led by a missionary.'

'From the tribes?'

'So I'm told. But that was a long time ago. *You* are from Esteberg.'

'That's right. How did you—'

'Secrets don't last long in a town like this, Inspector.'

I stared at the priest, who looked plainly back. 'Is Mrs Harsson a member of your choir?' I said.

'She is. As was her son.'

I was the first to break eye-contact, raising my gaze to the eaves. My mouth was dry and I felt a weariness cover every inch of me. 'I would like to speak with Mrs Harsson.'

'You don't need my permission, Inspector.'

'I would like you to be there.'

'Me? Whatever for?' he said.

'I want her to understand how important this is.'

Father Popov agreed to arrange a conversation between the three of us, and to leave word at the Horse and Hound. Mrs Harsson was apparently very old and frail; the Father believed she would be more comfortable if we spoke at her home. She was a devout volunteer in the church, though the Father's tone suggested her devotion was not always to the church's benefit. As a young priest he no doubt faced many challenges.

I returned to the inn and, after making enquiries as to Tabitha's welfare, I ate a modest meal in the common room. Mrs Lehner brought over the plate and glass of wine herself.

'There we go, *Inspector*,' she said, and was heading back to the bar before I could say a word. I glanced about the common room but found it unchanged: no one looked my way, no one whispered or sniggered, and there was no suggestion whatsoever that I was the topic of anyone's conversation. Yet, I felt exposed.

I made myself eat slowly, and sip my wine long after the plate was cleared away by the bored serving girl. I retired to my room as the tables were beginning to fill with the night's regulars.

Locking the bedroom door behind me, I let out a breath I hadn't realised I'd been holding. The room appeared unchanged. I checked all my belongings, all through the wardrobe, under the bed, and in the desk. In the bottom drawer I found the King's Bible. I recoiled, as if from the serpent himself. I closed the drawer, only to open it quickly once more. I took the bible out and placed it squarely on the desk, though I could not bring myself to look inside.

20th October 1721

An agreement was made with Mr Hennig. Alexsander was to play three times a week. Whatever the crowd asked for, he was to play. If the room was empty, he was to play. Mr Hennig didn't like sad songs but, and he shrugged expansively, if that was what the crowd wanted. Mr Hennig helped plenty of men and women drown their sorrows; some nights he drowned his own – just not in sad songs.

Alexsander went walking again. When he passed the painter's balcony he waved up to Marcus, but didn't stop to talk. He wasn't in the mood for talking.

Heading south he admired the stone animals of the bridge. He had to wait as two carts carefully manoeuvred past each other. For no reason he could understand, he shivered at the sight of the carts. I understood. He watched them both, going in different directions, until he could see neither. The sun came out and that warmed him.

Fearless, he walked into the forest. He breathed in deeply, actually enjoying the pine-laden air. There were no paths to follow, no signposts, and no *signs* of anyone having ever walked there at all. He strode confidently in no particular direction. He touched tree trunks, scuffed fallen needles with his boots, stopped to listen to the birds sing. When he grew hungry he ate from the small pack he'd brought.

At one point, perhaps it was midday, he sat against a tree and took out his fiddle. He practised for a long time. He played all the happy songs he knew, and all the songs he'd expect a small town's common room to call for. He practised the best drinking songs. And, when the sunlight turned softer with the afternoon, he played one or two sad songs – the kind Mr Hennig would shake his head at. By this time Alexsander had cleared the nearby forest of song birds and there was silence in the breaks between his playing. He enjoyed the silence, strange man.

I was glad to find myself back in the bed at the Horse and Hound, and not lost somewhere in an endless forest. Twilight had already descended, but the room's fire had been lit and provided ample light to wash by. I could only assume such a consideration was the work of Mrs Lehner, though I was slightly perturbed by the thought of her laying a fire in my room while I lay there sleeping. I would write to Alexsander and ask him to use a lighter dosage of ettiene for the duration of our stay.

When dressing, I caught sight of the bible on the desk top. It took me a moment to recognise it, and recognise why it was placed there. I sat on the end of the bed and stared at it. Soft brown leather, well-worn, and thin golden lettering. Then I recalled my vision.

The night before I had been too shocked, too confused, and too thrown by my conversation with Father Popov to consider what I had seen in any sensible manner. Now, in the silvery light of a growing moon, my first thought was of a warning. It was, admittedly, the most obvious conclusion – though no less correct for that. The four horsemen. Harbingers of destruction, each given a fourth of the earth to devour in their own ways.

I did not think Cornet Pitzmun was the actual horseman War, nor that the over-charging quartermaster was Famine. Not even the unsettling cart driver could truly be Death. They were only symbols placed before me for a reason I did not fully comprehend; not yet, and perhaps not ever. If they were meant to spur me into greater action and urgency in apprehending the person responsible for the horror at St Leonars prison, then the warning seemed disproportionately extreme. But if there was something greater at work in Drekenford then... I considered myself duly warned. I left the bible on the desk.

Mrs Lehner met me at the bottom of the stairs, as if she'd been lying in ambush.

'Evening, Inspector,' she said. I understood then that, no matter how often I might ask her not to, she would always use my title. 'There's a letter here for you.'

'A letter?' I pictured the King's seal, a recall to Esteberg, scant details of a captured suspect.

'Looks like the Father's seal if you ask me.'

'Yes, of course,' I said, doing my best to hide my disappointment. 'Is there coffee, Mrs Lehner?'

I read the Father's brief note as I broke my fast with buttered bread and a heavy, spiced sausage that I'd seen in the market. He had arranged for us to visit Mrs Harsson at ten o'clock.

I was about to step out into the street when I recognised a man slumped at the bar. He didn't look entirely disposed to company, but I couldn't help myself.

'I admire your day-brother's paintings,' I said.

He turned slowly, scowling. 'Then buy one.'

'I may just do so.'

'Buy ten, buy a hundred, he'd still be an idle, ungrateful leech,' the man said.

As much as I recognised the sentiment, given my own dissatisfaction with my day-brother's choice of occupation, his strength of feeling caught me off-guard. 'I'm sorry, I don't—'

He *harrumphed* and returned to his ale.

The night had a sharp feel to it, and a chill to the wind that regularly took me by surprise as I rounded a street corner or passed an alley. I gritted my teeth each time, crossed my arms, and swore I would be ready for the next icy blast.

I had a little time before my appointment with Mrs Harsson, so I made my way towards the manor where her son had purportedly worked. The same house from which he had stolen the silverware. Not the crime that I was investigating, but perhaps the catalyst for the crime that I *was*. I only had to ask directions once for the Eders' home and it was not difficult to find, being set high on the valley side. In front of the handsome house the trees gave way to a manicured garden so I stood, hands-on-hips, and admired the view as I recovered from the climb. The cold air did little to help the burning of my lungs, though the calm of what spread down the valley below was a greater aid. The warm lights of Drekenford proper and Fort Seeben on the opposite side, the dark glitter of the river, the blanket of forest – it was all quiet, all still.

Fort Seeben was particularly well-lit, with what I took to be a sizable bonfire. In my dullness it took me far too long to realise what the fire was for, but when I did I turned away sharply. Was there something sickly sweet on the air? With something bitter and ashen underneath? I brought my handkerchief to my face, hoping its perfume would rid me of scents and thoughts of charred, pox-ridden bodies. A quarter of the fort would go, so the cart driver had said. A fourth, so Death had said.

As feelings of my own uselessness rose I reminded myself that I had been given a task and I was carrying out *that* task to the best of my ability. A task given by the King, no less. I was no plague doctor. But I could not shake the feeling of responsibility, that I could somehow be the cause or to blame for what was afflicting the King's Dragoons.

The wind rushed through the trees and cut me down where I stood; merciless and unheeding of cloak and breeches alike it set my teeth chattering. And, perhaps more chilling, it brought the sound of laughter.

Shrill and hollow and strangely innocent, it echoed about the manor garden. I cast around for the source but I was alone and the house stood silent with only the porch lamp lit. The laughter grew in volume and hysteria. Beneath my cloak, I put a hand on my pistol but before I could make any efforts to load it I found there would be no need.

The two children, Victor and his sister Julia, came running around the corner of the house. I judged Julia to be chasing her brother and holding something disreputable in front of her. They both skidded to a halt as they noticed me.

'Hello,' Victor said, clearly embarrassed to be caught at play.

'What is in the jar?' I said, nodding towards his sister.

'Leeches,' she said defiantly.

'Another experiment?' I asked. I hoped that would dispel some of the boy's chagrin, but instead the colour of his cheeks darkened.

'They're for a doctor, *actually*,' Julia said.

'Is your father a doctor?'

'And a mayor.'

'*The* mayor,' Victor added.

'He sounds very important.'

'He's not home,' Julia said.

'I see, well—'

The door of the manor opened and a woman stepped quickly out. She was well-attired in a neat dark-green dress, with a heavy wrap of fur across her shoulders. It was only as she came to stand behind the children that I noticed they, too, were in fine clothes.

'Can I help you, sir?' the woman demanded in a none-too-friendly tone.

I bowed, removing my hat, and introduced myself as a king's man from Esteberg. The change in the woman was instantaneous.

'Ah, *Inspector*,' she said. 'How fortunate we are to meet so soon after your arrival.'

'I saw him before he even got to the inn,' Victor said.

'Quiet now, the adults are talking.' The woman's voice was like a knife: the edge was never far away.

'The honour is mine, Mrs Eder.'

She held out a gloved hand, which I took and mimed to kiss. Though I was no authority on high-society, I understood from my day-brother and his friends that a woman offering her hand in this manner was no longer fashionable in the capital.

'I am afraid we are to leave for town. Perhaps we could arrange a more suitable time for your company?'

'I would find that most agreeable,' I said, a little surprised to find myself matching her formality.

'Then we shall send an invitation in due course. Come now, children.' She herded them into the house and closed the door without as much as a glance in my direction. I didn't know quite what to make of her.

When I arrived at Mrs Harsson's house, Father Popov was already there. It was he that opened the door and ushered me inside. The house was small, with exposed beams that were so low I had to stoop. The Father led me through to a sitting room where a woman, whom I took to be Mrs Harsson, knelt tending a fire. I had to stifle a cough as smoke hung like rainclouds under the beams.

The room was plainly but neatly furnished, with a sturdy rug at the centre and two rocking chairs on either side. Father Popov crossed to the window seat and, careful of the drawn curtains, sat in a very deliberate, attentive manner. I felt suddenly that I'd walked into an orchestrated moment, like someone walking into a theatre rehearsal. My initial reaction was one of refusal, a wish to break away from whatever scripted lines the two of them had decided upon. So I knelt beside Mrs Harsson and picked up one of the heavier logs.

'Is it ready?' I said.

She pursed her lips. Her eyes were hard, and experience was etched deeply across her face. That the Father had described her as frail was its own little mystery; she was short, solid, and quite broad across the shoulder. However, she did not move particularly easily as she stood and shuffled to one of the chairs. I placed the log on the fire and felt some small pleasure when it started to take. When I turned to the room both the Father and Mrs Harsson were looking at me.

'Perhaps Father Popov explained why I asked to see you, Mrs Harsson?'

She remained silent, either not caring to answer my question or unaware it was a question at all. I was starting to wonder if Esteberg was the only place in Reikova where questions – and when to answer them – were clear and well-defined.

DAVID TOWSEY

'Your son, Gregory, and his day-brother, Jan,' I said. 'There has been an incident.'

'Aye,' Mrs Harsson said gruffly, her voice pitched as low as any bargeman on the Esterly river.

'You are aware of what has happened?' I said, unable to hide my surprise.

'Serves him right,' Mrs Harsson said, 'after wha' he did.'

'I... I'm not sure I understand,' I said.

Father Popov cleared his throat. 'Jan's sins affected more than just himself and his night-brother. Mrs Harsson was also cast out from her employment at the manor.'

'But you did nothing wrong,' I said.

'Course not. Them Eder,' Mrs Harsson made to spit at the name, 'they're no good. Thirty years I scrubbed an' washed tha' house. Then, gone.' She was rocking in her chair now, not frantically but steadily and I wondered if the rhythm was working to keep her temper in check.

'Forgive me, Mrs Harsson, but I must ask: at what hour was your son born?'

Father Popov winced, but before he could object Mrs Harsson answered.

'He was a night-baby, if tha's what you're askin'.'

'And his father?'

'Buried him two years back, God rest his soul.'

'I see. And your day-sister, did she and Jan care for each other?'

'Far as I know.'

The fire crackled and sputtered behind me, and it was growing a little too warm for comfort so I crossed to the other chair and sat. 'Did Jan or Gregory have any enemies in Drekenford? Anyone who would wish them harm?' I said.

86

Mrs Harsson glanced at the Father. 'Not tha' I heard,' she said.

'But you said it "served him right", what did you mean by that?'

'Just tha' – you do wrong, wrong is done unto you.'

'Is that the church's position?' I said to Father Popov.

'Jan committed a sin,' he said smoothly. 'He was judged guilty by his peers, and will be judged by the Lord Almighty, as will we all. Now, do you have any more questions, Inspector?'

'One. Did your son have a sweetheart, Mrs Harsson? Day or night?'

'Not tha' I knew of,' she said, looking down at her lap.

I judged she was lying.

'They are handsome men,' I said. 'Surely they caught the attention of a young woman or two, in a town as small as this?'

'Couldn't say,' she mumbled. 'Weren't none of my business.'

'I see. Thank you, Mrs Harsson,' I said, deciding against pushing her further, especially in front of the Father. But her reluctance clearly suggested the topic was one of some significance, and one I would return to.

Father Popov led me out, leaving the old woman sitting in front of the fire. She looked even smaller as I left, like she was curling in on herself. I felt a jab of pity then at the vulnerable loneliness of that room.

When we came to the church, the Father bid me goodnight and good luck with my investigations. Then, as if a thought had suddenly occurred to him, he stopped on the church path and said, 'You spoke of enemies, Inspector, but the Harssons have many friends in Drekenford.'

'Perhaps you might introduce me to some of them?' I said.

'Perhaps you might attend our services?'

I smiled at his neat work, and said I would try. I made my way back to the inn, deep in thought. Apocalyptic visions notwithstanding, I was beginning to believe this matter would not be resolved swiftly or simply.

The King, apparently, disagreed.

In the almost empty common room Mrs Lehner welcomed me from behind the bar, once again emphasising my title. The two men sitting at the bar sat straighter as if I were somehow about to inspect *them*. Those few at the tables eyed me warily. A warning bell could not have been more effective.

'Another letter came for you, Inspector,' she said.

I took the envelope from her, recognising the seal. I requested food and wine sent to my room.

'Important letters can't wait, Inspector. Don't you worry – you'll be taken care of here.'

I hurried upstairs and, with my door closed, I examined the seal. There was no sign of tampering. I sat at the desk, opened the letter, and read it slowly. Then once more, to be sure I understood.

War was coming.

In the chief inspector's terse and blunt way he confirmed that a second regiment of the King's army was due to join the dragoons at the end of the month, by All Hallows' Eve, and that Drekenford would then form the staging point for a large-scale offensive against the southern tribes. The King himself insisted that I use every method, source, and ability at my disposal to ensure the investigation be drawn to a conclusion before that offensive.

I carefully put the letter down on the desk, as if those heavy words were somehow fragile. What possible bearing could my investigation have on the King's wild ambition? I appreciated that magic and its misuse was concerning for the crown – hence my entire employment. But never in all my years had the King taken personal interest in the outcome of a case. And once again there was a hint of the impossible: that the King somehow knew of my visions. They were a part of myself I had never shared with anyone. Not even my day-brother appeared aware of them, let alone experienced them himself.

I was still dumbly contemplating this when there was a soft knock at the door. I folded the letter and then called for them to enter. The serving girl didn't look at me as she set down the tray.

'One moment,' I said.

She stopped by the door. 'That's all the beef the kitchen has.'

'And I'm sure it is fine. I wondered, did you know Gregory Harsson?'

'No.'

'Not even a little? Not even to look at?' I said.

'I know who he was, I'm not *simple*. He's a ways younger than me is all.'

'And his day-brother, Jan, did you know him?'

'How could I?'

She was being pedantic, of course, but she had a point. I let the silence stretch, though made it clear my attention was still on her. She could only manage so long before she said, 'I told my sister not to bother with Jan. He was too up himself, that's what I told her.'

'She didn't listen?'

'Does your day-brother?' she said. She didn't wait for an answer. 'Jan acted like working up at the manor made him special, different from me and mine.'

'But he wasn't.'

'And he was too young,' she said. 'Didn't matter how pretty he was.'

I leaned forward. 'Did your day-sister become involved with Jan Harsson?'

'No! Ain't you been listening? I told her what's what – just took her a little while to see I was right. But nothing ever came of it.'

'I see. My apologies for keeping you.'

She wasn't too gentle with the door when she left. I made myself eat, though I was too distracted by the image of a handsome, healthy Jan Harsson to take any satisfaction from it. And besides, the beef was poor.

21st October 1721

Alexsander was nervous. I couldn't remember the last time I'd felt that from him; when we were both younger men, that was certain. His palms were sweating and he had to clear his throat twice before he found his voice.

He was standing in one corner of the common room, Mr Hennig having moved some of the tables to give him more space. He had his fiddle, and a small lute was leaning against the wall. I didn't know where he found that. He also had the attention of everyone.

Perhaps that was why he was nervous. In Esteberg he had grown accustomed to indifference. During the first song he played he looked about the audience and, unsettlingly, found them looking back. He made more mistakes than he cared to count. Still, they clapped.

As per Mr Hennig's request, Alexsander avoided the tragedies and solemn songs. He ran through the jaunty tunes he knew, choosing a number typically played at harvest festivals. These seemed well received, and he tried not to notice when people did get up to leave. He took his break with a hearty lunch – better meat than I'd been served – and a mug of ale. I'd not known him to drink ale. I could only assume it was part of some desire to experience customs and produce local to Drekenford, before his wickedly demanding night-brother took him away once more. Wickedly demanding – that was how he described me to a half-listening Mr Hennig. It was one of those inexplicably vivid and distinct memories I had of Alexsander's day.

As the afternoon wore on Alexsander returned to his corner. More people sat listening, eerily attentive. He noticed the painter sitting at a table with two women, who smiled encouragingly. The nerves of the morning were gone, and he played well – as far as I could tell.

When he finished, Alexsander joined the painter and his friends. They spoke openly and freely and of things of little consequence. How I envied that in him. He also drank too much, for which he was unrepentant. As his new friends left he took some air; the square was quiet as the sun began its descent. On the far side a man was packing away an accordion, stopping briefly to glare at Alexsander. He supposed he'd stolen the man's audience and made to apologise, but the man hurried away. Alexsander was more troubled by this than he'd like to admit. But I saw.

I was woken by someone pounding on the door of my room. I stumbled out of bed, head swimming with ale and my breath stinking of the same horrid swill. I unlocked the door and was startled to find Mrs Lehner, candle in one hand, still in her nightdress. I looked quickly away.

'Inspector!'

'Mrs Lehner, whatever is the matter?'

'There's been— It's, I mean, it's terrible!'

'Calm yourself. What is terrible?'

'They say he's dead. They say, they're saying such terrible things.' She had no colour to her and was close to fainting, right there, on the threshold of my room.

'Dead? Who, Mrs Lehner? We need to inform the constable.'

'That's it, Inspector, that's the thing of it. It *is* the constable.'

Saying it aloud was evidently too much for the woman. I saw her knees go from under her and she started to sink, like a scuppered ship. I managed to catch the candle before the whole inn went up in flames, but for Mrs Lehner herself all I could do was slow her fall. I made sure she was in no immediate danger before dashing back into my room to fetch some water, with which I roused the confused and embarrassed woman. With my aid she walked back to her room and I assured her she was safe.

'They're waiting, Inspector,' she said, eyes as large and white as the moon ever was.

'I'm sure the thirsty of Drekenford can wait a little longer tonight.'

'No, there's men waiting downstairs. For you.'

I dressed quickly, then found these men at the bar, one gripping the top with both hands. He looked pale, and I wondered if he was as unsteady as Mrs Lehner. Three of them, in all, in cloaks and hats and their mouths set in singular seriousness.

'Inspector,' one of them said, offering me his hand. I recognised him from my first night at the inn: Victor and Julia's father, Mayor Eder. He had a firm, confident grip, and a smoothly shaven face. His dark, intelligent eyes sized me up instantly. 'I'm sorry to disturb you at such an hour, for such a thing as this...' Eder shook his head, somewhat lost for words; a state he appeared unused to.

'Lead the way, Mayor.'

'Yes, yes,' he said, waving for the other men to hurry out of the inn.

The streets were deserted, curtains drawn in nearly every house we passed, and only the lamps of the bigger streets were lit. We walked in silence; I was glad to see the men solid on their feet. When we rounded a corner, the modest crowd standing outside the constable's office was quite a shock. I had assumed I was being taken to his home. I had also assumed I was among the first few people to have heard of the constable's demise. The chief inspector had a saying about assumptions: if one didn't kill you first, you'd still be making them on your death bed. The chief liked making up such things, and delivering them as if they were accepted wisdom.

Mayor Eder ordered people aside, and as the crowd parted I caught sight of the young boy, Victor, among them.

'You shouldn't be here, Victor,' I said. 'Don't you have an experiment to be working on?'

'But *I* found him,' the boy said.

I glanced at the mayor, who gave a small nod. I followed the other men into the constable's office.

The room was cold. Colder than outside, that was the first thing I noticed. I couldn't recall if I'd felt the same chill on my first visit. One of the men blew into their hands and I resisted the urge to do the same. Instead, I turned to examine the heavy door: its edges were intact, as was the lock, and there was no damage or sign of it being forced open.

Mayor Eder handed me a candle in a porcelain holder and more were passed between the men. We four were the only people inside, except for the constable.

'Victor found him in the dark?' I said.

Eder seemed surprised by the question. 'I don't know, Inspector. But I do know the room was dark when we arrived.'

'And that was...?'

'As soon as Victor had run home and raised the alarm, so to speak.'

'Does he usually rise so early?' I said.

'He's a child,' Eder said with a shrug, a gesture of helplessness in the face of the mysteries of children.

'He is *your* child, correct? A night birth?'

'Yes, though perhaps that is a matter for another time?'

I stepped further into the room. The fireplace was still full of ash, though a small stack of logs was neatly piled next to it. The desk was as tidy as I remembered and, peering to the back, the cells appeared to be in a similarly normal state. The constable's chair was a little way from the desk and at an angle, as if pushed back in a hurry.

'Nothing has been touched. Victor touched nothing,' Eder said, as I looked about the room.

The constable was beyond the desk. Curled up on himself, agony writ across his body as clearly as it was across his face. Constable Webber, dead, but bloodlessly so – which led me to wonder if the cause of death was a natural one. But I doubted if the mayor would send for me if that were the case. Still, there was no blood on the floor around the constable. No blood obvious on his body from where I stood; the work of a knife or pistol shot would have bled horribly. From the shape of him a severe blow to the stomach made some sense if there had been someone else involved. A blunt, heavy instrument might have struck him hard enough to kill, and kill him dry. But something about that seemed unlikely; perhaps how neat and normal the rest of the room looked.

I knelt beside the constable. 'He worked both sides of the ettiene, yes?' I said.

'That's right, alongside his history of the town,' Eder said.

The constable's skin was as pale as Death's horse. His eyes were bulging so far as to be trying to escape the man's face. He had yet to turn putrid, no smell of rot in the air even as close to him as I was. Perhaps he had not been dead very long, but that was not how it looked to me, and there was a strange smell about the body. It tickled the nose but I couldn't place it.

His mouth was closed tight but there was something on his lips, a little fleck of white. I moved my candle closer, thinking it might be spittle or a froth of a kind. I made a noise of surprise.

'What is it, Inspector?' Eder said, squatting down beside me.

With a fingernail I carefully lifted the little triangle of paper from where it lay crusted on the constable's lips. But, instead of coming away with my finger, the paper pulled at the upper lip – it was part of a bigger piece, a piece inside the constable's mouth.

I leaned in closer. The jaw wouldn't be moved easily, but I did manage to peel back the lips. His mouth was full of paper. Rolls, scraps, pages, and balls, all stuffed deeply into the constable's mouth and throat.

The mayor swore, invoking one or two of the lesser known saints.

With some effort I pulled a balled page from the constable's mouth, but there seemed to be no end of it. The paper was dry, and much of its ink was intact. I opened the page out. A small, tight script ran in lines from one side to the other.

'That's his hand,' Eder said.

I glanced up towards the desk, but that could wait until I'd made a full examination of the body. I put a hand on Eder's shoulder to be sure the man was physically sound and not about to faint.

As gently as I could I rolled the constable onto his back. His limbs were stiff, but I managed to move his arms enough to get a better view of him.

The constable's throat and chest were filled to bursting. His neck was swollen and distended. When I undid the buttons of his shirt numerous tumours pressed out, apparently only held back by his ribs, and his stomach was similarly engorged. Pressing and probing the man's stomach I found nothing but solid, firm resistance.

'Good God,' Eder said. 'What could cause such a thing?'

I leaned back on my heels and thought whether lying to him would be a kindness or not. Eder's men were edging round the desk, their curiosity getting the better of them.

'Send your men out,' I muttered, deciding to tell the mayor the truth. The truth, at least, as I saw it.

'Inspector?' Eder said, but after one look at me he told the men to wait outside.

When they had gone, I said, as plainly as I could, 'This was witchcraft.' I did so because I judged the mayor to be a man of sound sense, a man not likely to fall into panic or hysteria when encountering the darker arts.

He had clearly steeled himself against a wound, against a death, of the traditional kind. This was much different. His eyes widened somewhat, but otherwise he kept his composure, under the circumstances.

'Help me turn him over,' I said. If the mayor was unused to taking orders, the strangeness of the situation overrode his natural inclinations. But what was to come next, I knew, would be beyond the man.

I unfastened the constable's breeches at his waist and above his knees, and proceeded to lower them.

'Inspector Morden! What is the meaning of this?' Eder said, a hand raised to his mouth.

With no more relish than the mayor, I lifted the constable's shirt and prised apart the dead man's buttocks. A more invasive investigation proved unnecessary – paper was clearly evident and in just the same abundance as the rest of the body. I returned the breeches to their former position and stood.

'I do not think a full dissection will be necessary.'

Mayor Eder gave me a look of such bewilderment, of such shock, that I worried he was but a breath away from denouncing me as some kind of devil. I guided him to one of the chairs in the hallway, a little way from the former constable. I told Eder to breathe deeply and focus his gaze on his own hands: something familiar and solid and safe.

I left him there and returned to the desk. It did not take long to find what I sought: missing pages. The constable's ledger sat squarely at the centre of the desk, the most recent volume in his chronicle of Drekenford. Other, older volumes were arrayed on shelves on the far wall but I had strong doubts I would need to disturb their slumber. This was a matter of recent history.

The ledger on the desk covered the last twenty-five years. It struck me in that moment that Constable Webber not only maintained a history of his town but, more immediately, his own life, both sides of the ettiene. His was perhaps the most extreme form of sibling diary I had ever come across. If I knew the man more, I may have felt more willing to speculate if such a record was born of curiosity, diligence, paranoia, or something else.

Of the twenty-five years, fifteen were cut cleanly from the book. The final entry, however, was still there: the night of my meeting with the constable, which was recorded in efficient detail. Then the gap and the next intact page was dated fifteen years previous, to the day.

I looked over to where Constable Webber lay, pain still so evident in every part of his over-full body.

The law devours its history.

That line from the Ritual of Berith, that Custodian Ignatius had shown me in Esteberg Cathedral's library, was clearly evident here. It was too neat, too grotesquely literal, to be a coincidence. There were more conditions – that was Ignatius' word – for the ritual to summon the demon, but I saw no evidence of them that night. Even so, I would require the text itself: Bartrey's *History of the Baalimine*. The book with the serpent-spine that drew me so, among those darkened shelves. I would request Ignatius send the text to Drekenford.

So decided, I put Webber's ledger down but in my distraction I knocked over the desk's candle. Unlit, and almost new, it looked just like those sold at the night market. Going to pick it up I noticed something marred its smooth wax surface: little pinpricks, not particularly deep.

I walked back to the inn, accompanied by Mayor Eder and his son, Victor. With their help I had roped off the entrance to the constable's office and securely locked the door. There was still a small crowd of gawpers and gossipers that wouldn't be moved by our insistence that there was nothing to see and that all was under the control of the correct authorities. They clearly believed neither to be true.

I wanted to question Victor, as he was the one who found Constable Webber's body, which of course meant his father should be present. When I said as much, the mayor appeared surprised, and looked down at the boy as if seeing him for the first time. I brushed aside his flimsy protests of there being much to do, but as we approached the inn the mayor became quite restless.

'We will discuss matters privately, of course, Inspector. I take it you have a room?' he said.

'I do, but I believe sharing a meal in the common room would set fewer tongues wagging. Are you hungry, Victor?'

The boy nodded with conviction.

We settled ourselves at one of the more privately situated tables, which reassured Eder somewhat. A number of other tables were occupied by diners, and though we drew curious glances it was no more than I had come to expect in the Horse and Hound. Mrs Lehner herself came to take our order. I was glad to see her recovered from earlier that night.

'Sirs,' she said, even going so far as to bob a small curtsy. 'Are we dining tonight?'

'I hope there is something other than beef on the menu, Mrs Lehner?' I said.

She looked surreptitiously to the mayor, before saying, 'The wild duck is *particularly* good today.'

We followed our host's suggestion and also ordered wine, though water for Victor. Mrs Lehner lingered at our table, visibly struggling to phrase the question she so desperately wanted to ask. Rather than rescue her from this state, I felt that if the woman wanted her gossip then it should not come easy for her.

'Is it true, what they're saying about the constable? Is it— Does it look suspicious?' she said, the last little more than a whisper.

'Mrs Lehner,' I said. 'The—'

'The necessary arrangements are being made, with a funeral likely by the end of the week.' Mayor Eder had evidently recovered some of himself.

Mrs Lehner put a hand to her chest, her cheeks flushing in shock, but managing to stay on her feet this time. 'What is the world coming to?' she said, gazing intently at each of us in turn as if expecting a definitive answer.

'Its end,' Victor said.

None of us knew just what to make of that. Mrs Lehner, for her part, retreated to the familiar safety of her bar, the orders of food and drink, and the glasses that needed polishing. These she took to with some fury.

'Do you believe that, truly?' I asked the boy.

'It is my scientific opinion, yes.'

I raised an eyebrow at that, but Eder appeared utterly unsurprised by his son's answer. How they sat together in that moment, father and son, gave me the impression this was a subject discussed to the point of its banning in their household.

'Perhaps you might show me your findings one day?'

He graciously acquiesced.

'But for now,' I said, 'I'd like you to tell me how you found Constable Webber, and why you were there at all.'

'I found him as you did: dead,' the boy said, his calm and even tone indicative of curiosity rather than any fear or potential trauma. Victor seemed unfazed by his experience, but I knew that could change with time.

'And how did you know he was dead?'

'I kicked him.'

'Victor!' the mayor said. I raised a hand to forestall any fatherly admonishment – such a thing could be quite distracting.

'Why did you kick him?' I said.

'Because he wouldn't answer me. I thought he was asleep, or drunk; the constable liked to drink, even early at night.'

'Now, Victor, stop these lies,' Eder said.

'I have evidence.' Victor reached into his pocket and produced a little notebook. 'My day-brother and I keep a record of all our shared findings.' He showed me neat, ordered pages in notably different handwriting.

'You work together on your experiments, both sides of the

ettiene?' I asked, failing to keep the surprise from my voice. I could not imagine Alexsander and I working so harmoniously towards a shared goal.

'Of course,' Victor said. 'There is much of scientific interest that happens during daylight hours.' He flicked through the notebook. 'As to Constable Webber... "Tuesday, August 15th, observed Constable Webber at bridge. He did not walk straight."' He turned the page. '"Thursday, August—"'

'That's quite enough!' Eder whispered harshly, glancing about the inn. 'You should not speak ill of the dead.'

Victor wrinkled his nose at such superstition.

'The constable didn't notice you kicking him,' I said, returning to the boy's narrative.

'No. And I soon discovered he wasn't breathing, on account of the pages.'

I stared down at the boy, who calmly stared back – as cherubic as a young scientist could be. In that moment I found him quite terrifying.

'And the purpose of your visit?' I said, moving swiftly on.

'Delivering mother's invitation,' he said. 'I have yours here.' He pulled a letter from a different pocket than that of his notebook, and placed it on the table. I imagined there were a great many pockets to be found about the boy. I looked down upon the letter as if the pale dappled stock was really the striped skin of an adder, and the red wax seal its murderous eye. I made no move to pick it up, but the spell was broken somewhat by the arrival of Mrs Lehner and our food.

Victor took to dissecting the contents of his plate methodically, working from left to right with dispassionate efficiency. His father ate hurriedly. Such a waste: the wild duck was superb, in a light plum sauce, and definitely of better quality than the food I'd been served before. I made a note to request 'the mayor's choice' when I next ordered.

During the meal I continued to question the boy. He was always clear and concise with his answers, taking time to think when he required it, which was not often. He recalled in detail the state of the constable's office: which was *exactly* as it was when I arrived. He would have made an excellent inspector.

When the meal was finished, Mayor Eder removed his napkin from his lap and stood. 'Inspector, I hope to see you at my wife's dinner party,' he said, nodding to the invitation that still lay untouched on the table, 'and, I hope, not before. But should you have need, my office will always welcome an agent of the King.'

'His Majesty is most grateful, I'm sure,' I said.

'Yes, well, come Victor.'

I ordered another glass of wine. I wanted some company as I thought.

The good people of Drekenford flowed in and out of the common room, a little more subdued than I had seen them before but otherwise much the same. Friends were hailed, drinks hurried and savoured, and jokes were told – though more often than not the result was a wry chuckle rather than raucous laughter. I watched them all without really looking, and they offered me the same courtesy.

The framer was at the bar again, this time engaged in an animated discussion with what I could only assume was a friend. Mrs Lehner was periodically rolling her eyes while pretending not to eavesdrop. She was a complicated woman.

I spent the better part of an hour there, considering the nature of Constable Webber's murder. It was positioned undoubtedly alongside the *interference* of Jan Harsson. The most obvious conclusion, therefore, being that both acts were the work of the same perpetrator, towards the same purpose: fulfilling the conditions required for the Ritual of Berith. But I'd fallen foul of obvious conclusions before. It was, however, a troubling idea that there might be *two* persons in Drekenford capable of such cruel sorcery. So, I decided to proceed as if pursuing a single entity until the evidence demanded otherwise.

Victor's description of the constable's office and the state in which he found Constable Webber was somewhat helpful. The boy had been clear that the desk and its contents were just as I found them, and that this was the only part of the room that was in any disarray – excepting, of course, the constable. The damage to Webber's ledger was rather self-explanatory – the law devours its history – but what caused the marks on the candle was less clear. Victor had made no mention of them, and that was interesting enough in and of itself. I didn't want to ask any leading questions. Instead, I left that line of inquiry for a later date; the boy may have simply not noticed the candle at all, or didn't think it worth mentioning. But I had my doubts.

When I finished my wine I stood and retrieved Mrs Eder's invitation from the table top where, like the snake I'd imagined it to be, it seemed to have made a shallow burrow for itself among the plates. Crossing to the bar, I found the mayor had paid for my meal and only my second glass of wine had been added to my account.

'I would like to look at your candles, Mrs Lehner,' I said.

'Candles, Inspector? Whatever for?'

The surrounding conversations came to a rather unnatural lull.

'Do you keep a store?' I said.

'Out back, yes. Got a box of them. From the market.'

'May I?'

'I'll bring them right out,' she said. She appeared to recover swiftly from her surprise, and hurried now to be part of whatever romanticised view she'd formed of my work. Returning with a modest card box, she straightened her apron before leaning over the candles and staring at their perfect, creamy surfaces. To be sure, I picked each up and, turning them this way and that, found not even a scratch.

'Are they safe?' Mrs Lehner said.

'As safe as anything we set a flame to.'

That did not reassure her.

'May I check the room?' I said.

She was reluctant, but eventually gave her permission, saying, 'Discretion, though, Inspector?'

'Of course, Mrs Lehner.'

And so I made the rounds of the room's wall sconces, which held two or three candles each in various stages of their short, thankless lives. I did my best to give an air of casual wandering to my work, nodding and smiling to those sitting nearby, but inevitably I did not go unnoticed. Many patrons followed my progress with mild bemusement which, despite Mrs Lehner's fears, did not develop into any kind of panic.

At the penultimate sconce I met my match: a particularly stubborn, waxed-in candle that was determined not to bare itself. To gain a proper purchase on the thing I had to commandeer a chair to stand on, much to the confusion of the two farmers sitting at its table. With a good deal of wrenching and twisting and muttered curses the candle finally yielded, though it had the last laugh: no marks. Nothing but smooth wax on its backside, and the flows of wax down its front were as natural as rainfall. Having returned the candle, I stepped down from the chair and lost my balance.

Stumbling, I caught myself on the shoulder of one of the farmers. He gave a grunt of surprise, but was otherwise unaffected. Mrs Lehner was at my side in an instant.

'Are you... bewitched, Inspector?' she said in an urgent hush.

'I am quite all right, Mrs Lehner, thanks to this solid fellow.'

The farmer gave a gap-toothed grin.

Mrs Lehner followed me to the final sconce, unable to hide her concern. There I didn't require the aid of a chair, nor did I find anything untoward. I said as much to Mrs Lehner, who was much relieved.

'Might that be the end of it, Inspector?' she said.

'I doubt it, but do not burden yourself with worry. I'm quite sure you and the inn are safe.'

'Well, that *is* some good news.'

I retired to my room and wrote to the chief inspector, advising him of Constable Webber's death. I left out none of the details, grisly or mundane, and reassured him that my investigation was proceeding as could be expected with such a case. I acknowledged receipt of his letter advising me of the King's wish for a swift resolution before All Hallows' Eve and the arrival of the second regiment. I also gave a brief summary of Drekenford's more notable citizens. I did not mention my vision of the horsemen.

I wrote to Custodian Ignatius, courtesy of Esteberg Cathedral, and requested he send Bartrey's *History of the Baalimine* as soon as possible. I suggested he employ a King's courier, a cost I was willing to account for personally, and reassured him of both the safety of the road south and the trustworthy nature of my host here in Drekenford. I hoped I convinced him, as I sought to convince myself.

When I finally put down my quill and capped my ink the sky showed hints of dawn. I stood and stretched and was surprised to feel something in my pocket: Mrs Eder's invitation. My earlier, fanciful trepidation was gone and I now admired the expensive stock and neatly pressed seal. The front bore my name in long, elegant cursive that continued in the letter itself.

I was cordially invited to a formal dinner, in honour of my arrival in the town of Drekenford, on the evening of the coming Friday. I was then asked to provide a swift reply, and was wished a most happy stay in their humble, little town, signed Mrs Eder.

Below, almost as if a post script, there was something else. Written so small I had to peer at the blocky, un-shapely letters and found myself forming the words aloud in an attempt to read them.

'Baa— Baalim— Baalimbemine der Ith.'

Light began to seep from those letters as I finished reading them. They were close to the title of Bartrey's book, but not quite the same. Then, with a tearing sound, the letters started to peel away from the paper.

I dropped the letter and could only look on as, now

face-down, the paper twitched and jerked as more letters prised free.

They crawled out from the pale, straight edges; ts and fs pulling themselves along the floor, their crosses like arms. Os and es and as rolled towards me. Ls, capital and lower, lumbered forward. And then some started to climb the bed, stabbing the sheets with their more flared stroke ends. I stepped back as I realised this inked migration was coming directly towards me, and that they were growing.

The letters closed in. Those nearest, walking along the top of the bed, were six inches tall now and larger with every passing moment.

I felt the wall at my back. I had nowhere to go as a t, now two feet tall, pulled back its dagger-tipped arm and swung for my hip.

My disbelief, and the sheer absurdity of what I saw before me, froze me in place. I did not even brace myself for the coming impact. I watched, ready to feel the stiletto strike of the letter. In a flash of madness I wondered if it was one of the ts from my title.

The t sliced through my coat as effortlessly as sheers through silk. But, as it thrust deeper towards my skin it burst into a puff of black smoke. Other letters, grown larger still, made similar strikes against my person but met the same end. I flinched each time. And then I noticed a hotness against my chest: my crucifix. I pulled open my shirt as more of the animated ink ended itself against my ward. The plain wood of it glowed as if on fire, and was just as hot to the touch.

I pulled hard, breaking the necklace, and then thrust forward Christ on the cross. I will admit the act of exploding the would-be assassins generated an almost childish exhilaration in me; so much so I was cackling uncontrollably by the time I had banished them all and the paper lay still. I remained triumphantly manic for a good few minutes, prancing here and there in the room like a prize-winning cockerel. I stamped on the letter, waved the crucifix, and even jumped onto the bed as a kind of territorial claim.

After longer than I'd care to admit, I regained my breath and composed myself. I stepped down and smoothed my hair. A cloud of acrid smoke hung at the ceiling so I crossed to open the window and, using my now hole-ridden coat, did my best to clear the air.

With my crucifix still in hand, I picked up the letter from the floor. No more assailants sprang forth. Very few words remained intact, the cursive letters streaking sporadically and insensibly down the page. I looked for a pattern there, or words left behind, but quickly found none. The blocky words I had struggled to make out at the bottom of the page were gone, the letter now ending in Mrs Eder's almost complete signature.

I sat on the corner of the bed and stared at her name. It would be a crude practitioner of witchcraft that signed their name to their abominable arts – crude, or arrogant. However, I couldn't be sure that it was her hand that brought the ink to life; I couldn't be sure of anything, not really. Perhaps, had I still been writing my letter to the chief inspector, it would have been my own words that turned on me. I would attend Mr and Mrs Eder's formal dinner, but I would do so with open eyes and my crucifix firmly in place. It was no ordinary necklace, but blessed by his holiness the Archbishop of Reikova himself. I would grace the next collection plate I saw with every kreer about my person, that I promised.

I readied myself for sleep as best I could and chewed my ettiene for Alexsander's sake, but sleep would not come. I lay awake with the window still open despite the chill and stared up at the ceiling. Events had moved so quickly since I was called to Jan and Gregory Harsson's cell in Esteberg: travelling with the dragoons, the pox that afflicted them, my visions of the horsemen, the murder of Constable Webber, and now the infernal letter. I wondered, then, were they all connected in some manner – above my own direct or indirect involvement? Could the same dark arts that killed the constable have brought down a pox on the King's soldiers? As I considered their connection, I recalled the figure of Death on her way to the fort. It was her presence that led me to believe the pox was no normal, unfortunate affliction, but some part of a larger design. I couldn't help but think, once again, that the visions of the horsemen may have been warnings. Warnings against my interference. How many people had been harmed or killed because of my investigation? How many more would suffer?

But it was too late. I had no option but to continue through to whatever bloody end awaited me. Awaited us. I fell asleep apologising to my day-brother.

22nd October 1721

Tired, but not angry, Alexsander had some understanding of the events of the night before. Some understanding of their significance and their dangers. Ultimately, that was his relationship to my work and he'd learned long ago not to probe too deeply into its darker aspects. So, instead he ate a lavish breakfast that he told Mr Hennig I would pay for. I couldn't deny him that.

He didn't have to play that day; a small mercy. He made and discarded plans as he finished his coffee. It was a beautiful day, judging by the sunshine that invaded the doorway of the inn whenever a new patron came in, squinting left and right as they did so. One such patron was a friend of his friend: one of the women he'd spoken to. The more attractive of the two. She had a strongly defined jaw and rather flat set to her lips, though this effect was softened somewhat by loose locks of hair that appeared to have free reign to do as they pleased. She took a table right where he'd played the day before, and kept glancing at him, her thoughts as plain as if she'd shouted them across the common room. He could take only so much of that strange tension.

He walked over to her and she became flustered. His smile held genuine warmth as he apologised, he wasn't to play today. He distrusted the disappointment this news appeared to bring.

He was, however, going to take a walk. Perhaps she might join him? He needed a guide in this new town.

I knew that to be a lie, but she did not.

They walked through the square and she led him to her favourite part of town: the church. 'It's so peaceful,' she said.

He didn't deny it. But as he stared at the altar at the far end he felt a chill. 'It's such a fine day, would you mind if we worshipped the sunlight instead?'

They meandered through the church's graveyard in a respectful silence. Then, back in the street, she asked where else he would like to go.

'Your next favourite place,' Alexsander said.

She took him to the bridge into Drekenford, the bridge with the stone animals. It was, evidently, a day of favourites as they spent much time debating the merits of each animal. She liked the bear, though it was a shame one of its glass eyes was missing and still, after many years, had yet to be replaced. He enjoyed the playful mischief of the baboons – was that an unfair choice, as there were two baboons on the same plinth? She thought not.

They stepped aside as a cart rolled along the bridge. The driver bid her good day. As she raised her face to look at Alexsander, with the sunlight flooding her features, I finally recognised this much-changed woman. This was Mrs Eder's day-sister.

He recognised something else, something much more powerful.

They spent the rest of the day together, later calling on the painter. He was, in my opinion, a rascal. They found him shirtless on his balcony, with an open bottle of wine beside his dry paintbrushes. Alexsander and he were sure to be firm friends. I was also sure to be waking with a hangover, but I doubted it was by way of punishment. Alexsander simply enjoyed enjoying himself.

They spoke at length of art, music, literature, and other forgettable methods of passing the time. This was how he chose to distract himself from the harsher realities of life. Rebecca – that was Mrs Eder's day-sister's name – had been pleasant company when they were walking, but came somewhat to life as part of a group. She argued passionately that support of the arts was a civic duty, as important as sewerage or the constabulary. She was preaching to the choir, of course, but that did not detract from her zeal. A zeal she maintained while those around her grew steadily drunk.

As the day drew to an end, she helped Alexsander back to the inn. He was to play tomorrow, he said, and he hoped she would be there. She said she would.

I decided to look once more at Jan Harsson's file – the one given to me by the late Constable Webber. I lit my candle, first making sure it was unmarked. Perhaps this verged on paranoia, but given the last thing I read had tried to kill me I felt such caution was justified.

It was with some trepidation, then, that I opened the file. To my relief the constable's cursive was nothing like Mrs Eder's; instead scratchy, short letters jostled for space along faintly drawn lines. It took me a little while to become accustomed to the style but once I could see the pattern of it the reading became easier, though no more insightful. The details of the stolen silverware – the crime for which Jan Harsson was imprisoned – were carefully documented, as was where the silverware was found. Mayor Eder was noted as the victim. Nothing was mentioned of Mrs Harsson, the mother, nor of Mrs Eder's role in the affair. From my brief meetings with both women I had no doubt they would have exerted considerable influence on proceedings. Drekenford was so far a town that enjoyed keeping records, but it also enjoyed keeping its secrets.

If there was a connection between Jan's crime and the

murder of Constable Webber, beyond the employment of sorcerous powers, it was unlikely to be found in the constable's own files. His records and histories were concerned with facts, not secrets. But in this regard I did have one weapon in my arsenal. I descended to the common room and took a stool at the empty bar.

'Up early this evening, Inspector? I'm the same after cold days.'

'And why is that, Mrs Lehner?' I said, feigning concern.

'My day-sister, it is, curse the woman! Never thinking of me; her hands get so sore, I end up pained the night through.'

'How dreadful. Just what does your day-sister do to get sore hands?'

Mrs Lehner tutted. 'She washes sheets – ours and the inn's and others' – says she likes it, simple work she says. But it's both of us that suffer for it.'

'I know exactly what you mean,' I said.

'Oh, from what I hear your day-brother is just wonderful.'

'But what he does to our *hands*; the callouses alone, Mrs Lehner. I think we share that kind of suffering, you and I.'

She beamed like a praised child.

'Awful business with Constable Webber,' I said. 'I'm sure you've heard.'

'Just awful,' she echoed.

'I only met him briefly, but he struck me as a warm, gentle man—'

'Oh, he was!'

'—and it's hard to wonder who would wish him such harm.'

Mrs Lehner nodded sagely. 'It's a hard lot, isn't it, Inspector? Hard to keep friends *and* keep the peace.'

'Eloquently put, Mrs Lehner. Would you say the constable lost many of his friends?'

'Over the years, I suppose he did. We had him in here, of course, from time-to-time. He and Stefan saw a lot of each other, if you understand my meaning, but then they had what you could call history.' She was enjoying this conversation far too much for my liking and, worse still, I was only to benefit from it.

'Stefan, that is the framer, yes? He and Constable Webber had problems?'

'Of the lady-kind. Of the only kind, really,' she said. 'She chose the constable.'

'I wasn't aware Constable Webber was married.'

'Widower. And that was the constable's fault too, depending on who you asked.'

'I see.' I tried to recall if Alexsander had been inside the framer's shop, or if he had seen anything in the painter's home that might be of use. But the memories were thin on detail and dominated by the strangeness of seeing the same painting over and over: I had an almost complete picture of *that* room. 'What of Mrs Harsson?' I said.

'Anna? Well, there was some bad business with her son. But he was sent away. Up north, I think it was, to...'

Mrs Lehner experienced an almost religious epiphany in that moment. It hit her with such force that she actually staggered, catching herself on the bar, and seemed to struggle under the weight of her own grin. I had, as my day-brother would say, over-played my hand.

'That's why you're here,' she whispered. 'Jan. Or was it Gregory?'

There was no use denying it; that would only fuel Mrs

Lehner's already blazing fire of curiosity. 'I know I can trust you with my secret, Mrs Lehner.'

She had the gall to nod seriously. 'Anna's a good woman. Don't let that hardness of hers fool you. She wept for weeks when her boy was gone.'

'And the constable? How did Mrs Harsson feel about him?'

She glanced to the door. We were still alone in the common room. 'Things were said. But that was just a mother's grief.'

'Gregory didn't die.'

'Sent so far away? It's as good as,' she said. I had to concede the truth of that.

I had my first leads. To call them suspects would be far too premature, but it was satisfying to finally be peering a little deeper into the depths of Drekenford and its community. All I had heard about the town before I arrived, from eminent Esteberg citizens such as the chief inspector and Brother Ignatius, was dismissive at best, disparaging at worst. I was starting to see first-hand that there was more to the town than northern prejudices might allow, both for good and for ill.

I returned to the constable's office, wanting one last look at the site of Constable Webber's demise. In part I was concerned that I had missed something, perhaps distracted by the strange and gruesome nature of the crime. And, following my conversation with Mrs Lehner, I was also interested in finding any materials pertaining to either the framer Stefan or Mrs Harsson herself.

I was pleased to find the cordon remained outside the constable's office, pleased too to see the crowd was gone and that one of the mayor's men was standing guard. His breath fogged the air and he was well-layered against the chill. He clearly recognised me and granted me entrance without so much as a hello. In fact, he made every effort not to look me in the eye. As he closed the door behind me, I wondered if the mayor had failed to keep tales of my examination of Constable Webber to himself.

There was a single lit candle by the door. I took it but did not light more. I wanted to see the room in small, four-foot square sections; that way I could focus on one thing at a time without distraction.

The hallway, where I had sat waiting when I first met the constable, was still empty except for its chairs. These were old and scuffed and more than one was damaged in some way. Leaning closer, I noticed they were the same chairs as those of the inn's common room.

I pressed on, finding the desk in the same disordered state as the night before. However, the constable's seat had been tucked back under. I thrust my candle forward to find an empty floor, and the constable's body gone. Rightly so, of course, but I should have been notified and advised where it was being taken to; I may yet have needed to examine the body again. I hoped the mayor and his men had not taken any further liberties without my consent.

Moving to the other side of the desk, I began leafing through its rather chaotic contents. The drawers were stuffed full of papers, files, and spare bottles of ink. The top of the desk was similarly burdened, and in no way organised that I could see; though I had long ago come to accept that one man's chaos is another man's order. Lifting stacks of paper revealed more pages, dried-out quills and, in one instance, a rotting apple core. If anything was to be gleaned from

Constable Webber's desk, it was that the man bore the wrong title: Archivist, Librarian, Chronicler even, would have been more accurate. I had to search long and hard before I found evidence of his work as a man of the law, and then I almost mistook the report of drunken behaviour as a potted history of a Mr Perlak's family's misfortunes.

All this mess also served to highlight the strange, calm oasis at the very centre of the desk, where the fallen, marked candle lay alongside the damaged ledger. To call them 'murder weapons' would have been difficult in front of a judge or magistrate, but that was my impression as I stared down at them in the weak light.

I carefully picked up the ledger and opened it. I skimmed through the ten years of Drekenford history that remained intact, but found nothing concerning either Stefan or Mrs Harsson. In fact, I found little of note concerning *anyone*. What possessed a man to record the intricate banalities of the everyday? I read his account of our meeting, noting the detail in which he described my clothing and manner. Apparently these marked me as remarkable – a foreign oddity was the implication, if it was not plainly stated. I smiled grimly at that.

Finding nothing of use in the ledger, I went to examine the candle once more. A seed of doubt had started to take root: had I really seen pinpricks in it the other day?

But as I touched its hard, slick surface I was overcome with dizziness.

I staggered, only just managing to catch hold of the chair and then fall into it before I went careening to the floor. I closed my eyes and tried to take steadying, deep breaths.

I saw the constable. I saw the candle. I saw them both, as

one, their image flickering interchangeably as they fell, rigid, to the stone floor.

Opening my eyes, I waited as the dizziness passed. As a young man I knew nothing of visions. But over my years as a Special Inspector I had experienced them with increasing frequency. Though I did not speak of it to anyone, not even my colleagues, the visions were often a boon: the forces I encountered were regularly beyond the realms of normal sight. The phrase 'it requires a thief to catch a thief' is not particularly popular with the constabulary. Its equivalent for my line of work is unheard of, unspeakable, and yet ever-present. I was not a witch. I caught and executed witches. But... was the power of my crucifix so different from that which animated inked letters? Were my visions so different from augurs drawn from flames, from water, or from darker sources? I shook such heretical thoughts from my head.

Feeling somewhat recovered, I turned to the floor by the desk and examined the flag stones individually. Before long I found what I was looking for: two small flecks of wax, and a streak as long as a finger. This is where the candle fell. Just a few feet from where the constable's body was found. My strange vision linked the two. Perhaps the candle was a conduit of sorts; a means of triggering the constable's grisly fate. And the dizziness it caused me could have been some remnant of that sorcery. Either way, the vision suggested the candle was of some significance. In all my years, they had yet to fail me in that regard.

There was also one other important, troubling aspect of the fallen candle: someone had returned it to the top of the desk.

Victor had made no mention of doing so, and I had no

reason to doubt the boy. That left the mayor and his men, and of course anyone who entered the constable's office without my knowledge and prior to my arrival. That was not a comforting thought.

Reluctant to touch the candle with my bare hands and risk triggering the dizziness again, I put on my gloves and cast around for some suitable container. In one of the drawers I found a pounce pot of good size and, sitting squarely on the chair, transferred the candle to the centre of the pot. The lid would not fit fully, but it was secure enough not to spill the pounce's fine powder all along the street; I planned to inspect the candle thoroughly in the relative safety of my room.

On my way back through the streets of Drekenford I made a resolution to face something I had been putting off: a visit to Fort Seeben. It would be easy to tell myself I had been too busy to go, that the investigation took precedence, but it would be a flimsy veil for my cowardice. In reality, the fort was an important part of that investigation.

I had so far thought it fortunate the pox had not spread from the fort to the town. Now I wondered if there were darker forces at work, either deliberately or inadvertently keeping Drekenford safe. If the pox itself was sent by witchcraft to afflict the King's Dragoons, perhaps the same sorcery stopped its transmission to the civilians living in the town? I had never heard of such a control of disease or pestilence. But then there was much about this case that, despite my years, gave me the feeling of treading new ground. If only I had Ignatius' library at my disposal… Instead, I endeavoured to see the fort, and the extent of the pox's ravages, for myself.

I made for the alley behind the inn, and then the stables. I passed a few awkward minutes as the stablewoman readied Tabitha; she refused my offer to help, having come to the correct judgement that I was less than capable with horses. Despite my insistence it was unnecessary, she walked me out of the alley. I did not give her the satisfaction of looking back.

Tabitha was, I believed, pleased to be out of her stall. Alexsander had the leisure hours with which to visit the mare, but I couldn't recall if he took her out particularly often. He liked to walk, alone or with company. I let Tabitha set our pace for the most part, only pulling her up once to let a cart join the main thoroughfare. This cart was painted gaudy colours and full of autumn produce.

We crossed the animal-bridge and, for the first time since making my resolution, I glanced up at my destination. Fort Seeben, raw as any scar I'd seen in my days, offered no kind of welcome. At least the pyres were no longer burning.

I pulled Tabitha to a halt at the fork in the road, alongside the strange stone marker – the long-legged house, as I thought of it. Someone had left a modest bunch of wildflowers at its base. I pondered the gesture as we climbed the winding track through the trees. As an offering to the fort, for what had become of the soldiers, it was almost insultingly small – there should have been fields and fields of flowers for their fallen. Rather, it appeared a more personal act. Mrs Lehner had mentioned soldiers visiting the inn on rare occasions. I would ask the colonel, if I was permitted an audience, if any of his soldiers had been known to form... attachments with the citizens of Drekenford.

I was quite relieved to be alone on the track. The steady sound of Tabitha's hoof beats echoed among the trees and went some way to dispel the eerie silence of those evergreens. I had to assume that all manner of beasts made a home of this forest but I had yet to see or hear any evidence of them myself. As far as I was concerned it was as dangerously barren and inhospitable as any desert, and it was this feeling that gripped me as the fort came into view. I understood, then, that the building of Fort Seeben was not just a kingdom's attempt to defend itself, but an attempt to tame its own landscape.

Yet in a month's time it would be more still: the staging post for an attempt to expand, to gain new lands to tame. The King's mad grab for greater domain, greater glory, all in the name of Reikova. To my mind, the only possible outcome for such a campaign was disaster, and I did not need any biblical visions to see that. The very lands of the south resisted northern control or influence, let alone the people themselves. A small consolation: I would be back in Esteberg well before the campaign began in full. I was just a witness to the King's opening manoeuvres.

The gates of the fort were closed. I was hailed by an unseen sentry, hidden somewhere along the wall despite the torches there. I gave my name and rank and requested an audience with the colonel. I was made to wait. It started to rain, which set the torches hissing and spitting; roughly the welcome I expected from the place.

Without sign or warning the fort's doors opened. Cornet Pitzmun stood there alone, small in that frame, small in the rain. If she was War, the second of the horsemen, she was much diminished in this place.

'Inspector,' she said by way of greeting. She looked haggard, with none of her previous enthusiasm or joviality. She was so changed I wondered if I'd been in Drekenford for years, rather than days. I didn't know what to say to the woman, so we proceeded to the main building in silence.

The colonel was, to my surprise, *not* reading a Romance when I entered his office. Instead, he was hunched over his desk consulting a number of different maps. He was squinting despite how well-lit the room was; poor eyesight being a hazard of habitual reading. I often struggled with the finer parts of maps myself.

When Cornet Pitzmun failed to announce me, I cleared my throat politely. The colonel didn't look up. Once again, I waited – though at least this time I was out of the rain.

Eventually, the colonel slumped back awkwardly in his chair and waved me forward.

'Inspector Morden. Still here, I see.'

'Yes, sir,' I said, remembering the colonel's odd approach to questions. 'I'm relieved to be able to say the same for you and your dragoons.'

'Are you now?' He suddenly stared intensely at me.

'The pox, sir,' I said.

'Yes... Those were a dark few days.'

'It's gone?'

'Along with a quarter of our number.'

'A fourth,' I said softly, glancing to Cornet Pitzmun. The woman remained standing to attention.

'What brings you here, Inspector?' the colonel said.

'My investigation,' I said. 'For a case such as this I need to understand every aspect of the town, of the community.'

'And you believe Fort Seeben is part of that community?'

'Don't you?'

'No,' the colonel said.

'But soldiers *do* visit the town, correct?'

'Not presently, for obvious reasons, but yes. In the past officers have been granted leave to spend an evening as they wish. I understand some chose to do so in Drekenford, though I have always discouraged it.'

'Why is that?'

He sighed, as a parent might when asked by a child why the wind blows, why leaves fall from trees, or why they can't remember everything their brother or sister does.

'This southern border is about to become a site of conflict.'

'I have heard of the second regiment,' I said, 'that is to arrive at the end of the month.'

'And badly needed they are too. How long this campaign will last, I cannot say, and I doubt the King himself knows. Nor does he, in his infinite wisdom, know what resistance the southern tribes will *really* present. Perhaps the town of Drekenford will be spared. Perhaps not. It is a mark on a strategic map; that is how my officers must view it.'

'I assumed the majority of the fighting would take place far from here,' I said. 'Drekenford is just a staging post, is it not?'

'Aye, for now. But with war, who is to say?' He stabbed a finger at his desk. 'I am not such a fool as to think we'll march a hundred miles south of here, and find the most taxing task the re-drawing of my maps!'

'Why go south at all?' I said, emboldened by the colonel's own fervour.

But I had misjudged the moment. The colonel cooled, his face no more animated than the animals of Drekenford's bridge.

'Though I may not personally appreciate the King's

motivations,' he said, 'it is my duty to enact them in the field. I would remind you of your own duty, Inspector.'

I considered, then quickly dismissed, a number of retorts – many of which were really accusations. I wasn't there to debate military procedure or the larger, philosophical points of warfare, even if biting my tongue left a bitter taste. Instead, I did as the colonel asked and returned the conversation to matters of my duty.

'Since our arrival,' I said, 'you're sure no officers have visited the town?'

'Quite certain. Those unaffected by the pox were far too busy.'

'How many officers died?' I asked.

The colonel was quiet for a moment, and I wondered if my question had been too blunt, callous even. But then this was a man who condensed the lives of hundreds of people to a 'mark on a map'.

'Five officers,' he said, eventually. 'The troopers fared worse.'

'Could I have the officers' names?' I said, thinking of the flowers laid at the bottom of the track. It seemed likely that whoever had left the flowers now mourned one of those five soldiers – a former officer's sweetheart.

'If you must. Cornet Pitzmun will provide you a list.'

'And when were the dragoons last stationed at Fort Seeben?' I said.

'Our rotations are every six months, Inspector. Now, if there is anything else?'

'I'd like to see it.'

The colonel frowned. 'See what?'

'Where you burned the bodies.'

The Cornet was also given this duty. She led me down the stairs and out into the night. The rain had stopped, the sky even clearing a little to show patches of stars. We passed where Tabitha was hitched and I patted the mare in what I hoped was a reassuring manner.

The fort was unnervingly quiet; between our footsteps the only sound I heard was my own breathing. I began to wonder if I'd misunderstood the colonel, and that it wasn't a quarter of his soldiers that had died, but a quarter was all that remained. When I mentioned the quiet to Pitzmun she shrugged.

'Most of the regiment is out training,' she said.

'In the forest?'

'Where else?'

This wasn't the time nor the place to discuss my dislike of southern trees. Though what I saw on the far side of the fort did little to help my antipathy towards them.

We passed through a single door, much smaller than the main gates, yet still guarded. The trooper nodded to Pitzmun and passed her a torch. I stepped out into a small clearing, where the treeline had been pushed back from the fort walls – a kind of no man's land. The ground was scarred and uneven and strikingly beautiful.

'I didn't realise there had been snow,' I said, before I could think, before I could stop myself.

Pitzmun's silence was as damning an admonishment as any I'd had since my childhood. But that was how it looked: like snow. It coated the jagged rise and fall of the pocked earth. It frosted the branches of pine for a good fifty yards in either direction. There was no breeze to stir it, to dislodge it, or move it on from this place; and a caustic, harsh smell dominated even that of the pine.

I glanced at Pitzmun. I saw, in the tightness at the corners of her lips and the dazed look to her eyes, that the young woman was struggling against the horror of what lay outside the fort. A constant, coldly picturesque reminder of what they'd had to do.

'The fires burned for days,' she said, in barely a whisper. 'You wouldn't think it took so long, but it does.'

She told me how the dragoons had dug pits, lined them with wood, and laid their comrades to rest. From Pitzmun's description I had no doubt the process was managed with the utmost respect and compassion for their fellows-in-arms. But they had not expected the ash.

'I've seen pyres,' Pitzmun said, shaking her head. 'Just as many bodies, if not more, burned. Never seen anything like this.'

I'd thought the airlessness of the forest to blame for the covering. But a gust of wind rose then, strong enough to sway the treetops and their branches below, but not the ash. I knelt and rubbed some of it between my fingers. It wasn't particularly sticky and crumbled at my touch as any ash would.

'The colonel won't come down here, not since the flames went out,' Pitzmun said.

I stood and stared at the strange scene before me. So still, so pristine despite its awful origin; I felt as if I stood at the foot of an enormous painting. A winter painting, as cold and callous and unrepentant as the season itself.

'What is to be done about it?' I said.

'Done?' Pitzmun said. 'Nothing. Even if the colonel could give the order to clear it, even if he thought such a thing possible, none of the troopers would do it. Would you?'

'No, I suppose not.'

'Whatever— Whoever's responsible, it's an evil thing to do.'

I agreed. 'The sword shrivels to flakes of snow.'

'What's that, sir?'

'Something I read, before I journeyed south.'

I recalled Ignatius, the library, and the Ritual of Berith with its conditions: the unfaithful lose sight of themselves. The sword shrivels to flakes of snow. The law devours its history. The stone moves on water. The broken heart bleeds gold.

There could be no longer be any doubt: the witch I sought was enacting the Ritual of Berith, one condition at a time, and in as ghastly a manner as was available to the imagination. First Jan Harsson's eyes, then Constable Webber's inexplicable demise, and now the unnatural ash.

I felt certain this scene, this gruesome tableau, was the very reason the soldiers were afflicted by the pox in the first place. So much death and suffering of the King's 'sword', so they were reduced to flakes of ash, to flakes like snow.

I *needed* Ignatius' book if I had any hope of pre-empting the ritual.

We returned to the main building and I was glad to be away from the trees. We passed the rows of empty tents. None of them were fastened with red rope, but then events had gone beyond that. A quarter of the dragoons dead, before they'd even made it to the border, before they'd even seen a southern tribesman. The King would not be pleased.

Pitzmun excused herself to fetch me the list of dead officers. I waited beside Tabitha, stroking the mare's side – more for my benefit than hers. She was solid and calm and dependable. I felt I was none of those things. The ashes had shaken me. Someone was keeping them frozen like that, among the trees, though I didn't fully understand how. Or, more worryingly, *why*. It seemed to be a kind of punishment, as if the soldiers hadn't suffered enough under the sorcerous pox. But why? Was keeping those ashes in place necessary for the ritual? That seemed unlikely. Instead, it felt more like a kind of cruel punishment – punishing the soldiers and, perhaps, me.

Pitzmun returned and gave me a slip of paper with the five names. Five officers, one of whom had a sweetheart in the town of Drekenford. I recognised none of the names, of course, and Pitzmun said her own officer was blessedly still among the living. She expressed this with such an earnestness I almost offered her a fatherly embrace, but managed to stop myself before I embarrassed us both.

I led Tabitha to the gate and bid the Cornet farewell. 'At least I won't be meeting any carts on the track this time,' I said.

'Carts, sir?'

'From the town. A strange woman, she said she was coming to help you with the pox.'

'We've had no visitors from town. Not at night, nor during the day, which I would say is just as well.'

'But... I spoke to her. I couldn't have imagined it – Tabitha didn't like her horse, she kept stamping the ground.'

'Perhaps she turned back,' Pitzmun said.

'Perhaps.' I looked down the dark track.

'Safe journey, sir.'

The gates of the fort closed behind me. I tried to calm my nerves. I led Tabitha along the track, between the ash-less trees, with one hand on her bridle and the other gripping my pistol.

23rd October 1721

Alexsander woke to find himself staring down the barrel of my pistol. I had left it on the bedside table; carried it all the way from the fort, through town, into the inn, and up to my room. I had still held it as I undressed, shifting my aim from the door to the desk, where the bible lay in silent judgement. I didn't trust any written word in that room. If it weren't for the ettiene he would have come to jarringly, sitting up in bed, pistol in hand. I have never professed to be a good night-brother.

He washed, taking extra care with our hair. He worried at the darkening bags under our eyes but had not brought anything to cover them. My fault. Chewing fresh mint, he dressed in one of our finer coats and descended to meet that day's audience.

Two men were sitting at the bar, where Mr Hennig was pouring one of them a drink. The rest of the room was empty. Alexsander ate breakfast, remaining hopeful. One of the men left. The other followed suit when Alexsander began tuning his lute.

'What's wrong?' he asked Mr Hennig.

The innkeeper shook his head.

'Where is everyone?'

'Some days are just like this,' Hennig said.

Alexsander slumped onto a stool at the bar. 'You're lying to me,' he said. 'Though I'm not sure why.'

'It's idle talk, that's all,' Hennig said. 'Idle talk of superstitious folk. Won't last.'

'About my night-brother?'

'We just don't get many of his sort, this far south, not this far from the capital.'

'We've been to remote towns and villages before,' Alexsander said. 'Drekenford can't be so different.'

'Can't it?' Hennig said. 'If you ask me, and you *are*, I'd say it's something about the shape of this town. Huddled in a valley as it is, tall, dark trees on either side. That gets to some folk. Even so, they'll get thirsty soon enough.'

'But what are they saying?'

Hennig looked uncomfortable, almost squirming, under Alexsander's gaze; it was strange to see such a large man act so. 'Just that he's bad luck, is all. That he went to see the constable and now the constable's dead. That sort of thing. Don't you pay it no mind.'

'They're right,' he said. 'My night-brother *is* bad luck. And I get the worst of it.'

'I won't be putting you out,' Hennig said. 'Just maybe not asking you to play, not until things settle a little.'

'And if I play in the square, will that empty too?'

Hennig shrugged.

Alexsander walked out of the inn, his instruments left behind. It was a grey, dull day, and there Rebecca was: sitting on a bench directly in front of the inn. She smiled and he forgot many of his frustrations.

'May I join you?' he said.

'I don't know. They say you're dangerous.'

'Only when made to play the harp,' he said.

'Oh?'

'It is a sound that cannot be unheard.'

'I like the harp,' she said.

'You were waiting for me.'

'So were they.' She nodded towards the inn where a handful of men were scurrying inside, each glancing at Alexsander as if he might try to stop them.

'In a larger town such a reputation would be a boon,' he said. 'I'd be an attraction.'

'Are you used to those things? Reputations? Attractions?'

'I have some understanding of them.'

'And turnips?' Rebecca said.

'Turnips?'

'They're a kind of vegetable.'

He laughed. 'I've eaten one or two – never cooked one, though.'

She lifted a basket to her lap. 'My confession: I was really waiting for the market.'

He accompanied her to the stalls, where he was utterly useless and she, she was ruthless. She bartered with every trader over the price of vegetables, honey, and sewing thread.

'If I ever need to buy a horse,' he said, in the calm between stalls, 'remind me to let you do it.'

'If you ever have the *means* to buy a horse, I'll certainly oblige.'

Before he could reply she turned to engage a harassed-looking woman over a tray of candles. He felt a sudden, inexplicable urge to take the candle from her hand. Not sure what he was looking for he turned it over, this ordinary-looking candle of dull yellow wax.

Both women were staring at him.

'Fine work,' Alexsander managed to say. They returned to their haggling.

He wandered among the small crowd of the market,

pleased that his reputation had not yet grown enough to put people off their necessities, as it had their ale. He stopped to admire some hand-worked goods: exceptional craftsmanship of household items all carved in wood and finely polished. The stall displayed smaller goods in the front, with larger items such as bookcases and wardrobes behind. He found himself enchanted by the simple but pleasing designs.

'Do you make instruments?' Alexsander asked.

The small man running the stall shook his head. 'Nothing so fine as that.'

'You are too modest. These are exquisite.' Alexsander picked up an intricately carved wooden chain, made of interlocking pieces, which had a spoon on each end. 'I've never seen the like. What is it?'

A small cough made him turn around. Rebecca was shaking her head.

'It's a wedding spoon,' the craftsman said, with a knowing grin.

Alexsander gave a cry and almost dropped the spoon, only just catching it before it hit the stone cobbles. He quickly replaced it on the stall and backed away, brushing his hands on his coat as if he'd touched something infectious.

'Don't worry,' Rebecca said, 'I'll make sure you get a good price.'

'That's quite al—'

'Sebastien,' she said to the stall-holder, 'my friend here is a poor, penniless musician. But as you can see he is not a man devoid of good taste.'

'He's the inspector's day-brother.'

'A thankless role,' Rebecca said. 'Maybe one day he'll find the peace and sanctuary of a good marriage.'

Sebastien regarded Alexsander carefully, then named a price for the spoon.

Rebecca set to work. Alexsander found the whole thing rather excruciating, but he couldn't leave. After an insufferable few minutes, a price was agreed that was almost half of the original figure. Alexsander handed over the coins as much to be away from the situation as anything else – his cheeks could not stand such a burning much longer. He was relieved to find the spoon was well wrapped so as to be hidden.

As they walked away from the stall, Rebecca slipped her arm through his.

'You are nothing but mischief,' he said. 'What am I going to do with a wedding spoon?'

'It's for a future attraction.'

I took the list of officer names to my best source of common knowledge: Mrs Lehner.

The bar was beginning to fill up. It was early evening and the light outside had already fled. Autumn nights were not my favourite – they teased of the warmer summer and promised nothing but the coming of winter. I found it a capricious and insolent season, without the honesty of what came before or after, and without the hope of spring. Alexsander liked the colours of the leaves.

Despite the press of thirsty men and women at the bar, Mrs Lehner was more than ready to assist me once again. She made a great pantomime of looking seriously at the meagre scrap of paper.

'How are your hands tonight, Mrs Lehner?' I said.

'My hands?' she said, clearly surprised by my question. Then she remembered our previous conversation. 'My hands, yes, sore again tonight, Inspector. But what can I do? My day-sister just won't listen to reason.'

'I'd say it's a rare thing – reason that is – during daylight hours,' I said. I gestured to the paper. 'Do you happen recognise any of those names?'

'Recognise them? Why, of course.' She nodded furiously. 'Willa, yes, she's a lovely, kind girl. Karl is a day-boy, but Mr Hennig always has a good word to say about him. Oh, Felicity is a *hard* woman. Always sits alone, she does.'

'Yes, Mrs Lehner, but—'

'Don't know this... what does this say here, is it Matherson?' She held the list out to me.

'I believe so,' I said. 'Second Lieutenant Matherson.'

'No. Never known a Matherson, Summer Lieutenant or otherwise.'

'Second Lieutenant.'

'What's that, Inspector?' she said, raising her voice and leaning over the bar. It was growing increasingly busy and loud in the common room. I thanked Mrs Lehner for her help. I missed her reply, but not her conspiratorial wink.

I hurried to the door; it was about time I paid a visit to Mayor Eder. I still had questions about his son, Victor, and I also wanted to know what had become of Constable Webber's body.

The streets were also busy that evening. Where they narrowed beyond the square I had to press between groups of labourers and workmen, muttering my apologies. They turned to stare at me. On the bigger roads I saw carts of them on their way out of town to the fields and forest beyond. Harvest labourers, I supposed, though in all honesty I knew little of what that actually meant. I assumed it was the stacking of straw bales, digging up vegetables, mending fences, that sort of thing. The kind of work that needed strong shoulders and leathery hands; I felt strangely conscious of my lack of either. I pulled my hat lower and picked up my pace.

As I walked I wondered at the little puzzle of Second Lieutenant Matherson. That he was unknown to Mrs Lehner, who kept a hawk-like vigil over her little field and all the thirsty mice that frequented it, was telling in of itself. An officer who, according to the list the Colonel provided me, made the journey from fort to town but did *not* visit the inn. In my understanding of soldiers – of people of any kind – the most likely motivation, if not drink, was a carnal one. Was Matherson the kind of officer to visit a whorehouse, or did he have a sweetheart in Drekenford?

Sweetheart. That thought triggered another: could one of the officers been involved, romantically, with Jan Harsson? I remembered Mrs Harsson's reluctance to talk of the subject. Would such a match have been the source of shame, of scandal? Perhaps if the officer in question had not been someone of the church, or they had gone to bed before marriage, or if the officer was a man and Mrs Harsson did not approve? I stopped myself. There were so many reasons for a relationship to be frowned upon, especially in a small town like Drekenford. But it was a possibility worth bearing in mind.

Mayor Eder's office was in the westernmost part of the town, an area that had an altogether quieter, more restrained character. Homes were tastefully decorated, streets well-swept and in good repair. On the neat pavements I met only governesses, either pushing large prams with well-wrapped parcel-babies or leading a string of eerily silent children. Eder's office was a large building fronted by substantial columns and a manicured lawn. My footsteps echoed on the polished stone of the entrance hall, where a great number of lamps – lamps, not candles – worked alongside large mirrors to dispel much of the evening's gloom. I spoke to an excitable young woman at a desk, who appeared positively crestfallen that I did not have an appointment.

'I'm sure the mayor would find a minute or two for me,' I said.

'He is *terribly* busy.'

'I don't doubt it. Upstairs I assume?' I started towards the huge winged staircase.

'Excuse me, sir! Sir? Ex*cuse*—'

'That's quite all right, Sophia,' the mayor called. He stood at the top of the stairs, one large hand resting on the balustrade like a count in his castle. A substantial pipe smouldered in his other hand.

I took off my hat and ascended, neck craned under his mayoral majesty. I found him much transformed from our previous meetings, the events surrounding which had shaken him. Now, he was on significantly firmer ground.

'Inspector Morden,' he said, his bass voice somehow managing to fill that enormous space. 'I hope no new disaster brings you to my door?'

'Not new, no, just the ongoing.'

'Well, in that case, you had best come in.' He gestured me through the large glass panelled doors. I entered a comfortable office that would have been the envy of any Esteberg official.

A soft, deep carpet was a welcome change to the cold stone, though the southern preference for dark wood and brass fittings was still evident. Brooding portraits of men and women of a mayoral bearing stared down at me as I sat.

'Do you mind?' Eder said, waving his pipe.

I told him I did not. And then he simply stared at me in silence for what could only have been half a minute, though it felt much longer. I withdrew my notebook with a deliberate care and wet the end of my pencil. I rarely had need of it, happily able to rely on an excellent memory for detail, but I found it useful for the impression it gave certain people: an atmosphere, or shared understanding, that what was said was being recorded and was part of my investigation. This established, the *absence* of the notebook could be just as useful.

'I just have one or two questions,' I said. 'You'll have to forgive me if they seem rather strange, or disconnected – this investigation has, as you know, grown more complex.'

'I see. Well, I will help in any way I can,' he said.

'I would like to see the constable's body again,' I said.

'I'm afraid that's impossible. His funeral was yesterday, Inspector. I'm terribly sorry, I assumed you'd known.'

'A small service at the church?'

'Exactly so.'

I pretended to make a note of this.

Eder frowned. 'He was buried in a family plot; the Webbers are a well-respected part of this community, Inspector.'

The mayor's implication was clear: I was not to trouble the constable's grave or those of his forebears. I had absolutely no desire to exhume the constable, but it served my purpose to let Eder believe he had won a small victory. I did my best to appear disappointed.

'I would have liked to examine the constable a final time,' I said. 'But at least I have my own observations, and those of two excellent witnesses.'

'Witnesses?'

'Yourself and Victor, of course,' I said. 'Should I need statements regarding what befell the constable.'

'Of course. Victor is... developing into quite an extraordinary boy. A shame the same cannot be said for my eldest daughter, Louisa.'

'I haven't had the pleasure of meeting Louisa.'

'No,' Eder said. 'I should not be so unfair. But my eldest child is less gregarious than young Victor, and less forthright than Julia. You shall meet the whole family, of course, on Friday; Margarete is very much looking forward to hearing news of the capital.'

'I hope I do not disappoint as a dinner guest.' I turned to a blank page in my notebook. 'Were all three children born during the night? That is to say, were they born of Margarete herself or her day-sister?'

'All night births, I'm glad to say. We've been very fortunate to avoid that *complication*. Though Julia was cutting it close – I remember the first light of dawn graced the room, just as she urinated all over the carpet!' Eder laughed without removing his pipe.

I made a quick note of the Eder family tree. I looked up and smiled. 'Do you, by any chance, know a Second Lieutenant Matherson?'

'Know a Second Lieutenant? No,' he said, 'I can't say I do.'

I knew he was lying. It wasn't that he was a poor liar, quite the contrary: he was smooth in his delivery of the falsehood – a smoothness that was obviously in keeping with his position. I felt certain because he questioned the rank, not the name. What was not clear, and what I could not push him to discover, was *why* he was lying. A small development, but an interesting one.

'I believe some of the officers from Fort Seeben visited your town on occasion,' I said.

'Well, of course, we show the King's Dragoons nothing less than the hospitality you yourself have experienced.'

'Do you also welcome the coming conflict they herald?'

The mayor drew on his pipe, setting the embers there ablaze. 'I have assurances the town is in no danger, that the fighting will be far to the south,' he said eventually. 'The King, in his wisdom, acts for the glory of all Reikova.'

'A final question. Are there many whorehouses in Drekenford?'

This, as I'd hoped, surprised him somewhat.

'Whorehouses?' he said.

'Dens of iniquity, brothels, perhaps even the private residences of ladies of ill-repute?'

'I know what you mean. And of course, Drekenford has its share of such places. Are there many? I couldn't say.'

'Perhaps you could advise me of the largest establishment?' I said.

'Inspector, *really*.'

'It would be a great help to my investigation.'

He drew from his pipe once more and was seemingly reluctant to answer. He looked beyond me to be sure the door to the office was closed. 'I suppose the place commonly referred to as "Lilly's" might be of some help to you. I have heard it caters to such appetites.'

As the mayor gave me the address, I doubted very much

that Second Lieutenant Matherson frequented Lilly's but it would at least be a start. I thanked Mayor Eder for his help, and left saying how much I was looking forward to the dinner party; my turn to lie. I fooled neither of us.

The sky had cleared somewhat so I took the opportunity to pay my respects to the late Constable Webber. On my way to the church I tried to make some sense of the many threads of the investigation. Whenever I seemed to be closing in on a lead it either slipped away or, worse still, splintered into two or more separate lines of inquiry. What began as one instance of the black arts had become two, then three if I were to count the attack on my own person. And yet I was no closer to discovering who was responsible, let alone their motivation to commit such heinous acts. Poor Jan Harsson, guilty of nothing more than petty theft, still suffered in a cell in St Leonars while I fumbled around in the town of his birth.

I tried to school myself into patience. I had learned, over many challenging cases, that my work could not be rushed. A steady, methodical approach eventually delivered results – and often essential information was to be found in the most unlikely of places. Unfortunately, Drekenford churchyard was not such a place.

It did not take me long to find the Webber plot; yesterday's bouquets still lay on the constable's grave. They were cold and colourless in the moonlight. I crossed myself, took off my hat, and spent a silent moment there out of respect. Though my interaction with him had been brief, Constable Webber had struck me as a rare man: a conscientious, diligent, yet caring small town constable. I had seen few such men in the past, and might never see another in my time. His gravestone echoed my thoughts:

Arthur and Gabriel Webber
1667 – 1721
Study to show thyself approved unto God,
a workman that need not to be ashamed,
rightly dividing the word of truth.

'Gabriel chose the epitaph himself.'

I turned to find Father Popov standing at a discreet distance. Either the young Father moved with some stealth, or I was in danger of losing my hearing. Both were disconcerting propositions.

'With his day-brother's blessing, of course,' the Father continued. 'He and Arthur were in agreement in so many things. I admired them for that. Though my day-brother is also a man of the cloth, we do not always see eye-to-eye.'

'They were young to be thinking of such things.'

'Perhaps.'

'Do you think he knew he was in danger?'

The Father spread his hands. 'I am not an inspector, Inspector.' He smiled sadly at his little joke.

'I had heard there were problems between the constable and Stefan, the framer.'

'That all happened a long time ago,' Father Popov said.

'Given where we are, it feels like recent history to me, Father.'

'I too saw Gabriel, at the end. Stefan is not a man without his share of sin, but I do not think him capable of such things.'

'And who would be?'

'I hope you will discover that, Inspector, for all our sakes. My congregation is worried. Scared, if I am honest.'

'And Mrs Harsson, is she scared?' I said.

'Not in any way you would recognise. But I know Mrs Harsson, and she shares all our concerns.'

'I see.'

'You should know that my congregation is mostly scared of *you*, Inspector.'

'Of me?' I said.

'I have done my best to allay their fears, to speak of your greater purpose, to explain that your very presence is part of our salvation. But fear is the Devil's blindfold. Take care, Inspector; in such dark times it is all too easy for people to place blame at the feet of an outsider.'

I heard Father Popov's warning, but I was not unused to such small concerns during the course of an investigation. The gossip, the rumours, the pettiness of the local populace – such as the kind of superstition that Alexsander had already faced – would not stop me. I would find the witch.

24th October 1721

To Alexsander's surprise, Mr Hennig asked him to play that morning. It may have been his painter friend's doing, who was the sole patron. Both Marcus and Hennig were dutiful in their applause.

Alexsander kept glancing at the door, until it grew so distracting he dropped three chords in quick succession. If his audience noticed they gave no sign but his professional pride could take only so much. He turned his back to the door, and the hopes she might walk through it, and gave his focus to the music.

When Mr Hennig put a plate on the table in front of him, he started as if from a daze and then finished the song.

'That's enough for today,' Hennig said. He nodded to the men peeking through the window. They ducked down when they realised they'd been spotted.

'Town like this, you'd think there'd be more than one inn.'

Hennig frowned. 'That's a terrible thing to say.'

Joining Alexsander, the painter raised a glass to his playing. 'You can play every day. Rarely get to drink alone when I'm not at home.'

'Why aren't there more inns in Drekenford?' Alexsander said. 'Folk here seem to like a drink.'

'Don't they everywhere? There was another inn. Burned down a while back, a tragic accident.'

Mr Hennig *harrumphed* from behind the bar.

Marcus leaned close and whispered, 'Not him. They say it was *her* that did it.'

The door swung open and, despite Alexsander's presence, Mr Hennig was soon busy taking orders and pouring ale. As the inn filled up, no one took a table nearby – they were surrounded by a moat of empty tables. Few would meet Alexsander's eye.

'She's not coming,' Marcus said.

'What?' Alexsander said, like a child caught with a hand in the biscuit jar.

'She says you only play the cheery tunes.'

'I don't know who—'

'She doesn't like the cheery tunes.'

'It's what Hennig wants.'

'There's no pleasing her. You'd better get used to that.'

'I don't know *what* you mean.'

'I'm sure you don't, that's the problem.' Marcus drained his glass. 'But don't worry – you weren't the first with one of those northern accents that she took a liking to. She knows her way round your kind, with your bumbling and your blushing.'

'I don't bumble, and I certainly don't blush.'

'You're doing it right now.'

'It's warm in here,' Alexsander said. 'And I've been singing.'

'Bumble, bumble, bumble.'

'What did you mean, I'm not the first?'

'Ah,' Marcus said, sitting back, 'I've said too much.'

'You've not said *enough*.'

'He was a soldier-type, I think, but refined. Knew his art from his elbow, at least. I liked him, and so did Rebecca, obviously. But eventually he had to go back up north, as you all do.'

'A soldier?'

'Yes, Alexsander, do try to keep up.'

'A soldier,' he mumbled once more. That seemed significant but he shied from the feeling, cursed man. 'How long were they together?'

'Gossip becomes you, did you know that? You look ten years younger.'

'Tell me.'

'Oh, very well. But not here. If I have to tell tales then I shall at least do so with decent wine.' Marcus stood and announced to an uninterested common room that he wouldn't water his roses with the swill they served there.

In the studio they drank and talked of everything *but* Rebecca. Sitting among half-finished canvases and those lucky enough to still be unblemished, without the threat of her arrival, Alexsander felt foolish for thinking of her. He was far too old for that sort of thing. All his great, sordid adventures were behind him. And yet, despite the painter's best efforts and the best efforts of his cellar, Alexsander's thoughts returned again and again to Rebecca, and her soldier. The affair loomed so large in his mind, I could not help but remember it as day turned to night. Though his assistance was unintentional, and my interest came with very different motives than his own, I was at least grateful for it.

Rebecca was Second Lieutenant Matherson's reason to visit Drekenford. Rebecca was, most likely, responsible for the flowers at the side of the track. And she was growing in my day-brother's affections – as distasteful an idea as that was. She was not a pious woman.

I lay in bed in almost complete darkness and stared at the ceiling. While there was some satisfaction in solving this minor matter, I struggled to see how it furthered my main investigation; except, perhaps, for ruling out a puzzling set of details. I could not connect Rebecca and her sordid romance with the officer with any other events, nor did it go any way to explain the strange happenings at the fort: the settled ash, meeting Death as she drove up the track, or the exact toll of the pox. If I were to suppose Rebecca had some mastery of the dark arts and that her relationship with Matherson had ended acrimoniously, perhaps it was possible to piece together a motive for such an extreme act. But it lacked the precision of what was done to Jan Harsson and Constable Webber – if Matherson were the target, why employ such a fickle, uncontrollable device as a pox?

Getting nowhere, I tossed aside the bedsheets and lit a candle. I opened the curtains but it was a moonless night, with a covering of thick cloud. At least it was dry. I took my time and washed thoroughly, and was pleased to find my finer clothes had been laundered just as I requested. Tonight I would be dining with the reputable part of the Eder family.

I had not seen Mrs Eder in a good few days, but I didn't think my growing knowledge of her day-sister would affect my behaviour towards her. Would Mrs Eder see me differently, however, knowing that my day-brother was all but courting her day-sister? In our brief meetings she had struck me as an entirely sensible woman; I assumed she would understand the fleeting and misguided nature of the romance, given the situation, and simply tolerate it as I did until events naturally resolved themselves.

I spent much of the evening employed in writing correspondence. I advised the attendant of my boarding house in Esteberg that I would be away for at least another week, likely two, and that I would be grateful if he could water my ettiene plant.

I gave the chief inspector a detailed account of my progress so far, though had to admit I was still some way from an arrest. I explained the shift against me in the common feeling of the town. I apologised that I had not been swifter in my resolution of this case, nor had I been a particularly successful ambassador for the crown. I concluded my letter with the solemn promise to resolve my investigation and bring the perpetrator of these unnatural crimes to justice.

I wrote to Ignatius once again. I asked him if he received my previous letter, and implored him to send Bartrey's *History of the Baalimine.* I considered telling the custodian of the horrors I had witnessed here in Drekenford that I believed were accounted for in Bartrey, but decided that would not help my cause. Custodians and librarians valued cool judgement and a calm hand when it came to their precious texts.

My letters finished, I changed into my finest breeches, shirt, and coat. My shoes had been polished by one of the inn's staff – whoever it was had done an exemplary job. I perfumed my hair with rose water and hoped Mayor Eder and his wife would make some allowances for my less than noble appearance, on account of my travelling and, most likely, my modest station.

The night had grown cold and as I rode through the streets I was glad of my cloak, though it did nothing to improve my appearance. I tried to recall Alexsander's forays into the higher social echelons of the capital: what he wore, how he carried himself, and the graces and airs he managed so effortlessly. But I knew such recollections were worse than useless – they only put me in a dark mood as I thought of Alexsander in my stead. We could not have looked or behaved more differently. My only consolation was that I could rely on Mrs Eder to appreciate *that.*

I found the tree-lined track to the Eder's house with relative ease and admired the gnarled and twisted intricacies of the trees that passed on either side of me. However, my interest in the strange, unknowable patterns made by their branches and scant remaining leaves was edged with a kind of horror. None held the symmetry of man's symbolism but there was something, just a hint, of the pentagram in those branches. The trees pulled at me, tried to tempt me and the mare from the path. I had felt such a thing before. I'd discovered a cellar where a coven gathered, one wall of which was covered in unholy icons. These were mounted on their own bizarrely shaped canvasses – bizarre until I realised they were not canvas but skin, dried and pulled taut as a drum. Each one a complete piece, cut from a single back.

I found the cellar after one of my visions. I'd seen a pentagram blazing on the coat of a pallbearer as a funeral procession passed me in the street. I made to put out the imagined flames, much to the man's consternation. The coven gathered beneath the morgue where the man worked. He was—

A bird took flight, its wings clattering among the branches. I flinched and, the trees' spell broken, I urged Tabitha on up the track.

The Eder house was a welcome sight. Its warmly lit windows spoke of sanctuary, of family, and of an open hearth that night. Having tied my mount at the post, I employed the polished brass knocker firmly. It was an imposing piece: a stag sporting a great spread of antlers that veritably snarled around the ring in its mouth. As the door swung inwards I imagined for a moment the stag was readying to charge.

'Good evening, sir,' a man said. He bid me enter and took my cloak. I judged him to be no older than myself but he moved with a bone-grating stiffness.

I was led down a pleasantly tiled hallway to the

drawing-room. There, as if I were a lord of great standing, I was announced.

'Special Inspector Christophor Morden,' the man said in a clear, clipped voice.

All eyes turned to me. I had, in all my years of service, rarely experienced such a moment of terror.

Fortunately, I was rescued by the hostess, Mrs Eder. She guided me through a room of finely dressed men and women, few of whom I recognised. My initial impression was of quite a crowd as I was whirled between groups of guests that chattered and laughed, both of which sounded like breaking glass to me. I wondered if I'd stepped into some kind of southern masquerade ball – many of the women tittered from behind black masks, though I was glad to find none of the men were so attired.

Yet my concern of having to dance was, thankfully, fleeting; the drawing room was spacious but certainly not big enough for that. And the crowd that had first sparked fear in me revealed itself to be no more than fifteen people.

I found my courage and my voice in time to be introduced to a small knot of people that included the mayor. I shook hands with the local magistrate, Channock. Since the death of Constable Webber, I would require direct dealings with the magistrate. When his wife presented her hand, I did my best to kiss it in a courtly manner. Both the Channocks were elegantly dressed and bore themselves with a dignity that, to my eyes, suggested aristocratic upbringing. My arrival produced a brief lull in the conversation that led me to believe I may have interrupted something. In a hurry to fill that lull, I asked the lady why she, and so many others in the room, wore a mask. Her thin, grey eyebrows rose above its lacquered edge.

'It is a harvest mask,' she said. I gave no sign of comprehension so she continued. 'Between the harvest festival and the winter solstice, a lady attends all formal functions masked. To bring good fortune, and good yields.'

'Yields?' I said.

'A simple, harmless superstition,' the magistrate said. 'The town's farmers swear by it, but in truth I think our ladies enjoy the game of it.'

I'd rarely found superstitions to be simple, nor harmless. In fact, they often functioned as these very masks did: hiding the dangerous, the cunning, or worse.

'Are such games not the same in the capital, Inspector?' Mrs Channock asked. 'At the King's court?'

'Perhaps, though I cannot speak for the court,' I said. In truth, I could speak for nothing: I was not in the habit of attending 'functions'. Once or twice Alexsander had been engaged to play, alongside other musicians, for the lesser nobility. But my memories of those evenings were fragmentary at best – he was often paid in wine for such performances.

'If not for the court,' Mrs Channock said, 'could you speak *of* it?'

'She means gossip,' her husband added.

Floundering, I was at risk of being terrible company. 'Well, the King's war has the city abuzz, of course.'

'Yes?' they all said as one.

'Some speculate just how sound His Majesty's judgement is in sending troops here,' I said, acutely aware of how poor I was at this. 'Some even question more than his judgement...'

'Is that so?' Mrs Channock said.

'Come, Inspector, you must think us dreadfully provincial in our hunger for gossip,' Mrs Eder said.

'Not at all,' I said a little too quickly. 'I have found nothing but warm hospitality and kindness in Drekenford.'

'Ah! Good, kind country folk,' the magistrate said.

I was about to agree when I noticed the mischief lurking at the edges of his mouth. 'The capital,' I said, addressing Mrs Eder, 'is a hard place of late, with little joy and scant civility. I confess, with each passing day I dread my return north.'

I thought my lie convincing, but its effect was not as I intended. My hosts looked awkward, almost embarrassed by what I had said, and I didn't know why. Perhaps they felt I was being overly open and honest – an odd irony for a lie – but it was the southern peoples that had a reputation for bluntness.

A passing servant carrying a tray of glasses provided much needed distraction. I took a glass of wine and found it sharp, but not unpleasantly so. It could have been river sludge and I would have smiled as I sipped it gratefully. When I turned back Magistrate Channock had been replaced by Father Popov, and Mrs Eder had been called away to perform her duty as hostess. The Father wore a more ornate set of vestments than I'd seen him in before and, blessedly, he looked as uncomfortable as I felt. We shared a small, knowing smile at that.

'—and I am sure there is no further danger. Isn't that right, Inspector?'

The mayor and Mrs Channock were both looking at me.

'Well,' I said, taking another sip so as to gather something that might pass for a coherent thought. 'I would urge caution, until I have apprehended whoever is responsible.'

'And will that be soon?' she asked.

I gazed for a moment at that matt black mask. 'I hope so.'

'Hope? But what good is—'

The magistrate's wife was interrupted by the striking up of a piano, which dominated the far corner of the drawing room. A high-pitched ditty was completed, likely designed to cut through, and then silence, the room's conversations. In the small pause after those tinkling notes I felt, once again, a strong discomfort with the situation. I was struggling to get a firm grasp of my surroundings, so dizzied was I by the kaleidoscopic mix of dresses, masks, and coats in the room. So dizzied I hadn't seen something as large as a piano. What hope, yes *hope*, did I have of spotting smaller, more significant details?

Into this discomfort stepped a young man with the voice of a fallen angel.

He sang acapella to begin; long, high, stretched sounds that I barely recognised for the words they were. My breath caught in my chest when the piano struck its first chord alongside him.

Mayor Eder leaned close to my ear and whispered, 'My daughter's fiancé.'

His hair was the colour I imagined the dawn sun to be. Even from halfway across the room his brilliant green eyes revealed the silks worn by the guests for what they really were: pale imitations. Without his voice he would have been a striking, if diminutive boy. With it he was a colossus.

He sang and though I knew the song, I did not recognise it at first. The arrangement was dramatically different and he put his stresses in such surprising places. If the effect had been anything less than breath-taking, it would have been disastrous. I felt a shiver along the back of my neck and when the song finished the room gave a collective sigh as if waking from a dream.

I applauded with such vigour I spilled my wine, but I did

not care. I saw ladies dab their eyes, removing their masks to do so, and beside me the Father was so moved the colour had quite drained from his face.

'Father, are you all right?' I said.

'Every time I believe I am prepared, that I know what is to come.' He shook his head.

'Astonishing, isn't he, our Olesca?' Eder said.

He sang twice more. I could have wept – it was too much, it was too little. I left the drawing room, a stranger on my arm, in a walking daze.

We followed the procession, my partner and I, into the dining room. She was dressed in a sprawling, tiered beige dress that resembled an extravagant cake. She made no attempt at conversation – I had the impression she was similarly affected by the performance. She sat to my left, her husband to *her* left, and the magistrate's wife was to my right. It was no small consolation that both ladies were married. I had worried some effort would be made to find me a match among the eligible women of Drekenford. Perhaps I was too old for that consideration.

I took my seat, an ornately carved work of spiralling heavy wood, and had just enough wherewithal to be impressed by the dining room. A huge hearth dominated the opposite wall and provided plenty of warmth and light in what may have otherwise been an oppressively and darkly decorated space. A deep green papered the walls, putting me in mind of the pine forests that surrounded the town. No doubt this was deliberate. Bursting from these vistas were a number of stag heads, stuffed, and even – for one or two of the larger specimens – gilded, the tips of their antlers leafed in gold. Like the Eder's doorknocker, I felt these hunting trophies aggressive in countenance.

'Ghastly, aren't they?' Mrs Channock said, causing me to jump.

I coughed to hide my embarrassment. 'Pardon, madam?'

'My husband helped bring down that big one, or so he claims.' She gestured to the stag that hung above the mantle. 'Should you need a good nap, ask him for the story. It is positively *biblical* in length.'

I smiled but said nothing further, not wishing to be rude about her husband nor my hosts. I was rescued from having to find a change of subject by my other dining companion, who introduced herself as Mrs Fredericks.

'Have you ever heard such a voice?' she said, looking rather intensely across the table to where Olesca was taking his seat.

'Never,' I said.

The magistrate's wife rolled her eyes and turned from our conversation; she had the air of a woman contentedly bored with life.

'Not even in the capital?' Mrs Fredericks said. Though she was masked as Mrs Channock was, I could tell she was a livelier, younger woman, who I doubted would ever become so jaded.

'I don't have the pleasure of such performances very often, myself, but my day-brother is a musician. I feel fairly confident the capital holds few voices such as we were blessed with tonight.'

'I've heard he has a very fine voice, your day-brother.'

'He will be pleased to hear you say so,' I said.

At the far end of the table, Mrs Eder stood and tapped her

glass. We all stood, and those whose glasses needed charging were attended to. A murmur of laughter rippled along one end of the table as young Victor insisted he be served, holding out his empty glass. I was glad to see him there – I hadn't noticed the boy in the drawing room. His father indulged him, much to the amusement of the men at the table. Their wives were quietly less enthused, I thought.

'Welcome, new friends and old, to our home,' Mrs Eder said. 'As the nights grow cold it warms the soul to see you all. And to our newest friend, Special Inspector Morden, we bid a *special* welcome, and God's speed in his vital work.'

I was toasted, which I found most uncomfortable. A gentleman I didn't recognise raised a further toast to our hosts, and then we sat as the soup was served.

'I imagine he will be quite jealous,' Mrs Fredericks said. She had taken off her mask for the meal, revealing a soft and kind-looking face.

'I'm sorry?' I said, not following.

'Your day-brother: jealous of not having heard Olesca sing?'

'I imagine he will,' I said. I tried to hide how much I enjoyed that idea, which had not occurred to me.

'Are you still wittering on about that southerner's butchering of our songs?' the magistrate's wife said.

Mrs Fredericks gasped. 'You can't possibly mean that!'

'I can, and I do. It is disrespectful what that boy does. I tell Margarete every time, and yet she still forces that southern bird to warble out of tune.'

Mrs Fredericks was stunned to silence.

'The only one more bored of his singing than I is his fiancée.'

Mrs Channock nodded at the young woman slouched in her seat next to Olesca. 'What does that tell you?'

I had yet to be introduced to Louisa, but my first impression was of a young woman disappointed by everything she saw; no doubt why the magistrate's wife felt such an affinity with her. Her long, straight hair covered much of her brow and half her face. She barely touched her soup, idly stirring it as a listless child might. Her fiancé did not look at her once, let alone speak to her, during the entire dinner. I wondered aloud how the two found themselves engaged.

'Odd couple, aren't they?' Mrs Channock said. 'Our good hosts say he came north to Reikova to make a fresh start, a new world. It was quite the surprise for us all when that included marrying the Eder's eldest.'

'I confess, I know little of courtship in the younger generations.'

'Do you confess a lot, Inspector?' She laughed. 'No need to look so alarmed. I quite enjoy confessions – I understand why Father Popov skips to work each day.'

'I can see I am outmatched, madam.'

'Then you see more than my husband.'

Mrs Fredericks had been following our conversation, wide-eyed and, I believed, against her better judgement. She almost choked on her soup twice. More dishes were added to the table, and I used the change of course as an opportunity to excuse myself and visit the bathroom.

I was the only one to do so. The butler who had announced me earlier now directed me along the hallway. I passed under the gaze of yet more stags – these were at least painted rather than stuffed. I began to wonder if this animal was an obsession of the mayor's, until I saw something, beside the entrance to a study, which suggested it was much more than that.

A vibrant tapestry depicted a coat of arms, dominated by two resplendent stags. I was no scholar of Reikovan history, let alone its heraldry, but even to my ignorant eye it was impossible to mistake the royal nature of the arms. Each stag wore a crown that bore an obvious resemblance to the King's own, and the heraldic shield itself was topped by the same crown. Mottos adorned the arms and ran along the edges of the thick tapestry, the lettering thin stitches of gold. They were almost sunk into the tapestry so I had to peer closely before I realised the mottos were in Ketts.

And to think I had been worried that my northern accent and mannerisms would embarrass me as a foreigner in those parts! Instead, I found myself sung to by a boy from the southern tribes, in a house festooned with Kettoman heraldry.

A polite cough from the butler down the hallway, undoubtedly for my benefit, reminded me of my purpose. I turned left, as instructed, but before I came to my destination I was presented with something of a dilemma: an open door.

And not just any open door, but that of the servants' staircase that ran both up and down. From the sounds and smells rising from below it was obvious that it led to the kitchens. The sterile silence from above spoke of bedchambers. I could not resist the opportunity to see more of the household where Jan Harsson had worked, especially from a servant's means.

I trod as quietly and carefully as I could on the plain wooden stairs. I winced at their creaks, paused at their louder groans, and left by the first door I came to – even though the steps continued upwards. I did not wish to stumble into a dusty loft.

To my relief I found the corridor empty. One door I came to was ajar. The room beyond clearly belonged to Victor; and I could say that not because it contained childish ephemera in a state of chaos, but quite the opposite. Everything in the room was meticulously ordered and placed entirely at right angles – be it on the shelves, on his writing desk, or the pillows on his bed. The floor was completely clear and the sole picture gracing the walls was a crude but detailed framed sketch of human anatomy. Beyond, I could see through an adjoining door a very different situation. Given the colourful detritus, I assumed it to be Julia's room.

I left the open door and continued down the corridor. Here portraits of great men and striking women gazed down at me, each and every one passing judgement on my intrusion. They were but a momentary relief from the prevalence of stags, because when I looked closer the animal could be seen in one form or another everywhere – breaking from a distant copse in one portrait of military bearing, a gem-encrusted broach in another more domestic example.

Passing the last room on the corridor, I thought I heard my name. I stopped and listened, every muscle tensed. There, again, a high pitched whisper: *Christophor*.

It crept out from under the closed door. I reached for the handle and was suddenly back downstairs, walking into the dining room.

My day-brother was beside me.

I looked at him, and he at me, almost as a reflection might. But there was no doubt it was Alexsander. The way he held himself, the smile that was always lurking at the edge of his mouth, the stoop of his shoulders – too lazy to stand up straight. He wore his finery better than I. We walked together back to the table, where we sat next to each other.

Laughter and chatter abounded and I felt a warmth, a genuine *camaraderie* among the diners and their hosts. But it was felt as one might the heat of a fire: at a distance, from an essential remove, lest I interrupted that warmth to dire consequences. There was no such sensation between my day-brother and I.

My apology for our absence fell on deaf ears. The magistrate's wife, laughing almost maniacally at something her husband had said, turned to me, her mouth cavernously empty of teeth.

Empty, too, were the sockets of her eyes.

I started backwards, knocking into Alexsander. He was similarly shocked by the sight of Mrs Fredericks, who was weeping blood softly into her soup bowl and saying something to herself, over and over. I could not hear what, exactly, above the laughter. All the diners were without their eyes and most carried on as if nothing were the matter. I tried to stand but the magistrate's wife gripped my shoulder with the weight of an avalanche. It was then I saw the two white pips of teeth crowning in the eye sockets, as they had in the Harsson boy's.

At the end of the table Mrs Eder stood and crushed a glass between her hands. Only one of them bled but did so profusely, cascading blood onto the table, which silenced the room. Her head sported antlers that stretched high towards the ceiling. Impaled on each point was a letter, still sealed. She turned to me, her eyes blazing like full hearths.

Alexsander touched my hand. I did not want to see him again, nor acknowledge him in any way. He was not there.

Could not be there. He was an intruder in my night. But I did follow his gaze to the southern boy, Olesca. He was not eyeless, and nor did his eyes burn with fire. He simply looked from my day-brother to me, and back again. His calm, innocent demeanour was a chilling shock amid the demonic laughter, the blood, and the ruined finery. He opened his mouth and said, 'Sir?' Clear and toneless across the banquet hall's ruckus. 'Sir?'

I blinked.

I was reaching, my hand alone, for a door handle. I was in the corridor upstairs, with the butler beside me.

'You dropped this, sir,' the butler said, offering me something shrivelled and blackened.

'I'm sorry, what did you say?'

'You dropped this, sir,' he repeated.

I gazed at the man, his cliff-like face betraying nothing.

'Thank you,' I said. He offered the object to me again and I had little choice but to take it. A heart, or it once was, so putrefied had it become. Small, but perhaps still big enough to be a man's, and pricked with pins. The end of each pin was covered in candle wax. 'Thank you.'

The butler escorted me back to the dining room. If it weren't for his stoic presence, I may not have entered – even though I heard none of the raucous laughter of my vision. There was also none of the warmth. The magistrate's wife was dissecting a small game bird, possibly a quail, her eyes both definitely in place and intensely focused. Mrs Fredericks appeared quite relieved by my return.

She was talking to me, but I did not hear her. Instead, I looked about the table: at Mr and Mrs Eder; their children; the fiancé, Olesca; and at the serving staff that stood behind them, that carried dishes to and fro, that entered almost unseen.

One of them was my witch.

I left the Eder house under an almost full moon. The rest of the dinner proceeded without incident, with nothing more than the barbed comments of Mrs Channock to navigate. When the men retired to the drawing room, the women to the parlour, I took my leave professing no taste for whiskey and my day-brother's pressing duties. If my hosts understood such a lie, they were too gracious to show it, and instead Mayor Eder feigned disappointment. I was the only guest from the august gathering to leave early.

The path wound down from the top of the valley, with loose rock and broken branches making slow going of it. I had not drunk beyond what was polite so I had the sense to let Tabitha choose the way, and do so at her own pace. I tried to clear all recollection of the actual dinner, the to-and-fro between Mrs Fredericks and Mrs Channock, from my mind. Instead, there was much to take from the evening; I understood that at least, even though I understood little of the specific details. The shared vision. Mrs Eder transformed. The boy, Olesca, watching on. No. Watching *us*.

I stopped Tabitha at a break in the hedgerow, the woods behind me, and looked out to the fort on the other side of the valley. It gained a kind of shape from the few lit camp fires and the teasing smallness of lamps. But that shape was too slight for the fort. It was shrinking, had been from the day I arrived, although now it was very clearly shrinking back from the ashes of itself.

Those ashes caught all the night's light, but especially from that of the moon; a light that shared the ashes' colour and coldness. It would have been somewhat pretty if it weren't so terrible. That was the way of things.

I hoped they had stopped burning bodies at the fort. I knew better than to hope there were no new bodies to burn.

A crack sounded across the valley, like a single rifle shot in the still night. Except there was something more wooden to the noise. I found it curious. Tabitha felt more strongly on the matter. With no urging from me she skittered, almost lopsidedly, back onto the track. Then, with a fear no Reikovan thoroughbred has known, she galloped as fast as the rocky trail would allow.

Another crack followed behind.

I tried to call to the horse and pulled on the reins but it was no use. I could only cling on.

More reports came in the night, followed by slower, longer booms – like the thunder that trails behind lightning. Those booms seemed to shake everything, even my fogged breath and the billowing cloud coming from Tabitha. It wasn't rifle fire. Cannon, perhaps.

Still clinging to the horse's neck, I saw thick black lines snaking their way along the wall beside the track. Stones and mortar vibrated, visibly shook, before giving way. More and more debris fell onto the track. If it were a race between us and the failing wall, we were losing.

Tabitha did her best but was soon bloodied up and down her legs. The air turned with the smell of it; first a sharp note and then it became impossible to escape.

I coughed and spluttered.

And then the wall collapsed completely, like a dam

bursting. Out and out it poured, whatever had been behind, dark as pitch but flowing like wine. It crashed onto the trail and, at last, I managed to regain some control of my mount. I turned us as quickly as I could from the disappearing track and blundered into the woods.

Thorn-filled bushes and low branches grasped at me, more than one taking its own little piece. Tabitha was evidently already too cut and bruised to care. We were away from the flooding torrent, at least. But there was no river there. And the smell. There could be no mistake it was blood, but old and thick and wasting.

Deeper into the woods, we were guided by what little light pierced the canopy. It was an old part of the forest. None of the tall, regimented pines that grew by the fort flourished here. Instead it was home to the bitter and twisted trees, the names of which were lost to common folk. Trees that man had yet to put to use. Or, most men.

Tabitha would not slow. Her breathing was like a broken bellows, wet and wheezing with it. I fared little better. The ground rose to a small clearing. On the opposite side, just for a moment, I saw something – someone – on the branch of a tree. A flash of flesh in the moonlight. As impossible as I knew it to be, I saw they were lying naked there, at least twenty feet from the ground. An arm dangling. And then, at a gallop, we passed directly below. A smell cut across the blood and leather and horse. A cloying, tacky smell of burning wax. There, then gone.

She screamed.

Grating and high, then at once low and guttural, my horse screamed. A sound like no other. Its rhythms harsh and wrong. Such pain there; a pain devoid of comprehension. She bucked and tossed her head, slowing, as if to dislodge something. I leaned down, near her now frantic eyes.

Her lip had split. Drawn back over her teeth, I could see a tear in her upper lip as if it were cheap fabric. Juddering and jerky, the tear grew an inch as I watched. Then there was another. And another. Up past her nose, now. Flesh peeled back under its own weight. How she screamed.

Helpless to help her, I tried to dismount but she would not let me. Perhaps it was pure panic, or perhaps she did not wish to suffer alone, but she picked up her pace once again. Could she outrun it, as she had the breaking wall? The wall that tore and cracked like her muzzle.

But it didn't stop. All up her face bloodied strips of her fell away, revealing muscle and bone and teeth. Huge teeth, so far back I had never seen them before, now lined red. With every toss of her head more of her was lost.

To my shame I shrank away as the tears crested her head. Terror rippled through her even as she ran. There was so much of her gone, so much stripped. Muscles distended and bulged and then broke loose.

Finally, she could take no more. She stopped, abrupt, and threw me from the saddle. She may have saved me then from whatever had taken her. Whatever had flayed my horse alive.

I struck a tree hard enough to blacken my vision. It returned only briefly, enough to see the final throes of Tabitha, flesh gone and innards failing her. Selfishly I wished the black to take me from the death of a friend, and it did.

ALEXSANDER

25th October 1721

I've seen the moon, whatever my night-brother might think.

Pale and full; that's how it was that morning when I woke in the forest. Struggling above the treeline it was out of place, of course it was. The moon didn't look right against the washed out blue. It was as confused as the rest of us.

I had dead pine needles for a bed and a huge, exposed root for a pillow. I ached in every joint – every part of me where bone met bone. I was wearing thin, and had felt it for some time. My mouth was so dry I wondered if I'd ever drink a drop again or if that was it: I'd become a desert creature with scales and a grittiness in places that used to be soft.

I went to curse Christophor but stopped. I could recall enough of what had happened. So instead I rose unsteadily to my feet with the help of the tree trunk. There was no telling who had the rougher feel, me or the tree. It didn't help to have the moon staring at me the whole time.

I found her ten or so paces away.

I didn't want to look. I choked back a sob, and glanced away to the trees; it wasn't a sight any man would seek out, but I had to. We both cared for her.

She was strangely neat, if such a thing could be believed. Lying there, but not sprawled or crooked or ungainly in her last. I didn't think that should be possible.

A full horse skeleton stripped completely to the bone and arranged in front of me.

She appeared so... false. She couldn't have been real. The whole scene spoke of artifice, perhaps even the artistic. A sculpture or painting – it had the unnerving mix of flatness and depth that a quality painter could produce. I felt compelled to touch her.

A leg. That's where I started. Somehow that was safer, less intrusive, perhaps even approaching a normal thing one might do. The smoothness of the shin from the knee down – though even in such a moment it occurred to me those weren't the right words. Those were my words, words for me, not her. Christophor might have known, but I didn't. I ran my fingers the whole way down to her hoof. I had no idea they were so complex, so full of moving parts that were now stilled. It was a foolish ignorance but I simply hadn't thought on horses' hooves before.

I touched more bones before my morbid curiosity was sated. All were smooth in that most natural of ways. I continued to marvel at that, right until I approached her skull.

And there it was: the whole reason we were there. In that forest, somewhere near that village, hundreds of miles from where we should have been. A hollow eye socket.

I felt for the jagged pip of a tooth, of course I did; it was impossible not to wonder. There was nothing here that could be reasoned, or that could be considered coincidence, or that would be so unusual as to be disbelieved. Tabitha and that boy in St Leonars prison couldn't have been further apart, and yet my night-brother and I had briefly entered their lives, and that was that. But there was no tooth.

I stood and realised how helpless and useless I was. The

right thing would be to bury her but how could I? With my bare hands? I didn't like the idea of leaving her in such a state but there was little else for it. One small consolation to the whole despicable thing: I doubted her bones would become food for scavengers and the like. No, whatever evil had wrought this would be keen to preserve their message. I could tell so by the lack of smell – no rot or decay or similar markers of death. These were separated from the skeleton of Tabitha. The rest of her was not so cared for.

Gore marked a trail back along the forest floor. It glistened where it caught the morning sun and meandered briefly, like a stream, where it met roots or a rise in the ground. The smell was ferocious. It was cooking, this offal and organ and muscle. The sky may have been bright enough, clear enough, to show the imposter moon but the heat was nothing so natural. I approached with a hand over my face and still the stench stung the back of my throat.

The mess bubbled like a simmering stew. It was true for as far as I could see down the trail of bodily destruction. Elsewhere the forest floor was entirely normal, but where the flayed parts of Tabitha had congealed there was a hellish scene. It popped and gurgled and groaned without shame.

My night-brother, either wilfully or by necessity, appeared not to think on the terrors and evils he witnessed. I couldn't be so hard, so closed. How could anyone? To see a living creature reduced to such a state by some wicked design, let alone an animal I considered a kind of friend, was beyond my ability to consider dispassionately. That was one of the many differences between Christophor and I.

I felt things. He pushed them away, or avoided them altogether.

I wouldn't avoid the full, gruesome truth of what befell Tabitha. Let Christophor do what he would with my memory of the matter. If he had a shred of courage – the kind of *real* courage that came from deeper feelings – he would return later that night to see it for himself. But I knew he would not. So, I stared at that horror enough for the both of us.

Eventually, I judged neither of us would ever forget and I turned to go. That was when I saw her heart.

It came to the surface and bobbed there, like an apple in a barrel. Such a mocking motion for something so huge, so vital, it was enough to make me cry out.

I felt a stab in my own chest. I clasped a hand there and bent double against the pain. Everything tightened and I couldn't breathe. I staggered, hitting a tree, and forced my eyes open. I gulped at the air but could do nothing with it. There was something else, pressing against the palm of my hand. Something in my shirt pocket. A hard lump. As soon as I registered it, the pain was gone. Tentatively I lifted the object out.

My own heart.

Such a dark and withered thing, how had I let it become so?

Then I saw the pins, and the tattered ribbons, and the clumps of hair. And that sight reminded me I still lived and breathed, albeit barely, and that my heart was right where it should be. Three hearts, two to be seen. How many lost beyond saving?

If it weren't for Christophor I would have thrown that pierced monstrosity into the other nastiness and been done with it. But then, if it weren't for Christophor I would have done a lot of things. As it was I put it in his heavy coat, which was as far away as I could get it while still being about my person.

I didn't feel right about leaving the remains of Tabitha like that, but I couldn't stay and there was little I could do about it. The smell would have driven me off eventually. With no better idea of where I was, or which direction to take, I followed the trail of Tabitha's destruction hoping to find a way back to the track, and the village beyond. Though the sheer amount of animal was undeniable it was soon behind me and I was surrounded by featureless forest. I became aware of the calls of birds as if I'd passed through some sort of barrier or border into a new part of forest, one that was home to more than tragedy. I was soon lost there.

I couldn't recall ever being in such a vast, pathless place. Esteberg was a sizable city but everywhere you went there were roads and pavements, alleys and lanes. Ways directed to you by convenience or necessity. Even on the ride south there was never any doubt where the track was, whether it crossed hills or forest or field alike. We took paths for granted, I thought, or at least my night-brother and I did.

My only idea was to keep the sun on my right as best I could, so I had the hope of travelling north. At least I knew the forest was finite in that direction. To the south, who could say? I had to stop and check the sun often, which also served as an excuse to rest. My thirst soon became all I could think about. It throbbed through me, sometimes soft, sometimes strong enough to cause me to stumble. And always, everywhere, were the pine needles. On my hands when I picked myself up. Finding the gaps in my shoes. Tickling my ears as they fell from… where? The branches, you fool, but then why did they feel as if they fell from my own head? My unbrushed thatch.

Thatch was rich. I had thinned out so much these last years I felt ravaged. My few remaining curls were, to a man, embarrassed by their conspicuousness, like dancers stuck in the middle of a ballroom with no hope of a partner. Vanity in the old is an unforgiveable thing.

I wiped my brow and tasted my own salts. The sun was reaching its zenith and I hastened my steps, momentarily certain that my one guide would soon be lost to me. Then I stopped, relieved I still had the wherewithal to laugh at myself. I sat in a shaded spot and waited for the sun to become useful once more. I couldn't see the moon.

After a few wasted hours I resumed my course north, or so I hoped. Each step felt torturously slow and it occurred to me I might never get out of that forsaken place. But I wouldn't give Christophor the satisfaction of knowing I had been the one to kill us with my ineptitude or lack of stamina. No, I'd rather sleep until we became his responsibility. It was his fault we were here after all. His fault—

I heard a different song than the birds. A voice, drifting through the trees. My salvation or damnation, who was to say between the two? I followed the sound as I was bid, sure in the knowledge that the melancholy, wordless tune was for me and me alone. Not wordless, I realised, and then I saw flashes of white through the trees. The Lord's angels, perhaps, come to escort me heavenwards despite my night-brother's sins. Despite my own. Like a fool I began to recount them, finding all manner of ways to trivialise or explain my indiscretions until I realised there was no need. They would know me for an old heathen who drank too much and cheated poorly at cards, who slept with married women and felt not a drop of remorse. They knew it all and more.

I glanced back at the dark forest, the choice obvious before me – as clear a metaphor as either testament ever managed. I chose to have it done with. Arms spread wide I walked towards the angelic host.

The singing continued as I stepped beyond the treeline. My divine salvation became more earthly as I realised the white I'd spotted was not in fact robes, but bed linen.

Enormous sheets swayed in the late afternoon heat. I was at the base of an incline that led up to the back of a house, which glistened along the bottom with the glass of a greenhouse. After long hours in the forest this homely scene felt so strange to me – just as the moon in the daylight sky, I was the imposter here. But my thirst couldn't be denied. I skirted the sheets, still hearing the unsettling song.

He saw me first, I thought, because when I stopped he was staring at me around the edge of a coverlet. Eyes of a green to make all the trees of the forest envious. He was so short I mistook him for a very young child, but his face, the way he held himself, his confidence all spoke of a man at peace with who he was. That, not the eyes, struck a spark of envy in me.

My throat was too hoarse to speak. In those moments of silence I realised he had been the one singing. Had I heard him before, elsewhere, or was that Christophor? But what would he know of such a voice, uncouth as he was?

The young man opened his mouth, but instead of singing, he screamed.

So low a sound, so deep compared to the singing, it didn't

seem real, not at first. His demeanour didn't change at all; he continued to stare, slightly curious, this green-eyed man. Until Rebecca appeared in the garden. Rebecca pushed her way between the hanging sheets, and the man stopped his screaming. As if nothing untoward had happened, he turned and walked away.

'Alexsander, what—' She looked me up and down, taking in the full state of me. 'What happened to you?'

'I—'

'Never mind that, come inside before you scare any more of the children.' Rebecca took me in hand and, I'm ashamed to say, I leaned on her for much of the way up to the house. She led me into the handsome and well-looked-after greenhouse. Everything inside – the walls, the floor, the plants themselves – had a slick, hot wetness.

Without preamble she began checking me over, turning my face this way and that. She found dried blood on my hands and up my arms. I watched on, mute, as she pressed and prodded until she satisfied herself that either I was done with my bleeding or the blood was not mine. In truth, I couldn't be sure myself which was the case.

Eventually, I managed to croak a request for water and she hurried off, commanding me to wait there. But I couldn't wait. On a window sill, beside a plant with spiky, purple-tipped leaves, was a watering can. Holding it above my head I poured until I almost drowned.

'I suppose it's all from the same well,' Rebecca said, a glass in her hand. I drank that too. 'Now, tell me what happened.'

I recounted Christophor's flight through the forest, his being thrown from the horse, and my waking up in the embrace of a tree.

'And the horse?' Rebecca said.

'Gone.' I did not want to disturb her with any details of just how.

She shifted her apron. I hadn't properly taken her in until then. She was wearing working clothes and her hair was tied back with a handkerchief.

'I've interrupted your day,' I said, by way of an apology.

She waved away my concern. 'Come with me.'

We walked through a maze of carpeted corridors, some of which I recognised; Christophor had investigated those corridors just the night before. The details were a little vague, but his feeling of unease wasn't. I felt much the same under the gaze of the stuffed stags and large, old-fashioned paintings of severe men. I was glad when we passed through the pomposity of the family home and into the servants' side. The walls went from an overbearing dark green to a clean white, and the furnishings became plain and functional. Perhaps it was my imagination, but Rebecca seemed to find the change more comfortable also.

'Who was the young man in the garden?' I said.

Rebecca didn't slow her pace and didn't answer. Instead she opened a door on a room that was all but empty except for a metal bath and a stool. She ushered me inside and said, 'Olesca.'

I knew that. Of course I did. My night-brother was so taken with him, with his *singing*. Olesca.

'But that's his night-brother's—'

'That's right. Apparently in the southern tribes they only have one name, the same name, both night and day. Two personalities, one body, one name.'

'That must be difficult,' I said, eyeing the steaming, half-full bath.

'They see it as a thing of power, to be in such harmony.'

'Harmony. Yes, like a chorus or choir it was. Can you believe such a sound came from one man?'

'I can,' she said. 'And I know what you're doing. You can still talk and wash.'

'Are you sure this is really...'

A flushed-looking serving woman walked in with another bucketful of hot water, tipped it in, and left without a word.

'If you could see yourself, Alexsander. You're covered in mud and blood and half the forest.' She reached up and produced a sizable twig, as if from thin air; it had some of my hair still stuck to it. 'I want to be sure you're not really hurt.'

'I'm fine,' I said, but she saw my lie for what it was. I glanced from her to the door.

'Aren't we both a bit old for that kind of silliness?' she said, moving a towel from a stool and sitting down.

Reluctantly, I began to unbutton my shirt. I eased it from my shoulders, wincing as aches flared into sharper pains. A tempest of a bruise covered my upper arm and as far as I could see along my back.

'He could have broken your neck,' Rebecca said.

'It's not the first bruise Christophor has given me.' Loosening my trousers with blood-encrusted fingers I let them fall to the floor. My back to her, I stepped into the bath and hunkered down like an animal. Even so, the warmth of the water was a relief.

'Come on now,' she said softly.

I leaned back and felt the shock of the cold metal, but soon became used to it. I closed my eyes and could almost forget where I was, what had happened, and who was in the room with me. But then I felt her touch my shoulder. She washed my back; gentle when she needed to be, and without a word.

Though I didn't know her as well as I might, I'd not known her so quiet or so serious as then. I wasn't sure I liked it.

Before long the water started to resemble a pond. Rebecca left and then returned with some borrowed clothes – not the mayor's – that almost fitted me. I accepted them gratefully. When I was dressed, she insisted she walk me back to the inn.

'That's ridiculous,' I said.

She gave me a withering look. We managed a compromise: she would walk me to the end of the track. I waited for her in the front garden.

The Eder house had a stunning view of the village and the valley. The low sun spread a slow fire through forest and street alike. Fort Seeben, a place that seemed to haunt my night-brother's thoughts, sparkled inexplicably. It was beautiful but I shivered looking at it.

'Hello.'

I glanced down to see a well-dressed young boy. He too was gazing out at the valley. The Eder boy, I knew, though we had never been properly introduced.

'Hello. I'm Alexsander.'

'Patrik,' he said. He held out his hand. Such an adult gesture it took me a moment to remember I was to take it.

'You're very lucky to live here, Patrik,' I said, immediately aware of how condescending that sounded.

'They won't let me go over there.'

'Where?'

'Fort Seeben,' he said. 'My night-brother and I would very

much like to know why it appears different to the surrounding forest. We have our theories, of course.'

'Of course,' I said.

'And we keep a record of our findings,' he said, tapping one of his pockets.

I was no expert when it came to children, but they were often a curious and wide-eyed audience when I would practise in the parks of Esteberg. This was a less innocent, more calculating curiosity.

'*My* night-brother likes his notebooks too,' I said. 'But I never understand a word he writes.'

'The fort is a matter of refraction, I bel—'

'Come now, Patrik, stop bothering Mr Morden,' Rebecca said. She put her arm around the boy, but he squirmed away from her embrace.

'No bother,' I said. 'Though I fear I was in danger of learning something.'

'Mr Morden is a musician. It's that wonderful?'

'Hmm,' Patrik said. 'The trees must have something on them, some sort of coating that the army—'

'Patrik, that's *enough*.'

I was taken aback by the firmness of her tone. This obviously wasn't the first time Fort Seeben had been a source of contention.

'Where is your sister?' Rebecca said.

'Reading somewhere,' he said, waving back at the house. 'She reads Romances,' he told me, saying it such a manner to make his disdain clear.

'Go find your sister and then get ready for bed. The sun has almost set.'

'What can one learn from *Romances*?'

'Patrik! Bed!'

I smiled at the retreating boy. 'I imagine I could learn much from that little boy.'

'Yes,' she said. 'He misses little.'

'Charming,' I said, offering my arm. Rebecca strode off down the track without waiting for me. Had I done something to offend her? Or *not* done something she had expected? The bath was far from how I had imagined the first time she was to see me naked, but she had been so insistent. As I took in the many windows of the Eder house, I realised all our previous encounters had been in town, safely away from her home. This was different – she held responsibilities here, she was a mother of sorts. Such a place had no room for a flirtation with a wandering musician from the north.

We walked under the shadow of the covered track, trees banked against a low wall on one side, and trees stretching off into the forest proper on the other. Looking for long at the forest made me uncomfortable but I also couldn't help searching for any signs of the destruction of the wall, and where Christophor had strayed from the track the previous night, when he still rode Tabitha. I saw no evidence of the terrible experience, none of the bloody mess I had woken to that morning. Eventually, I could take no more and sought a distraction.

'Olesca... he is smaller than I imagine most southern tribesmen to be,' I said.

'Have you met many from the tribes, living in the capital?'

'One or two. But now I think of it, they weren't particularly tall. All the stories and paintings I've seen have big men in them,' I said. 'Big men shaking their fists, or charging with a spear, or atop something monstrous. No women.'

She gave that some thought. In the shadows she had a sterner aspect to her – something I'd seen flashes of before, but this was more total, more like the impression I had of her night-sister. The formidable, as far as Christophor was concerned, the formidable Mrs Eder.

'Those paintings and stories say more about us, than about the tribes,' she said.

'And my songs?'

'They say very little at all, from what I've heard.'

'You wound me, madam,' I said, smiling. 'How do you know so much of the tribes?'

'When he's not singing, Olesca likes to talk of home.'

'My night-brother was quite taken with his voice.'

'But not you,' she said.

'Well, I've heard more foreign singers than he has.'

We had reached the end of the track, and the trees gave way to two-storey buildings with tall, sloping roofs. The pavements felt a welcome relief.

Rebecca kissed my cheek by way of farewell. Not a cold gesture, but one that I took to reinforce my earlier feeling; this was a line in the sand. Beyond that line, in sight of the Eder house, whatever we felt for each other was secondary. Unwelcome. So I would keep to my side.

'Look to yourself, Alexsander,' she said. Her simple, unguarded sincerity was hard to ignore. 'Don't let your night-brother dig you both an early grave.'

I glanced at the treeline. 'Neither of us are much for digging, least not with our hands.'

Christophor wanted to go find her. He knew it would be impossible, a fool's errand, and one only made in an attempt to ease his own battered conscience. He paced as he thought it through. There were other ways to honour the dead, other means, he decided. The very reason he was sent there in the first place, for instance. She was just a horse. Worse had been inflicted on the men and women of Drekenford. Worse, Christophor thought, but he knew he was lying to us both.

When uncertain or shaken he turned to his work. He wrote letters – one of which was to the King. Another to a librarian. Christophor made requests, apologies, excuses, and promises. He was comfortable with none of them.

That night he barely left his room. The busybody, the woman downstairs, pushed food on him from the corridor. She craned her neck to see just what he was doing. If she had seen she wouldn't have understood. Very few could.

He was dissecting the pinned heart. Cursing the south, his scant resources, his clumsy day-brother, he cut into the scarred and dried tissue. What he found there, I couldn't say, but he was not happy. That wasn't unusual.

But I'd rarely known him so scared.

26th October 1721

When I opened my room door I was met by Mr Hennig.

'Ah, glad I caught you,' he said. He had clearly been waiting for me in the corridor – his lie obvious in his over-selling.

'Caught me at what?'

'I, I—' he stuttered. The conversation was not going as he'd planned, as he'd practised.

'I'm not to play today?' I said.

Mr Hennig grimaced. 'There's a back entrance, you see, with its own stairs and such.'

'Really, that is too much, Mr Hennig. I pay for my room, my food, my wine, just as your other patrons.'

'I let you through that common room there won't *be* other patrons.' He angled himself to give me little other option. I met his gaze. He had the decency to look me in the eye, at least.

'And what of my night-brother, does he—'

'What happens at night ain't none of my business. None of my business. Sometimes we day-lighters are more superstitious, more jittery, that's all.'

'The daylight isn't to blame for this town's shortcomings, Mr Hennig.'

'There's no one to blame, is there?' he said. 'People are just the way they are. Wherever they are.'

I opened my mouth, but decided against debating the ethics of superstition with the innkeeper. He was only looking after his livelihood. I would have to look after my own.

I straightened my light autumn coat, wishing I'd taken the time to make myself more presentable that morning. Some mischievous part of me came close to knocking on the doors of the other rooms and causing a ruckus. Instead, I hummed a sad tune for Mr Hennig, he who had no time for sadness in his common room; a sad tune of a man left friendless and penniless and destitute by his no-good night-brother. It was a favourite of inns in the north.

The stairs were tight and uncarpeted – a servants' staircase if I'd ever seen one. So it came as no surprise when I almost bumped into a young girl of abnormally large teeth coming the other way. She carried a mop and bucket and a good few pounds, none of which helped as we shuffled and squeezed our way past each other. I apologised, she blushed, and we left it at that.

At the backdoor I heard the rumble of the common room, which was punctured by a drunken cackle. Drekenford was starting early, or so I thought. But when I stepped out into a bright but not warm day I found the sun higher than I expected. It had been a difficult few days. And what did *I* have to be up early for?

I turned away from the stable and tried not to think of Tabitha and her grisly fate. I wandered along busy streets and empty alleyways, paying no heed to where I was going or to what end. Whatever day it was, it was not market day.

This was the first time, that I could recall in our decades together, when Christophor's work had prohibited my own. It made me think: how else had I been affected? What positions or opportunities had been denied to me because of him? Companies, orchestras, quartets that had turned me down – and there had been a fair number of those – had always done so on reasonable grounds, or so they said. But as I remembered those conversations, how the directors shook their heads with pursed lips and a certain look in their eye – was that my night-brother lurking there?

Not for the first time I felt foolish. I thought, after all these years, I understood the way of things and how people navigated this world. But in truth I was as ignorant and as naive as a silk merchant's favourite daughter.

What to do? My feet decided for me, and they decided on

something a merchant's daughter could not do: get drunk in the middle of the day.

I climbed the steps to Marcus' rooms. He was home, though not in a full state of dress. He opened the door and frowned.

'If you're looking for the workhouse you need to follow the river's flow to the edge of town. Big place, it is.'

'So you've heard?' I said.

'Not so much as a mouse farts without me hearing it in this town.'

'What's that you're drinking?'

He made a show of surprise, as if I'd magicked the glass into his hand. 'This? This is for thinning my paints.'

'Let me in, you rascal, before I ruin your chances of ever selling another painting.'

The slim painter admitted me entrance with an exaggerated bow. 'A little notoriety wouldn't hurt,' he said. He fetched me a glass and a shirt for his back. I told him not to on my account, but apparently it was the painting that kept him warm on such days – not the wine.

We took to his balcony and he brought cushions for the chairs. For some time we watched the toing and froing of the upstanding citizens of Drekenford. It was, in its way, fascinating. Men and women and children all hurrying along, and managing to do so somehow despite their personal burdens. For many those burdens were all too evident in the hunch of their shoulders, or cut of their clothes, or way their gaze wouldn't sit still. Perhaps it was my mood, but looking down on them all I could believe they had the direst of secrets, every one.

'If I wanted a bellows for a companion,' Marcus said, 'I would have brought one up from the cellar.'

'Bellows?'

'You're breathing as if your very life depended on it.'

'Doesn't it?'

'I suppose it does.' Marcus raised his glass to his lips.

'I don't know what I'm supposed to do,' I said.

'Why should you *do* anything?'

I looked at him, this slight but muscular man of roughly my own age. His habits had treated him more roughly than my own; existing, as they did, on both sides of the ettiene. The lines across his face were deeper, the veins of his cheeks and nose more pronounced, his teeth stained as much as he might try to hide it. I looked, because I had no answer for his question. Not really.

'Has he taken your instruments?' Marcus said.

'No.'

'Chopped off your fingers?'

I would not dignify that with an answer.

'Does he chain himself to the bed at the end of each night, or lock the room in some elaborate manner, or—?'

'I take your meaning,' I said, before he could really warm to his subject. 'It is not the same to simply *play*, it is my livelihood.'

He snorted at that. 'Alexsander, you know how this goes. You will be gone from this place in a week, maybe two. Whatever professional pride has been wounded will heal. You'll soon forget Drekenford, until a lady mentions a distant relative during a card game and you'll say, "Yes, I sojourned there once, a lifetime ago."'

'Perhaps you're right.'

'It's rare, but not unheard of.'

'And what until then?' I said.

'Why, do what anyone does when they have the illusion of time on their hands: indulge your vices.' He refilled my glass, his hand shaking as he did so.

I thanked him, but made a decision in that moment *not* to follow his advice. I would not spend the next handful of days drinking myself into a stupor until I fell into the first warm embrace my purse would pay for. No, I would pursue a less predictable course of action. And the more I turned over the idea the more it took root. Its tendrils crept between my teeth and around my tongue, knitting my mouth uncharacteristically closed. They spread down my throat and collapsed my lungs until I felt short of breath at the power of the idea. From there it could only spread lower. My legs sent jouncing and jiggling, and my feet tingling at unseen needles.

Marcus sat back, the small smile on his face suggesting he thought his work done, his friend mollified, his company on this lonely balcony assured.

Instead, I began to wonder how I might aid Christophor.

'I want to help catch a witch.'

'What do you know of witches?' Marcus said.

'More than I'd care to.' I wondered if I should have kept my newfound purpose to myself. But Marcus was determined to have company, and determined that company would *talk*. 'I've been there for every case my night-brother has worked, after all.'

'How's your night-brother on the fiddle?'

'Atrocious.'

'And what makes you think you'll be any better as an inspector?'

'I've no plans on joining the King's constabulary!' I said. 'Just helping in whatever small way I'm able.'

'When I'm not seeing Stefan's drudgery-filled nights, I sometimes dream of mountains.'

'Mountains.'

'And the climbing thereof. If I were to fetch up at the foot of a mountain in a sturdy pair of boots and clutching some kind of polished stick, with obvious intentions, I'd be in less danger than you,' Marcus said, glancing out over the balcony. 'At the very least, *I* would know where to start.'

'You may be right, you—'

There was a welcome knock at the door. We had reached that stale part of the day when friends risk becoming a chore. I peered into the gloom of Marcus' rooms. I could just make out someone divesting themselves of a coat and bags. And then, out of the dimness, I saw her calm face, her easy smile.

I shot back in my seat, pulled myself upright, and re-buttoned the top of my shirt. I touched needlessly at my poor excuse for hair and smoothed my eyebrows with a licked finger. There was nothing I could do about the wine on my breath, except perhaps steady my breathing. A task easier said than done.

'I saw you two pickling yourselves,' Rebecca said reproachfully, stepping onto the balcony. 'And decided to join you.'

Marcus carried through one of her canvas bags, which boasted fruits and a little pie each. 'I hope, my dear, you come bearing sense as well as victuals.'

'I couldn't carry enough of either for you, Marcus.'

'It's not me that has a need.'

'Oh?' She turned to me. Again that smile.

Evidently we were back to an easy rapport. Back to our

in-town selves, and how we had been before I stumbled out of the forest behind her house, half-dead and the other half delirious, until she gave me water. Until she... bathed me. Heat rose in my cheeks.

'He's blushing,' she said.

'That could be the wine,' Marcus said. 'Our friend here is drinking himself into, and then out of, a bad idea.'

'Do you have any other kind, Alexsander?'

'Not of late. No one does.' I said this too quietly, too sincerely, and the mood turned.

'Well, you better tell me then, if you're going to.'

By way of building up to do so, I told her of Mr Hennig's banning of my music and of my public use of his establishment. I made my lack of purpose more than clear. And then I said, 'So, I plan to assist my night-brother.'

'And not just with his dirty linens and drawers!' Marcus said, though we both ignored him.

She looked at me for what felt like a long time. 'Won't that be dangerous?' she said eventually.

'It might be.'

'And what hope of success do you have?'

'Hope? More than I have right to. Perhaps more than my night-brother has, in fact.'

'Alexsander, don't do this.'

'That's what I said!' Marcus crowed.

'Let your night-brother handle his business.'

'"What happens at night is none of my business,"' I said in fair imitation of Mr Hennig, which was lost on them. 'But it is our business, is it not?'

They looked uncomfortable at that as both considered their respective siblings.

'I've seen enough prisons and hangings and the like to know 'the importance of harmony.' I held up a hand to forestall Marcus and said, 'Not just through my night-brother's eyes. I don't mean to cause him any difficulties, quite the opposite.'

'And what if the very thing he requires is your inaction?' Marcus said.

'Then so be it, let him say so. Otherwise, I will help his investigation.'

'That's very brave of you,' Rebecca said softly.

'Come now, Rebecca! I imagined you able to talk him away from this ridiculous notion.'

'I saw the horse,' I said. 'I didn't see the woman in the prison, or your own constable, but I saw the horse for myself. I hadn't grown fond of it the way my night-brother had, but still. To know that can be done to a living creature... How can I do nothing?'

We all made attempts, in our own ways, to rescue the day after that. We laughed too hard. Drank too quickly. Pursued arguments too readily. All in vain, of course. Long before sunset we made our excuses and said our goodbyes.

Rebecca lingered at the bottom of Marcus' steps. She started to say something, and then stopped.

'Are you all right?' I said.

'Be careful, Alexsander.'

'Rebecca, wait—'

But she hurried along the street. The hood of her coat was pulled up despite the mild afternoon. Even I, in my wine-soaked state, could tell she'd said all she had to say on the subject. Perhaps that was the best I could hope for – that my decision gave no more need for discussion or cautionary words.

Feeling sorrier for myself than I had before arriving at Marcus', I took to the streets again. At least Christophor's notoriety hadn't denied me the run of pavements and parks and the shops. I was drawn to the smell of a bakers but for some reason found the abundant stacks of ruddy, wholesome loaves in the window too much. I needed somewhere to match my darker mood. As I passed sweetshops, toymakers, florists, jewellers, and the like, I wondered if Drekenford had been transformed into some benign idyll before my very eyes. Or had it always been so *jolly*?

I found a kind of grim safe haven in a curio shop. With windows almost entirely blocked by displays, and an apparently miserly approach to lighting their oil lamps, the shop was as gloomy and dusty as a church. The proprietor was a small, disinterested woman with glasses that could serve as wagon wheels.

Every surface undulated and churned, a sea of porcelain and wood and imitation gemstones. It hurt to look at for long, the gaze could not find anywhere comfortable to sit; it slipped and fell among cut-glass and tarnished silver. I made the mistake of hoping to touch something, anything, to stop the sense of rolling waves. My fingers came away dusty and confused.

'Can I help you?' the woman asked.

'I hope so,' I said. 'I'm looking for a gift for my night-brother.' I had not realised that was really the aim of my wandering until I said the words aloud. I wanted something to accompany the note I would write to him.

'A gift, for an occasion?'

'More of a peace offering.'

'Good gift-giving,' she said, warming to the subject, 'requires some thought.' She tapped her lips, which sent her bangles into fits. 'What was the nature of your falling out?'

'Oh, well, I'm not sure he would see it as such. We've simply had a differing... direction, over the years. Different priorities.'

'Interesting.'

I stared at this singular shopkeeper, who courted the air of a fortune teller or seer.

'Your night-brother, does he have any vices?'

'No,' I said.

'You answered rather swiftly.'

'Of our differing directions, his was virtue.'

'A religious man?' she asked.

An impression flashed before me of men on horseback, fields blazing behind them, all inexplicably inside Drekenford's own church. I felt the weight of his crucifix on the back of my neck. He had a bible locked in a drawer – locked away by a sense of terror as much as wards and cylinders.

'It's complicated,' I said.

'It often is.' She gestured around the shop. 'If not vices, and not virtues, what else?'

'He does collect...' I didn't know how to say it without sounding ridiculous. In truth, I didn't know the correct terminology.

'Yes?'

'He collects eggs. But not the kind you eat,' I added quickly.

'Blown eggs. Well, why didn't you say?' She turned and began moving boxes and crates crammed behind her small station. Finally, she placed a velvet-lined tray on top of the counter. I looked down at perhaps fifty eggs of various sizes and colours, feeling as lost as I ever had in my life. I made a noise to that effect. 'How long has he been collecting?' she said.

'Since we were boys.'

She gave me a look of incredulity. Well, did Christophor know what strings I employed on my lutes? What reeds I favoured? What varieties of red or white I would or would not drink?

'That one looks nice,' I said, pointing at a large egg with reddish speckles.

She ignored me. 'You won't find anything here that a man collecting for so long doesn't already have.'

'What is the use then?'

'He will appreciate the thought, I'm sure.'

'Are you,' I said.

'Even if he already has a set they may be of lesser quality that he hasn't managed to replace. Here,' she said, lifting a little tray from within the tray. 'Bullfinches are common enough, but he'd have been lucky to find better than these.'

'They're very pretty.'

'I imagine you have no idea which nesters he favours?'

I shrugged helplessly.

'Well, the engravings on the bottom there will mean something to him I imagine.'

'I'll take them,' I said, and did my best to remain impassive as she conveyed their price. I had been in the wrong business all this time. She packaged them with appropriate care and asked if there would be anything else. I cast my gaze once more around the flotsam and jetsam of the shop. I wondered if I should find a gift for Rebecca, but was exhausted by the thought of having to choose. And then a thought came to me.

'Do you have any bears?'

It took her only a moment to absorb my odd request. Then she was a whirlwind about her own shop. She returned to the counter with a pack of bears: one made of sack-like material, two of porcelain, and a small stone carving. As sweet as the sack bear was, the stone was more appropriate.

'Could you—' I began, before stopping myself. I could remove one of the bear's eyes myself. I had already confused the shopkeeper enough for one day. 'The bear is her favourite,' I said.

Christophor read my note more than once. His surprise was sharp, but I should not have expected any less. He could not, it was clear, fathom why I had made such a decision, and why now. With a kind of care that can only come from experience, Christophor picked up the eggs and admired them. The woman in the shop had steered me well in that respect, at least. I had half-wondered if she was taking advantage of a man as much at the mercy of his cups as his ignorance.

Christophor gathered himself and made to leave the sanctuary of the inn. Through the front door. Evidently the village's superstitions and prejudices were not strong enough to deny the *Special Inspector* himself. Or perhaps he simply had the strength of will to ignore such shackles – shackles made of gossip, whispers, and weak-minded decisions. I envied that strength, doubly so because I saw no way to find it in myself.

Mrs Lehner was pleased to see him up and about, and called a hearty greeting from behind the bar, which she could barely see over. He was wary of her, though it wasn't obvious why.

What was spurring him into such a frenzy wasn't obvious either. Was it Tabitha's fate? He did care for that horse. Was it the ever-increasing sense of guilt that came with each day that passed without the completion of his duties? Was it my note, with my threat of involvement in his affairs?

He ghosted his way through the streets towards the track that led up to the Eder's house. He made no effort to find a break in the treeline, or any evidence of the site where he and Tabitha had left the track that night. He kept his head down and lengthened his stride.

He was worried he wouldn't be able to go back to the house. He was worried he would be too scared. That was why he hurried himself.

Unwilling to use the stag brass knocker, he rapped briskly on the door and tried not to fidget as he waited. The house was well-lit with candles in most of the windows, upstairs and down, and lanterns on the porch. Eventually, the door swung inwards to reveal the butler.

'Special Inspector Morden.'

Our name had never sounded so lifeless.

'I would like to speak to either Mayor Eder or his wife.'

'You do not have an appointment.'

Though it was not a question, Christophor withdrew his badge from his coat pocket by way of an answer.

'The mayor is attending his offices,' the butler said.

'Mrs Eder then.'

The butler became very still. Moments passed. Then he appeared to shudder. 'Very well,' he said, 'if you will accompany me to the parlour.'

For the third time in so many days Christophor was walking along the corridors of the Eder household. The experience wasn't becoming any more pleasant with each visit. In fact, this time they felt positively tight, the paintings and tapestries and the like were closer than ever and the air strained. Mrs Eder was waiting for him.

'Thank you, Henry,' she said, dismissing the butler. 'Welcome, Inspector, what a pleasant surprise to see you again so *soon*.' She didn't offer him a seat.

'I'm afraid I am here on official business this time, Mrs Eder.'

'In that case, my household is entirely at your disposal.' She reached for a bell on a side table, but he stopped her.

'Perhaps I might ask you some questions, before speaking to your staff.'

She arched a brow at that.

'I won't keep you any longer than necessary,' he said. He produced his notebook and pencil, an act timed with the same precision and ritual as you'd find from a conductor who stands before their orchestra. 'I must first apologise.'

'Apologise, Inspector?'

'I should have brought my questioning to your door earlier, but I'm afraid events somewhat overtook me. You'll recall Constable Webber, and no doubt—'

'Terrible business. And a man so well-loved, so much a fixture of our community.'

'Yes,' Christophor said. 'Though I understand there was an issue between the constable and Stefan, the framer.'

Mrs Eder scowled. 'Inspector, gossip may be a necessary evil when entertaining, but I choose not to sully myself with such things in private.'

'Sadly, that is where much of my investigations lead.' He scribbled uselessly on a full page. 'Were you the one who discovered Jan Harsson's theft?'

'No,' she said. 'That was Patrik and Victor between them.'

He flicked back a few pages to his Eder family tree. 'Your son, born a night-child and not cared for by your day-sister.'

'I wouldn't say that.'

'What would you say, Mrs Eder?'

'Rebecca may not be married to an Eder, but she does *care* for our children. She lives here and helps when she's able.'

'Patrik and Victor discovered the crime. How?'

'You've met Victor at least,' she said. 'He and his day-brother have an inquiring, and determined, mind. I've often thought, were we in the city, one of them would make an excellent addition to the King's constabulary.'

'I dare say their talents might be wasted there. Regardless, can you say *how* they came to realise Jan was the thief?'

She sighed, appearing somewhat conflicted. 'By turns they hid in the dresser,' she said eventually, an odd mix of pride and shame in her voice. 'Day and night for over a week, I believe. They kept a meticulous log of who took what, when, and why. Jan Harsson was the only member of staff to make... What they called: "Unsolicited, singular-directional withdrawals." Inquiring, and determined, as I said.'

'And yet Constable Webber's report made no mention of Victor's "log"? Perhaps he was too proud to admit the assistance of a child?'

'I wouldn't care to speculate.'

'No.' Another flick of the page. 'But you did dismiss Mrs Harsson, Jan's mother, following the incident.'

'That was a shame. We had grown quite fond of Mrs Harsson over the years. But, as I'm sure you can imagine, the situation was untenable.'

'Did Mrs Harsson cause any problems following the arrest?'

'Not that I'm aware of. But it was the *situation*, you understand.'

'The gossip,' Christophor said flatly.

'As you say.' She picked up the servant's bell. 'Now, is that all, Inspector?'

'For the time being, though I would like to speak with your staff. One at a time, if you please.'

'Of course.' She rang for the butler. 'Perhaps you would be more comfortable conducting your interviews in the servants' quarters.'

It wasn't a question, and soon Christophor found himself being led back through the corridors to a room he would rather not have known. An empty bathtub stood in one corner, and two low stools were in the centre of the otherwise bare room. He made sure to position himself with his back to the bath. I believe he was blushing somewhat, until the first of the servants was ushered in.

The whole business of it felt unnatural to me. At times the conversations had the stilted air of bad theatre. The majority of the servants were meek as mice and unable to meet Christophor's gaze. The men answered in monosyllabic mutters, the women in squeaks. Every one of them looked grateful to be dismissed. Christophor's notebook stayed in his pocket.

That was, until the head chef strode into the room.

A large woman, but none of her gone to fat. She sat heavily on the stool and leaned forward, one arm resting on each leg. She stared Christophor right in the face. Stains speckled her rolled-up sleeves, some of which were undoubtedly blood.

'You've got until the dinner service needs readyin',' she said by way of greeting.

Christophor cleared his throat. 'Did you know Gregory Harsson, or his day-brother Jan?'

'Yes, I knew 'em.'

'Personally, or simply professionally?'

'Both.'

'Do you believe Jan was guilty?'

'They said he was.'

'Do *you* say he was?'

The woman glanced to the door. 'That, and between them more, I'd say.'

'More?'

'There's other things to be stealin' in a house like this, if you catch my meanin'.'

'I'm afraid I don't.'

'Things that don't need carryin' out under a coat or the like,' she said.

He pondered that little riddle for a moment. 'Might those things be more willing to walk themselves out?'

'I'd say so, and on more than one occasion.' She straightened a little. 'I didn't like it. I told Gregory so. Told him to think of his day-brother, of what *he* might lose. I didn't like it one bit, and the mother knew, too.'

'Mrs Harsson?'

'Oh yes, she knew, nothin' got by *her*. But I was meanin' Mrs Eder. The young 'uns made a poor secret of it. But I s'pose that's the way, when you're that age.'

Christophor was slow to it, but the pieces did come together; the eldest Eder daughter, Louisa, was bedding Gregory. Someone well beneath her station.

'Louisa,' he said under his breath. The chef gave one last look to the door, and then nodded.

'Wasn't right, what happened to Jan. Just 'cos his night-brother went and did somethin' silly.'

There was finally call for the notebook. When Christophor was alone in the room he wrote down the name and stared at it for a long while. He underlined it, slowly, deliberately.

'If you are going to be of use, Alexsander, ask the questions I cannot,' he said to himself, to me.

This I remembered clearly and distinctly, as was his intention. He was demanding to know more about Harriet, who was day-sister to Louisa. A day-sister he could never reach; but she might provide answers that were impossible at night. For some reason he did not want to question Louisa or Olesca directly. Perhaps that would jeopardise the investigation, or expose him somehow.

Either way, he was starting to understand but there was still more to know of the incident that had started this case, this hunt for a witch among the high and low of Drekenford. He now felt certain Gregory and Jan Harsson were sent so far away to reduce the risk of an Eder family scandal. But what spurred the witch to further punish the boy? For that, perhaps I could be some help.

27th October 1721

However, the world is not as open to a musician as it is a *Special Inspector*.

Especially a musician without patron or employment. Without a modest crowd of onlookers, even. I knew if I were to set myself in the square, at the fountain perhaps, and simply practise – practise, not play for an audience – I would be chased off on some pretence or another. How could it be that I suffered more from Christophor's work than he did? And how then was I supposed to help with that very work?

I was without direction or purpose, a familiar state at least, but I knew one thing: I would not visit Marcus. I would not spend another day in a comfortable stupor, in good company and with easy distractions. I would *not*.

Unless, of course, it was done with purpose.

I didn't recognise the woman waving at me from across the street. I would have sworn that before judge, mob, even God himself, but I waved back nonetheless. She was standing in front of a baker's, a wicker basket in the crook of one arm and a slightly older woman at the other. She hurried over, all but dragging a less enthusiastic companion in her wake.

'Mr Morden?' the woman said, with a strong hint of doubt.

'Good morning,' I said, smiling to each in turn. 'Have we met?'

'Well, no, not really, but I recognised you. I know— Well, I mean to say our night-siblings have met. I'm sorry, this is really rather presumptuous, but I saw you and, well I did wonder, I—'

'Beatrice you're babbling,' her companion said sternly. Beatrice proceeded to perform the finest impression of a beetroot I'd ever seen. 'I am Mrs Channock, and this is Mrs Fredericks. We met your night-brother, Inspector Morden, at a function held by our esteemed friends the Eders. You may recall the evening?'

I recalled much more of it than I would like, but I did my best not to let that show. Instead, I took their offered hands and said, 'Charmed to finally meet you both in the favourable light of day.'

'Yes well, I imagine you are a busy man, Mr Morden, and we—'

'Would you join us for afternoon tea?' Beatrice said.

'Beatrice, *really*, you forget yourself.'

'No I don't. Would you, Mr Morden? That is, if you are not too busy?'

I could do little to deny such an earnest, guileless face. But I could do my best to profit by it.

Beatrice Fredericks lived in a townhouse on a tree-lined street in a well-to-do area of town. I expected as much from a well-to-do young lady, but I was not expecting such tasteful touches throughout. The decor – from the lightwood entrance hall through to the spring-patterned parlour – was understated, but considered. Touches of gilding were employed to compliment, not dominate, the space and light. Ample room was allowed around the plainly upholstered high-backed chairs and table.

As I entered the parlour the smell of polished wood was offset by a wonderful scent. I looked about me and soon spotted the source – a large potted jasmine dominated a dresser close to the door. I turned to my host.

'That is simply a wonder, Mrs Fredericks.'

'Beatrice, please, and thank you.' She blushed once more, but a blush of the self-congratulatory kind. 'My plants are somewhat of an obsession.'

'I have rarely seen such a pleasant and tastefully applied obsession, Beatrice.' I circled the room, stopping at a colourful little tree. 'And what is *this* wonder?'

'You have an eye for a woman's weakness,' Mrs Channock said, arranging herself at the table.

Beatrice cleared her throat. 'That is something special my husband—'

Was there a note of emphasis there?

'—brought home from one of his trips east. He travels a great deal.'

'How unfortunate for him,' I said. 'But his loss appears to be your gain.' The potted tree was an explosion of red and yellow bell-shaped flowers. When I blinked they appeared to dance and merge into a flickering inferno.

Beatrice came beside me and unconsciously removed a dead flower from the back of the plant. 'I've never had it flower so late. But then these are strange times, don't you think?'

'Are we to have tea?' Mrs Channock said. 'Or do you only water plants, not people, in your parlour?'

'I had hoped to wait for our other guests.'

'Other guests?' I said, taken aback by the hope this kindled in me.

'It's an ambush, Mr Morden,' Mrs Channock said. She guffawed at her own jest – not a sound I was expecting from the woman, but she did so naturally. 'Don't look so terrified. We won't ask you to perform.'

'Oh, but would you—?'

I was saved by the butler announcing Mrs Merringway, Johanson, and Parn. Introductions were made. Judging by the expressions of these married women in their middle-years, it was they who felt ambushed. I was very much aware of my singular masculinity in a parlour full of many-layered dresses. I was not unused to the company of women – it certainly didn't render me a panicked mute as it did Christophor – but I was not typically the lone representative of my sex. It was quite the burden.

When the butler entered once more I felt hope again, stronger this time, strong enough to recognise its provenance. I wished Rebecca to walk through that door. I wished she would do so wearing a finer dress than her market clothes, her hair arranged in some unexpected way – ringlets, perhaps, cascading down one shoulder. I wanted to both recognise her and find her new there, in a relative stranger's parlour. But it was not to be. Four more names, none of them hers. Four more married women, none of them discernible from the next.

'She won't be joining us,' Mrs Channock said, cornering me by the little tree. 'Not that she was invited.'

'I don't know what you mean,' I said.

'No? Most of the town does.'

'You make a simple friendship sound so sordid, Mrs Channock.'

'I wouldn't take it to heart. You're not the first, and you won't be the last.'

'Mrs Channock—'

'And who would blame Rebecca? None in this parlour, certainly. We all appreciate a pretty little thing brought from far away.'

I tried to stop myself and not rise to the goading of a magistrate's wife. But I was weak. 'Some of us have to impress without a uniform and sabre.'

It took her half a breath to catch my meaning. 'Yes, Second Lieutenant Matherson was handsome, little good it did him.'

'I imagine no event of note in Drekenford escapes you, Mrs Channock.'

'We live in a fairly small town.'

'Come now, no need for modesty,' I said, determined to make use of this vile woman, and to move the conversation away from gossip of which I was the subject. 'What, for interest's sake, did you make of the arrest of the Harsson boy?'

'The Eder servant? Only that it had little to do with silverware.'

'So I'm beginning to understand. Warming beds was perhaps beyond his duties? Especially that of Lou—'

'Don't,' Mrs Channock said, raising a hand to cut me off. She glanced around the parlour in what I took to be a genuine state of anxiety. But there was only the polite chatter of women taking tea. Suddenly my mouth was quite dry. 'Don't. I've found certain names have a kind of power of late.'

'I would not have taken a magistrate's wife for a superstitious woman,' I said.

'And what of a constable? One who said a few names

until someone put more permanent words in his mouth.' She looked at me with a chilling calm. 'That floppy-haired girl and her southern gander were the reason the Harsson boy was sent north in chains. My husband signed the papers, but they were the reason.'

I repeated that piece of information in my head, over and over, hoping it would help confirm some of my suspicions for my night-brother. 'I did not expect to see anyone from the southern tribes here in Drekenford.'

'There are plenty of theories about that, I can assure you. Some say he simply wandered out of the forest a few years ago, and into the Eder house.'

That was a possibility I could picture only too well.

'Once there, their eldest insisted he must stay, that she would marry him. Personally, I've never seen the kind of spine in *that* girl that would "insist" on anything.'

'It does sound a plausible explanation. He—'

'Plausible? *Plausible*? A boy barely tall enough to reach the table wandering through however many hundreds of miles of forest? Alone? Which part of that sounds plausible to you?'

'Well.'

'No. I may not subscribe to the belief that their proposed marriage is a secret union between southern tribes and a maligned – frankly forgotten – house with Kettoman roots. Who could think such a union would really threaten the King?'

'Who indeed.'

'But it is between those two unlikely extremes that the truth lies.'

For once I was lost for words. This appeared to satisfy Mrs Channock, as if that was her intention all along. The question of Olesca was certainly puzzling – a southerner who, like myself, was so far from home. Was one part of him more comfortable, more accepting of the situation, than the other? Did he, by daylight, long for the nomadic life of a tribesman? Or did his night-brother walk barefoot on the slate flagstones of the Eder kitchen and feel at home?

But, perhaps the most puzzling aspect of it all was the general sense of acceptance the town seemed to hold for a southern tribesman in their midst. The place was so quick to turn against Christophor and I, and yet here was a young man from an entirely different world. Was it simply that he wore clothes of our fashion, combed his hair, and spoke Reikovan without an overbearing accent? Was that enough to accept him as one of our own? Granted, without the self-inflicted bodily deformations, and the immodest traditional clothing, and the unknowable ritualistic celebrations it was easy to forget where the man was from.

'He is alone,' Mrs Channock said quietly.

I blinked at the woman. 'I'm sorry?'

'It's clear what you are wrestling with. He is alone. That's why we have all turned the other cheek. He is alone, and that is not how we think of the southern tribes. We cannot conceive of them as individuals.'

If I was in any doubt that Mrs Channock was a formidable woman, it was no longer in question. I might have taken days, weeks, or perhaps I would have never consciously reached that very conclusion: Olesca was alone. The southern tribes were a mass. A sprawling, uncontainable mass that knew nothing of borders or cities, walls or boundaries, fields or plough. There was no 'alone'.

Mrs Channock shifted as the sunlight caught the silver of

her bracelet. 'Being from the capital, what, do you suppose, the King would say?'

'We are not officially at war with the southern tribes.'

'Officially.'

'But it would be a scandal worthy of any drawing room discussion.'

'Would it.' She stared at me levelly. 'My great-grandfather fought and died in an unnamed part of the world. My family had nothing to bury. My father also took up arms against the enemies of the crown but, judging by the stories he told me when I was a girl, his regiment became somewhat lost. My whole family's contribution to the greatness of Reikova was battling insects the size of birds and naming rivers after the King's children.

'When have our wars ever been "official"?'

I had no answer for her, of course. Only gossip. 'Some in the capital say the King's actions are harder to predict of late. Unstable, is a word used on occasion.'

'Perhaps,' Mrs Channock said slowly, 'His Majesty is at risk of being under the influence of *foreign* powers?'

'Powers. I'm afraid you've lost me, Mrs Channock.'

'Evidently.'

In fact, I was becoming more confused and disoriented with each passing moment of the conversation. I felt the need to return to matters more closely at hand.

'The serving boy we spoke of earlier,' I said. 'He was sent north because of... romantic entanglements with the floppy-haired girl, as you called her.'

'That's right,' she said.

'It is strange, is it not, that Mr and Mrs Eder approve so strongly of the match between the girl and the southern tribesman? Strongly enough, perhaps, to manufacture a charge of theft?'

'I've witnessed stranger occurrences, *Inspector*,' she said.

I raised my teacup in salute to that. But I also determined to spend the rest of the afternoon discussing topics such as draperies, ballads of the modern variety, and the definition of a 'solarium'.

Was there a tap at the door, or was it the sound of receding footsteps that woke him? Christophor was cautious in opening his own bedroom door so early in the evening. Bleary-eyed, but his grip on his pistol was firm enough. He expected Mrs Lehner, or the serving girl, or a tray left by one of them. A heavy southern breakfast.

Instead it was a parcel, wrapped in brown paper with the seal – the King's seal – unbroken.

He looked uselessly up and down the corridor. Noticed, for the first time, how it listed slightly to the left and considered briefly the value of knocking on other guests' doors to ask if they had seen or heard anything. Had they seen a clandestine deliverer of parcels? Instead, Christophor locked the door behind him and put the parcel on the desk.

He stared at the seal.

This had all begun with the very same: the crest of Reikova. A symbol that should swell a heart with pride and strengthen even the weakest of resolves. His hands shook as he broke the red wax.

The paper parted to reveal books. Books, bound by string

and still layered in dust along the tops. Books no one read, only referred to. And yet, there was one page clearly marked by an incongruously clean, white slip of paper.

He placed this book reverently to one side and examined the rest. These he had not requested, but seemed to know. The names on their covers, Poul and Hendricks and others meant nothing to me. In none of the texts were there signs of tampering or censorship, for which he was glad. Even as a Special Inspector of the King's constabulary some knowledge was forbidden to him. He knew his limits, his boundaries. In some ways enjoyed them.

The slip of white paper was like a beacon.

He opened the book on that particular page. He read lines that were familiar to him, but made little sense to me. Did they reassure him? I could not tell.

'Stone cannot move on water,' Christophor said firmly. 'Hearts do not bleed gold.'

Cannot and do not. And yet he knew otherwise.

He added layers of uncertainty and doubt to the treacherous geography of this case. It was that geography, and not the streets of Drekenford through which he drifted, that he concerned himself with that evening. He needed to take some air and to be away from the books he had waited so long for.

Just when he was beginning to understand this case, another complication appeared. He was confident of the arrest and exile of Jan Harsson – of the reason given and the real reason behind it. But that knowledge begot more questions, the most pertinent of which being: who engineered the situation? Mr or Mrs Eder, the parents of the girl Jan was consorting with? A serving boy was obviously not a good match for their eldest daughter. But then neither was a tribesman. Or was it Olesca, the young man who was himself betrothed to that daughter? He did not have the same sway with the local authorities, but his motive was just as strong. Motive: that was Christophor's word. In this instance, it could have been jealousy, combined with fear of losing his match with a northern noble woman. Or perhaps there was the young woman herself? Louisa, having grown guilty or tired of her own infidelities endeavoured to have them sent away. And last of the immediate suspects was Victor, who by his own mother's admission was responsible for catching the boy's thievery. What did he know of his older sister's indiscretions?

This was what occupied Christophor as he lost himself in unfamiliar streets. That, and a book I did not understand.

28th October 1721

I surprised Marcus by arriving at his doorstep before midday. When he opened his door he was working his mouth in the way of a man just woken; a man just woken from a chair, fully clothed, and surrounded by empty bottles if I had to guess.

'What's wrong?' he said by way of a greeting.

'Nothing that wasn't wrong yesterday,' I said.

He squinted up at the cloud-filled sky. 'Is it even eight o'clock?'

'Ten,' I said. 'I need to come in.'

He stepped aside. His shirt was unbuttoned, and his fly

similarly so. His sun-darkened skin looked as dry as parchment, as did his close-cut hair. But I had been ungenerous: glancing into his lounge I saw only one finished bottle of spirits beside his favoured chair. Age was catching up on us all, in our own ways.

I surprised him a second time by not making my way towards the balcony. Instead, I turned inwards towards his studio space.

There was an almost total darkness in there, with only a sliver of light squeezing beneath the shutters. If only Drekenford's singular inn could manage the same with its shutters, a guest might manage to sleep beyond the dawn. Though, perhaps like Marcus and I, most guests relied on libations to achieve that.

He gasped when I threw the shutters open.

'Just what's taken hold of you, Alexsander?'

'I don't know,' I said, turning about the room. 'That's to say, I don't know the word for it. I don't know if there *is* a word for it. A feeling, I suppose.'

'I don't trust feelings.'

'Quite.' I strode back towards the door. 'But will you indulge me?'

'Will I need to do anything?'

'Rarely. This is the first? 1693?'

'Well, I made sketches and such previously.'

'But this is the first finished painting?'

He nodded.

I stared at the view from Marcus' balcony and experienced a strange moment of vertigo, of dizziness, brought on by the sensation of being in two places at once. In clumsy brushstrokes the far side of the valley was covered in evergreen forest, the nearest rooftops peppered the middle ground, and the streets held blotchy passers-by. I looked everywhere and nowhere. I worked methodically from side-to-side, then top-to-bottom, not knowing what to look for in particular but sure there was *something* to be found. I let my gaze lose its focus and the view softened. Marcus' early ineptitude was covered as colours found each other, blending and bending, until I saw a closer approximation of the town of Drekenford. I moved on to the next painting.

The same, of course, but already different. Marcus had made progress within the year; even my uneducated eye could see that. He took a slightly more detailed approach to the roof slates, tightened his show of the forest, and kept his streets empty – perhaps until he could do the people justice. The first steps towards a more playful use of light and shadow were evident. This trend continued throughout the next handful of paintings, until 1700.

I looked at the painting, and then at the painter.

'Did you... did your night-brother paint this?'

'We had bad storms that year,' he said.

On closer inspection I saw, yes, it was still the day before me, despite the impression of candles in windows under a blackened sky.

'A poor start to the century,' I said.

'Was yours much better?' he asked, sounding genuinely interested.

I thought back those twenty-one years. I remembered being in Esteberg and at a garden party for the whole day. Just who was our host I couldn't recall, but we toasted the clock striking twelve. Made the best of it, though few could hide the pangs of envy that our night-siblings would see in the new century proper. I managed with some decorum only because I knew Christophor would *not* make the most of it. Those were his busiest years as he began systematically removing his own necessity as a Special Inspector, one poor soul at a time.

Normality tried to resume in Drekenford in 1701: a pleasant springtime view was my impression. Flowers in window-boxes, somehow brighter than they were in previous years. A crispness. Spring lambs cavorting in the streets would not have surprised me.

'You overcompensated this year,' I said.

'I was young.'

'Not that young.'

I gave each of the following paintings my attention, noting the slight changes in season that suggested Marcus finished his painting early or late that year. One such late painting was 1717, which I almost disregarded until I stopped, mid-step, caught between two years.

'What's this?' I said, waving at the canvas.

The floorboards creaked and popped as he came to stand beside me. He said nothing for a moment, but did lean a little closer to the painting.

'The river.'

'River? Where?' I said. I glanced back along the line, certain I hadn't seen anything that could remotely represent the Dreken river, even in Marcus' style.

'Where they didn't want it.' He drew a line that snaked from the edge of the painting, ghosting behind buildings and streets, until his finger left Drekenford behind. 'That was the year they changed the course of the river. Changed a lot of things in town, that did.'

'But what for?'

'Oh, I don't know. They probably gave a reason at the time, but damned if I can remember.'

'Why does anyone move a river?'

'It did used to flood badly, back when I was a boy,' he said. 'There was talk, though, I remember that much.'

'Talk?'

'Talk. Thirsty work it is too.' He turned and disappeared into his modest kitchen. He returned with a weak white wine and two glasses. I watched him spill a little on the floorboards, and then accepted the glass from him. He drank without fanfare. 'Some said they moved the river, tore up half the town, spent all that money, just so they could build the bridge.'

'The animal bridge,' I said. I moved through the years and, now I knew what to look for, I could see the small changes wrought on the town, even though Marcus' balcony didn't command a full view of the river or the bridge. The river could be seen in the absence of a few otherwise insignificant buildings, the new prominence of others, the subtly changed shape of the streets of Drekenford. The bridge was a grey mark on the extreme edge of each painting – in some cases it was covered entirely by a more intrusive frame. But invariably it was there, after 1717.

'Who are "they", Marcus?'

Either my unexpected question had dealt him a third surprise, or perhaps he was surprised at the naivety behind the question, because he raised an eyebrow in response. 'How many people do you think could do such a thing in a town like this?'

'The mayor would have to approve, of course.'

'Did more than approve. Made the whole thing happen, I'd say.'

'But why *then*?' I said, gesturing to the other paintings. 'Why not build a bridge to celebrate the new century?'

Marcus shrugged, as if to say one might as well question the movement of celestial bodies or the whims of a lover.

I stared at the small brass plate, 1717, and something tickled the back of my throat. I coughed but it wouldn't be moved. I coughed until water came to my eyes. 1717. Missing the mark, Marcus slapped me between the shoulders. Somehow I retained control of my glass. And then I realised, and cursed myself an ignoramus and a drunkard.

1717 was the year Olesca walked out of the forest.

She was waiting for me at the inn. Not out front, of course, but at the rear entrance to which I was banished. Rebecca knew that much – and much more. I was not expecting her, and we had not made plans to see each other. She was sitting on a barrel, as if she worked a river barge and had just come ashore for the usual reasons. She looked beautiful in the light of a setting sun.

'I was starting to wonder if you were warming someone else's bed,' Rebecca said. Her coy smile was far from girlish. She took my hand and led me inside, up the stairs, and right to the door of my room.

'How did you—'

'Sshh,' she said.

With her there the room was transformed. Everything I had come to take for granted was different. Lesser. I was embarrassed by our sparse, utilitarian living. But she made no comment, said nothing in fact as she stood before the bed in her blue dress, looking at me.

'Something to drink?' I said.

'To steady the nerves?'

'I seem to remember someone telling me I was too old for that kind of silliness.'

She helped me out of my coat and then began unbuttoning my shirt; it was happening so quickly, but I did not stop her. Her hands were cold, causing me to inhale sharply as she traced a finger down my chest. She lingered at the fading bruises and cuts. I watched her as if she were on the other side of the valley, so far away, touching someone else – an old man, with sagging purpled skin. I made to draw away, but she stopped my vanity. She pulled me down to a kiss. There was warmth there, at least.

Stepping back, she loosened the many bows and knots that made a labyrinth of a woman's dress. Eventually it fell to the floor. Layers of white undergarments followed. Naked, no more conscious of herself than she had been sitting in the common room, or haggling in the market, or pouring another glass of wine on Marcus' balcony. Unchanged by that moment, yet I was so very changed from when we'd first met. And she was to blame.

I gathered her to me. Felt the press of her breasts against my chest. Her breath on my neck.

Though new to each other, we knew what we were about. We took to the bed in no hurry. There was light left in the day.

She became a different shape as she lay beside me. It was my turn to trace lines on her. My hand between her legs. She moved in a rhythm, rucking her hips, and I followed. With her eyes closed, I could have almost been forgotten, until she gripped my chin, my cheek, and then my hair. She kissed me, harder now, insistent. I was not to stop.

I felt her shudder. And then once more, before she pushed me onto my back. I stared up at her. Marvelled at the loose hair against her shoulders, the rise and fall of her chest, and, more than anything, the feeling of her.

Her hands raked me as she worked both our bodies.

'You were. Always. Needed,' she whispered.

I felt us both tense. She pressed her forehead against mine. And then she was gone, far away, to the other side of the bed where inches were like miles between us.

I stared at the ceiling, and the shadows stretching across its length. The only sound was our breathing. It wasn't how I'd imagined it would be. And I felt foolish at that – it was the thought of a young man, someone with their naivety intact, who hadn't seen enough of the world to dent their idealism. I twisted and turned even as I lay still. I didn't want to lessen what we'd just done, but there was too much I didn't understand.

Rebecca was snoring.

I turned to her. She was fast asleep, even without the chewing of ettiene. Before too long her night-sister would wake. But there was nothing I could do about that. For once my night-brother would wake up staring down the barrel.

I eased myself out of bed, not wanting to disturb her, and chewed my leaf. I helped him that much, at least. On the window beside the plant was the little bear I had bought for Rebecca. There hadn't been a chance to give it to her properly, no right moment for a gift between us. This wasn't the right moment, either. But still, I tucked it into the front fold of her dress, not knowing when I would have another chance. In truth, it was a relief not to have to give it to her myself. Something told me we would not give gifts to each other. I'd made a mistake buying it. That wasn't the nature of what we had.

When I returned to the bed, Rebecca lay with her back to me. I reached out but didn't touch her. It was enough to know I was needed.

Christophor came to with Mrs Eder on his pillow. Our whole body tensed, and that was enough to wake her. She withdrew slowly.

Neither of them were shocked. But they both seethed. In their own ways they were witnesses to the whole affair, from start to finish, powerless to stop the lives of others. She covered herself as best she could, her back to him, as she dressed. He did the same. Not a word was said. They clung to the shred of dignity in that silence. She closed the door without so much as glance back.

He sat on the end of the bed and tried to remember the last time he'd woken beside a woman. And harder still, when he'd last fallen asleep beside one.

He spent the majority of the evening looking for something. It was difficult to determine just exactly what that *something* was. He wouldn't think on it for long. Was he trying to hide it from me? Such a thing was possible, I supposed, by his guarding of his thoughts – wilfully making it harder for me to recall them. I hadn't been aware of Christophor ever doing so before, but then I wouldn't if he'd been successful. Of course, a simpler explanation could be that whatever he was avoiding was too difficult to countenance, even for a hardened, pig-headed Special Inspector.

He was cold as he combed the streets. The sky was starlit and winter-clear. He should have found his witch by now and discharged his duty. He was outstaying his welcome.

That was how it felt as he passed men and women about their business on streets such as... I couldn't tell exactly where in Drekenford he was; the night still had its shadows and he didn't pause to look at signs. But wherever he went people saw him and then pursed their lips and shook their heads.

Christophor had more than enough experience of the animosity of a local populace. But typically that came after arrests, accusations, trials, and the like. It was a quick shift in the wind: people who were more than willing to help bring a witch to justice would, hours later, be keen to see the back of him. Drekenford had decided against the first part of the bargain. It made him wonder how badly things might go before the end. So far he could still walk the streets unimpeded. That was something.

He went to the river, looking up and down the deserted banks. He followed it as far as he was able towards the stone bridge, before a property's rear wall forced him back into the warren of streets. He found the bridge similarly empty of whatever he sought, which evidently wasn't short tempered cart-drivers or their longsuffering draft horses.

Christophor was almost back at the inn when he stumbled across the very thing he'd been searching for. It, or more accurately *they*, were standing in the covered entrance of one of Drekenford's larger smithies. Their attention was total. The hot light from the forge gave them a devilish hue and their eagerness positively cackled in the air about them. Victor and Julia Eder, two children singular in purpose.

'I've been looking for you,' Christophor said.

'Hello, Inspector,' Victor said without looking up.

He joined them in watching the smithy at work. Though his knowledge of the craft was not extensive, it did strike him that he was seeing something unusual. It wasn't horseshoes or blades or ironmongery of a traditional kind that had the large, aproned man bent over his station. Instead it seemed to be more intricate work.

'Do you often watch a smithy at his business?' Christophor said.

'Only when we're paying him,' Julia said, his intrusion clearly wearing her patience thin.

'I see. And what are you paying him to do?'

They exchanged a look. Slowly Victor turned to him. 'To aid us in an experiment,' the boy said, expressionless. A chilling child. He would make an excellent magistrate, so I thought.

Christophor considered this, and decided a gamble was appropriate. 'This wouldn't happen to be your *secret* experiment, would it?'

'I told you not to tell him!' Julia said.

Victor winced.

Christophor was unduly proud of himself for outmanoeuvring two children.

'This isn't the *whole* experiment, just a single phase,' Victor said.

The smithy straightened and, bringing a square of metal to his face, blew on his work. 'There we are, Master Victor,' the smithy said, showing the boy the still-hot piece. 'Is that about the right of it?'

Victor moved as close as he dared against the forge's heat. Christophor followed him. Man and child stared at a six-inch square of scoured metal, engraved into which was what looked like a nest of overlapping circles. In the centre were the letters V and M.

Christophor recognised a witches' mark, an apotropaic mark, when he saw one – he'd employed many of his own making over the years. A ward against the evil eye. A keep-away that, on occasion, bore talismanic letters of the Virgin Mary.

'Victor?' Christophor said. 'What need do you have for such a thing?'

'Not here, Inspector,' the boy whispered.

The smithy looked nonplussed. But his demeanour improved dramatically when the boy handed over a silver kreer.

'Fine work, Mr Baerson, sir,' Victor said. 'When can we expect the others?'

'Tomorrow noon be appropriate?'

'The evening would be better.'

'Right you are, Master Victor. Evening it is.'

Victor offered his hand, which was swiftly engulfed by the smithy's. Apparently satisfied, the boy passed the square of metal to Julia and then set off down the street at a purposeful pace. He didn't look back. Julia and my night-brother followed in his wake.

Their destination was obvious, but there was not an insignificant part of Christophor that hoped he was mistaken. Perhaps the mark was somehow related to Victor's study of the Dreken river? Perhaps the boy feared the influence of dark magics was affecting his experiments there? Perhaps...

But with every corner turned and every street crossed, they drew closer to the start of the track. They passed a bakery, a sweetshop, a wooden toymaker, and each time Christophor felt the faint flutter of hope at the bottom of his throat. Then, as they came to the same spot at the base of the track where he'd stopped that night, he abandoned that hope. He opened his mouth, making to object, but the children continued onwards when he had paused, faltered. He had no choice but to follow.

Even then, miles upon miles of forest lay available to them, just to their right. He knew all too well how easy it was to lose oneself in there. Though he generally felt ill-equipped to read children, he could tell by the set of their shoulders, the fact their gaze never wandered, and how they leaned into the incline of the track, that their intentions were set in stone. They didn't utter a word the whole time.

Just where had this foreboding come from? I had not sensed it in Christophor when he interviewed the Eder staff. He had spent most of an evening in the house, some of which was in the company of Mrs Eder herself. Was it a growing apprehension that he was in fact correct in his suspicions? Or, was he coming to realise his error? Could it be that my efforts were having such an effect?

These were not his thoughts, though he was equally distracted. There was something in that night, there in the relative quiet that was only broken by the sound of their shoes against the rough track. No sound came from the forest. There was no breeze to disturb the branches or encourage their leaves earthward.

He noticed Julia first. She had stopped and turned to him and was taking his measure. He was breathing heavily while they could have been made of wood. He felt oddly self-conscious under her gaze. Her straight blonde hair framed her face in such a severe way; she had the air of a girl already aware of the extent of her jurisdiction, of her powers. He doubted Julia Eder would ever over-play her hand, ever misjudge a situation, or ever be denied that which she really desired. But those things, her open, guileless face seemed to suggest, would be few in number.

'Well?' Christophor said, surprised by the dryness of his voice.

Victor sighed at his sister. 'He's the King's Special Inspector, Julia!'

'Exactly,' she said.

'He already knows what we're about.'

Christophor wasn't used to being discussed as if he weren't present. He didn't quite know how to respond.

'He mustn't see where we put it,' she said.

'Just what do you—'

'Agreed,' Victor said. 'But I will share our findings, Julia, if they prove pertinent.'

The girl gave that considerable thought, before nodding. She turned and continued on towards their home.

'You must forgive my sister,' Victor said softly. 'Since Olesca appeared from the forest, she has developed a distrust of outsiders.'

'Has he ever hurt either of you?'

'Nothing so crude as that, Inspector, no. He simply changes those around him. Our parents, our siblings, even the staff.'

'But not you or your sister?' Christophor said.

'We're just children to him, below his interest.'

'And what *are* his interests?'

'A new beginning,' Victor said, but before he would elaborate he hurried to catch up with Julia.

The Eder household came out of the clear night, monolithic in its defiance of forest and sky alike: trees wilfully kept at bay, stars extinguished simply by its existence. It was lit at the front only by the moon. The side that could be seen from the track offered the glow of a single candle on the ground floor. To Christophor it slumbered malevolently, huge and malignant, high on the valley-side and overlooking its town. *Its* town. That was the direction of feeling, and it lay behind the sense of darkness that emanated from the building: ownership.

Did the children feel it too? If so, they showed no sign. Instead, Julia took up a position of almost military significance: a visual crossroads that took in both directions of the track, the house and its grounds, and the forest – as far as could be seen. Victor began counting paces from the treeline in. The boy stopped at fifteen, just as he was lost from sight.

'Victor?' he said, entering the forest himself.

'Here, Inspector.' The boy waved from between two trees. 'My studies have shown that fifteen paces is, on average, the distance required to become fully hidden in a forest.'

He stared at the boy, at a loss for words.

'Of course, that is a gross simplification. Variables such as the season, deciduous as opposed to evergreen forest, the ocular capability of the subject... I have extensive charts, should you wish to learn more.'

'Another night, perhaps. Why are we here, Victor?'

'Why? To observe, of course. Which requires an observation post.' Victor walked from tree to tree, looking back to the house when he came to each one. He bobbed and ducked his head, birdlike, only to move on again in as much of a straight line as the forest allowed. From time to time he looked up, just another motion in this odd dance? No, Christophor eventually understood: the boy was checking the branches, those that had large enough and low enough branches to be useful as an 'observation post'.

If my night-brother found the situation even faintly ridiculous, he gave it no thought. He had encountered characterful individuals of all kinds in his occupation, but few with the drive for scientific endeavour and logic of this pre-pubescent boy that he now followed through the forest.

'Aha! Mark this tree, Inspector.' Victor stood waiting; he meant it literally.

Christophor carried a small knife. He wouldn't have said it was for such eventualities, but in truth the marking of a tree was closer to its usual employment than anything more martial. I had seen it used to pry open jewellery boxes, pick up objects without touching them, and scratch all manner of surfaces. Now, it was used to scratch VM – denoting once more the Virgin Mary – into the bark of an unsuspecting tree. Not just a mark, but a mark against witches. Victor approved.

'Why here, Victor?'

'I have already explained, to observe.'

'Yes, but *what*?'

'Well, what can you see?' the boy said.

I did not expect such patience from Christophor, but he looked about him. The forest offered little, yet he could make out a surprising amount of the Eder house. The observation post was directly in line with the plane of the front of the building. The side was obscured in places, but mostly that was the higher windows and the roof. And of the rear it had an almost complete view of the moonlit greenhouse doors.

The doors.

He glanced down at the boy.

'You're watching the entrance and exits of your home.'

'Correctly deduced, Inspector.'

As if on cue Julia entered stage left, striding towards the house.

'I might not agree with her caution, but I must insist you turn your back. She will only make trouble,' the boy said. He sounded genuinely embarrassed by the situation. But once again my night-brother obliged these children.

Christophor remained turned towards the expanse of dense forest for some minutes. In such a place, in such darkness, he knew only too well that the mind could play all kinds of tricks. My night-brother, a King's Special Inspector, a man who brought justice and liberty from tyranny in his wake, began counting the leaves of the nearest branch.

At thirty-four he was relieved of the task by Julia herself. The three of them stood by the marked tree. Victor had a notebook and pencil in his hands. What was on the page was difficult to make out, but it had the appearance of a linear organiser of sorts.

The children settled into their watch with more discipline and patience than any soldier we'd met.

'The apotropaic is at one of the doors,' Christophor said.

'Correct,' Victor said tersely. Evidently, experiments were not for idle chitter chatter.

'And the smithy is making you more?'

'After our initial findings, we intend to increase the scale of our investigation.'

He chose his next words carefully. 'This is not an experiment for gathering information on passers-by, is it?'

Moments passed. He wondered if they hadn't heard him.

'No,' Julia said, eventually.

'Tell me, Julia, how long have you suspected someone in your own home?'

She looked him in the eye. 'Ever since they began bedding our father.'

As it was before, so it was again. Christophor examined what was given to him, this time by the blunt and unflinching delivery of a child, and found it able to reinforce an existing idea. He did not press Julia for more. He might claim decorum and decency would not allow it – but I'd known him to countenance worse when a case required as much. Instead, he took his own meaning from the girl's words: that Rebecca was bedding Mr Eder during daylight hours, just as her night-sister did under the moon. It was the simplest, easiest conclusion to reach, and it was all the more wrong for all that. But he already had a low opinion of Rebecca, a woman he saw growing in my affections.

He left the children to their vigil and returned to the inn.

'See?' Christophor said into the mirror, as he chewed ettiene. 'See what kind of vile woman you carry on with?' He said it thrice over to be sure of my hearing.

But I had other ideas just who was bedding Julia's father.

29ᵗʰ October 1721

I had arranged to meet Rebecca for luncheon at one of the more reputable establishments in Drekenford, called simply The Orangery. I assumed our coming together the day previous hadn't altered our plans, nor altered too much else between us. But I did find myself wondering about the whole afternoon; especially how she had been so clear in what she wanted, and how much that had taken me by surprise. Not that I wasn't willing. I chased these thoughts round and round, until eventually I had to occupy myself with something else.

I was no closer to convincing Christophor that he was pursuing the wrong person. Where I found compelling causality, he saw coincidence. Where I found information of interest, he saw the frivolous. We were both looking for evidence strong enough to convict someone of witchcraft, and I understood the severity of those charges and the punishments they brought. But I had to begin somewhere, did I not? Really, I was just following his example from over the years: cases of this kind did not fall from the sky, fully formed, into a man's lap.

Christophor was once taken with a sculptor he happened across, in a remote village somewhere north of the capital. He stopped and watched the man work at the stone for an hour, maybe more. Chip by chip, with no obvious guide or plan – at least not that Christophor could discern – the sculptor revealed the beginnings of a face from the pale marble.

My night-brother was entranced. For my part, I was most impressed that such a feat could be achieved in the dimness of candlelight. But for him it was a more significant experience, I might almost say it was spiritual. He didn't understand why it held him with such fascination, of course, but I did. It was a metaphor for his own work, and a rather obvious and trite one at that.

But in spite of that triteness, I could not deny feeling something similar. I knew, in much the same way I knew the sun shone beyond my window and that winter was only months away, that Olesca was the source of all this horror. Olesca was the witch we were hunting. He was the calm demeanour waiting inside the stone, and every piece of information I could gather was simply one more blow of the sculptor's chisel.

With that endeavour at the forefront of my mind, I began rifling through Christophor's drawers. One contained only letters: those from the capital directly addressed to him, organised in no particular manner that I could tell, and those – fewer in number – from the citizens of Drekenford. There was also not an inconsiderable number of draft letters of his own. These were interesting.

My night-brother was not one to openly admit his failings, nor could he easily ask for assistance. I held the evidence of such in my hands. Letters begun in a clearly forced joviality turned abruptly to an awkward request for aid, and then ended just as abruptly. Even simple requests for books from the Reikovan library were torturously drafted again and again. Those drafted to the chief inspector were tragic. Perhaps a casual reader would not see the fidgeting, the distraction, the self-doubt that was as plain as day to me. Perhaps the chief inspector would not see it either. But if he knew Christophor half as well as I did, he would at least recognise the distress masquerading as functional correspondence.

I looked up from the letters to see my reflection in the room's mirror.

'I'm sorry, Brother. But if I'm to be any use in this, certain boundaries will need to be crossed,' I said. 'Many already have.'

Chances were he would recall my intrusion when he woke later that night, but just how he would feel about it I couldn't say. I put the letters back and continued my search. Eventually, I found what I sought: a candle.

For my purposes, it was *the* candle. Taken from the desk of the late Constable Webber – not that I ever met the man – and transferred to this desk in an unattractive pounce pot: a distorted wooden egg, quite tasteless. I removed the lid and stared down at the candle, which was fat and the colour of honeyed milk. I recalled Christophor's sense of apprehension regarding this plain object. So much of my days now seemed mired by such feelings. Part of me longed to be rid of his world, for it to cease creeping its shadowy tendrils into my own, to return to long days of music and drink and laughter. But he had taken them from me. I put the lid firmly back on, not caring if I marked the candle itself, and left the room carrying it.

There were two chandlers in Drekenford, one a shop and one a market stall, a discovery made possible by asking the first person I met in the street. They also provided directions to the shop, a Williamsberg and Sons – it not being a market day. The shopfront was handsome and well-cared for. Everything was polished ferociously and the heady smell of worked wax was evident even from the pavement. A bell rang above my head as I entered. Behind the counter was, I assumed, Mr Williamsberg. He glanced up at the peals of my entry. But it was my pot that garnered his attention.

I placed it carefully on the counter and, with some showmanship, lifted the lid.

'We *do* sell candlesticks and holders,' Mr Williamsberg said, gesturing to the shelves of wood, iron, silver, and gold-plated wares.

'And of fine quality too, I imagine. Did you make this candle, sir?'

'I'd say as much.'

'You're quite sure?'

Williamsberg grunted, before lifting the candle from its powdery cradle. I took half a step back, anticipating all manner of mystical happenings: billowing green smoke, devilish flashes, Williamsberg swooning or, worse, falling stone dead in his own shop.

The chandler held up the base of the candle for me to see. Initially I was none the wiser, but looking more closely I could make out something at its centre. A mark. A 'W'.

'Aha!' I said. 'But you knew before you'd even looked.'

'I know my craft.'

'Quite so, quite so. And what of those holes in the side of the candle, hmm?'

'Sir,' he said, his tone rather patronising, 'what people do with my candles once they've bought them is entirely their business.'

'Pounce pots and pricks all along the sides. I imagine you've seen it all, Mr Williamsberg.'

'Just how can I help you?'

This was the crux of it: just how was this balding man going to help me? I could almost hear my night-brother's laughter as I floundered for a course of action.

'Well, as you can see, some of your fine wares have been quite abused.'

'So you say.'

'I'd like to replace them for my friend, but as a surprise.'

'Right then.' Mr Williamsberg did not appear to be a man well versed in the art of friendly or romantic surprises. It was unfortunate that I was to prove his cynicism well-founded. He lifted a crate of candles out from below the counter. 'How many?'

'Excuse me?' I said, somewhat taken aback.

'How many candles will you be replacing in this *surprise*?'

I waved my hand dismissively. 'That's just the thing of it; I don't know. Do they have a regular order, something of that sort? The Eders?'

'That they do. Not due for a week or so, but I can put some aside.'

'If you would be so kind.'

'No kindness to it. I'll take payment now,' Mr Williamsberg said, running a finger under his nose.

I produced my coin purse and began counting out the named figure.

'They'll all be here when the boy comes to collect 'em.'

I stopped.

I gazed down at the copper-pressed face of the King of Reikova and tried to think. Traitor that I am to myself, my only thought was of what Christophor would do in such a moment.

'Aren't they a little heavy for the youngest Eder boy?' I said in as off-hand a manner as I could manage, and still staring at my coins.

'Ain't the little one that comes. It's the *southerner.*'

We shared a moment then, Mr Williamsberg and I, in our mutual distaste of the young man in question. I did not doubt that his feeling was motivated by baser prejudices, and I took no pleasure in our meeting of opinions. In fact, it was an ugly thing. But I was so convinced of his guilt that I was quite caught up in the sentiment.

Olesca came to collect the Eders' candles. And he did so, I was certain, because he used them as reagents in his dark arts. He pricked his candles and sent forth his curses and others suffered. Surely Christophor could see Olesca's guilt writ large in such matters?

'The family will be grateful,' I said.

Williamsberg grunted by way of agreement, and our transaction was completed. I bid him good day, but he'd already put me and our business from his mind. I left with the impression of a man weighed down by his share of burdens. I hadn't even seen any evidence of the eponymous 'Sons'.

The rest of my morning was concerned with a different son. A line of inquiry, Christophor would have called it. But unlike my night-brother, I didn't have to spend hours looking for this boy – he found me.

'There you are, Alexsander,' the boy said. I was crossing the square in front of the inn, contemplating just where I might find the very person who hailed me. I was starting to distrust such convenient coincidences, which had grown more frequent since I decided to help find this witch.

'Here I am,' I said, squinting against the glare coming from the fountain. The square was fairly quiet, despite the fine weather. 'And here *you* are.'

Patrik gestured for me to join him in sitting on the fountain's edge. Once more I was struck by how mature, how confident this little boy was for one so young. Christophor had more dealings with the boy's night-siblings, of course, but I had some recollection that both Patrik and Victor shared a great deal in their characters and interests. They shared knowledge, too, in the little notebooks that bulged squarely in the boy's pockets.

'What brings you to the fountain on a fine day like this?' I asked.

'You. I was waiting until you'd finished your business at the chandlers.'

'You were spying on me?'

Patrik shook his head solemnly. 'Observation is the greatest part of any scientific undertaking.'

'I wasn't aware I was of scientific interest,' I said. I seemed unable match Patrik's seriousness, unable to keep a sardonic edge from my voice. Though I was aware enough to realise the irony of my childishness given our respective ages.

He took a notebook from one of his pockets. 'Yesterday you visited the painter, Marcus, but did not spend the whole day on his balcony. You returned to the inn, and met my mother's day-sister, Rebecca. There you—'

'You *have* been sp—' I coughed. 'You've been observing me very closely indeed.'

'Not just you – we've been following your night-brother too,' Patrik said.

I tried to remember Christophor's various interactions

with the Eder children, having little more than fragments and flashes of their meetings and conversations at my disposal. But the feeling that came through strongest from my night-brother was of respect: surprised at first, begrudging later, and then finally something genuine and unfettered. I wondered how he would feel about their 'observation' – he was the one who sought them out, not the other way around.

'May I ask why we are of such interest?' I said.

'Because you are the King's Special Inspector.'

'*Christophor* is, yes.'

'And you are assisting him,' Patrik said plainly.

'He might say otherwise.'

The boy looked away, as best as I could judge towards the Eder house on the valley's slope. 'We do our best for our siblings, don't we, Alexsander? But it can be hard.' He turned to me. 'I came to show you something. Something my night-brother and Julia don't think we should share with you.'

'Oh?'

'Julia doesn't trust you, and that weighs heavily on my night-brother. But I am not so close to my day-sister. So...' Producing a different notebook, he opened it on a marked page. It held a neat table of numbers that meant nothing to me. 'This is the river,' he said.

I stared, uncomprehending. But he was patient with me.

'This column is the date.' He tapped the leftmost set of numbers. 'This is the time our handkerchief took to cover fifty meters. And this is the estimated water speed.'

There were roughly twelve entries each year, beginning in 1716. The numbers were low that year. But even a dullard like me could see the numbers were consistently going up each year, if not each entry.

'It's getting faster,' I said, stating the obvious.

'And we don't know why.' Patrik lowered his voice. 'That is to say, we can't find a *natural* reason for it to do so.'

I thought back to my recent revelations of Marcus' paintings and the Dreken river. 'But 1717 was the year the river's course was altered.'

'That might explain the increase for that year, or even the next. But four years in a row?'

'Something else happened in 1717,' I said.

'Yes.'

'Something that many people here think defies logic.'

Patrik closed the notebook. 'Do you know what my night-brother and I argue about the most, Alexsander?'

A number of facile responses occurred to me, but for once I kept them to myself.

'We argue between determinism and causality. Do you know what that means?' he asked, without even a hint of mockery or condescension.

'No.'

'Victor believes there is a chain of events stretching back to the beginning of time. That one event begets the next, and so on, until here we are, talking here in the square, right now. That all these events are linked.'

I frowned, struggling to follow this young boy. 'And you do not believe this?'

'I believe that what I *believe* doesn't matter. What matters is individual causality which can be observed, quantified, and proven. And so we argue.'

'But you can't prove why the river is still getting faster,' I said.

'No, I can't. There is no clear cause, just the effect. So, I leave it to Victor and his chain of events. I leave it to you and your night-brother, who also see a chain of events.'

'1717, the year the river changed course, and the year Olesca came into your home.'

Patrik stood and pulled his little jacket straight. 'Enjoy your lunch, Alexsander. The potatoes there are very good.'

I was still so occupied with the boy's science lesson, I didn't realise his implication before it was too late and he was off across the square. I sat there for some time, on the edge of the fountain, trying to understand the swirling eddies around me: the speed of the river, the pricked candles, the boy from the southern tribes, and so much more besides. How did Christophor do it? How did he stand it with each and every case? I should have kept to my instruments, or just drunk away my days with Marcus. I used to be a simple creature, in the pursuit of pleasure.

Fortunately, my growling stomach reminded me of my main purpose that day.

I arrived at The Orangery before Rebecca and found it quite an unexpected delight. A little under half the tables were occupied, and were so taken by a rather refined sort of patron. More than one woman was engrossed in a book, reading without interruption even when sipping their infusions. A pair of gentlemen conversed on occasion over their broadsheets. As I waited for Rebecca I felt at quite the disadvantage, un-assailed as I was by the printed word.

Instead, I admired the furnishings. The Orangery, in keeping with its namesake, was a light and airy space. Windows placed cunningly in the high ceiling gave a great deal of light. Potted citrus trees flourished, under obvious attention, even in the autumn. Not only did they give a marvellous aroma to the place but their colour was wonderfully understated when embraced as the centre piece of an aesthetic. Too often in the capital, whole rooms were garishly coloured orange, yellow, purple, or gold. Such rooms were dominated by heavy dark woods, ornate sideboards of the most oppressive kinds. Here, light wood prevailed. It was so out of character for this dark and dingy Drekenford. My mood was lightened just sitting there.

When Rebecca arrived I surprised us both by embracing her enthusiastically. None of the readers appeared to notice.

'Why haven't you brought me here before!' I said, pulling out her chair for her.

'Not so long ago you were busy at midday.'

I sat with an *oof*. 'How easily you wound me. Can a man not enjoy his unemployment?'

'You seem cheery enough. But,' she said, narrowing her eyes, 'it's not wine.'

'*I* have had an encouraging morning. The sun is shining. My companion has arrived.'

'Promise you won't break out in song.' She picked up her menu.

'As you know, my dear, I make no promises.'

A waif of a waitress attended our table, and Rebecca ordered before I could manage so much as a how-you-do. We would be having the local Rowslin to drink, and partridge, with a light accompaniment of fruit.

'They have good Rowslin here,' Rebecca whispered, as if afraid the secret might spread. 'Not that swill Marcus gives you.'

'Oh?'

'I've requested the 1717, since you're in such a good mood.'
I stilled myself. '1717?'

'Don't look so aghast, it is not so very expensive.'

'A good year, was it?' I managed to say.

'The last of the good years, if you ask me. They're too sharp of late. I once drank a 1672, in more refined company, and it was quite exquisite.'

'Refined company.'

'Yes, dear. It means—'

The wine arrived. I declined the offer to sample it. As the girl poured my glass I had the urge to dash it to the floor, feign an accident or fit and then order an ale. I did not want to so much as sip a taste of wine from 1717. I stared in horror as Rebecca raised the glass in toast.

'To the last of good things,' she said with a smile. I offered something weak in return.

As she drank I could taste nothing but my own bile.

I looked at the ceiling, at the potted trees and their fruit, at the other guests and the staff – anywhere but her. She had dashed my good mood against the side of her ill-fated bottle and found the glass less brittle. Worse still, I knew my night-brother would find such shifting feelings amusing. In a few short hours he would smile condescendingly at himself and understand this to be part of the job: small hopes beset on all sides.

'Alexsander?'

I blinked, and she came into focus again. This beautiful woman, only a few years younger than I but wearing those years far more gracefully.

'You were grinding your teeth,' she said. She made a show of checking if the other diners had heard.

'It must be complicated,' I said, 'having children.'

'Children?'

'I know some keep occupations both sides of the ettiene, but many don't. My night-brother has no music in his soul.'

'Alexsander, I don't un—'

The words of the girl, Julia, to my night-brother rang in my own ears in that moment. Though I knew I should, I could not ignore them. 'But with children, what choice do we have? They need parents day-and-night, don't they?'

'Well, of course,' she said, shifting in her seat.

'You carried them, didn't you? Starting with the eldest, of course. I forget her name...'

She mumbled something. I leaned forward.

'Harriet!' she said.

'Harriet, day to Louisa. Remind me, it was a night birth though, wasn't it?'

'Yes.'

'And conception?'

She was no longer wrong-footed, she was once more the forthright woman who had advised a travelling musician of his dropped notes. 'I am not married to Mr Eder,' she said, firmly.

But my blood was up now. 'Not married, no.'

'If you have something to say, Alexsander, then do so. We're both too old for games.'

I lowered my voice. 'Are you sleeping with Mr Eder?'

She did not answer right away. I could see her considering the question, as she might a curiosity from a foreign land. Unexpected, but familiar in parts, and presumed harmless until it proved otherwise.

'I am not intimate with Mr Eder. And I never have been.'

'Rebecca—'

'No, you asked and I shall answer. My night-sister is married to the man. When they married, his day-brother was unmarried, but I had no interest in him. The feeling was *very* much reciprocated, if you take my meaning.'

I did. It had been my suspicion that Mr Eder was sleeping with Olesca during their daylight hours; my suspicion that *this* was the meaning behind Julia's claim. It was also one more piece in the puzzle of why a tribesman was so at home in a northern household.

'I'm sorry,' I said, 'I shouldn't have—'

She silenced me with a gesture. 'When my night-sister decided to bring children into this world I raised no objection.' She sipped her wine. 'I was younger then. I assumed I would one day want to do the same. And most likely with a man my night-sister did not approve of. It sounds ridiculous, I know, to view such a thing in terms of "good will". But what choice did I have? Does any woman have?'

I nodded, but in all honesty I had given the matter very little thought. In Esteberg mine was not a world of children, of parents, of their concerns. A child was only notable when a cause of scandal.

'Mr Eder has always been respectful and discrete with me,' she said. 'And I return the favour.'

Our food arrived, and I was grateful for the distraction. I believed her, of course. I had believed her before she even answered. Christophor was wrong about so many things. But that is the nature of doubt, isn't it? From small beginnings, hints, suggestions, it lodges itself like a splinter. From there it corrupts and pollutes gradually, in no hurry because it is assured of its success. I felt it, sitting in the light and airy

Orangery, felt it in my chest as I struggled for breath between mouthfuls of oily potatoes.

I should not have opened my mouth. I should have stilled my tongue, or better yet, clamped my teeth down on it. I should have speared another potato and stuffed it whole into my mouth. Instead, I said, 'And what of Matherson?'

Rebecca finished chewing, laid down her cutlery and stood to leave.

'Wait, stop, I shouldn't... I didn't mean to...'

'What, Alexsander? What didn't you *mean to*?'

But I had no answer. I'd known what I was asking.

She snatched her coat and left.

Other diners glanced at me over their broadsheets and book-spines. I dithered, unsure what to do. I had no appetite and the barely touched glass of wine was tantamount to self-poisoning. I looked to the door, and then back at the empty seat opposite.

Tossing some coins onto the table I hurried after Rebecca.

The good weather had brought the townsfolk of Drekenford into the streets. Coming out of The Orangery I stood on tip-toes and shaded my eyes to look in both directions. I caught a glimpse of her, of her maroon coat, turning a corner a hundred yards or so distant. I must have made quite a sight, a man of my age, hurtling down the busy thoroughfare calling, 'Make way! Make way!'

I rounded the corner where I had seen Rebecca and continued my caterwauling. I found her standing amid a bemused group of respectable citizens. She had been admiring the window of a shop.

'I was a fool,' I said, between great gasps of breath.

'Yes,' she said. 'And no.'

'It was improper of me.'

'As long as I've known you, when have you been anything else?'

I started to object, and then noticed the group of men and women – and children – listening attentively all about us. I made sure they noticed my noticing. Most then had the good grace to go about their business. But one man grinned encouragingly at me, as if his presence was some kind of support. His wife had to all but drag him away.

'I'm trying to apologise,' I said.

'And I'm trying to decide if you need to.' She shook her head. 'I said we're too old for games, and then I storm out of a perfectly good meal.'

'I thought the partridge was dry.'

It was good to hear her laugh. We started up the street, arm-in-arm, with no destination decided.

'Why shouldn't we share that part of ourselves?' she said. 'I'm not ashamed or embarrassed, are you?'

'I suppose I am. At least, a little.'

'Why?'

'There are times I wish I'd acted differently,' I said. 'I'm not entirely proud of who I once was, or what that person did.'

'That doesn't sound unusual. We all have regrets.'

'Tell me yours.'

We were greeted by another couple walking in the opposite direction. I smiled and wondered how we looked to them. With every step we were further from the centre of Drekenford, leaving shops for houses, and heading east along the valley.

'Matherson,' she said, 'I regret leaving him.'

That pricked me somewhat, but I pushed those feelings away; the man was dead. 'There was nothing you could have done.'

'That's not what I mean.'

The road was beginning to gradually slope upwards, and take us out of the town completely. We were now among carts rather than fellow amblers, but if Rebecca cared she showed no sign.

'I loved him, but he scared me.'

'Scared you? Did he threaten you? Hit you?'

She stopped. 'No! Look at you, with your hackles up; there's nothing here that needs defending.'

'Then…?'

'I was scared for the same reason I was in love: it was what he made *possible*. That I might leave here and never return.'

'What was so frightening about that?'

She looked up at me, incredulous. 'Well, everything.'

'But he was stationed at Fort Seeben, wasn't he?'

'He was offered commissions elsewhere. At first he refused, for my sake, but that could only last so long. In the end, I was the strong one. In the end, it didn't matter. I could have been with him.'

'You couldn't have known what would happen,' I said, holding her hands in mine.

'That's the great comedy of it all, isn't it? To think we could change things if we'd just made different choices.'

'Different isn't always better.'

'What of you, then?' she said. 'What do you feel that you shouldn't?'

I set us walking again – it was not a conversation for standing, and I doubted I could look her in the eye the whole time. To tell it entirely would need more of the day than we had left to hike up the valley and beyond. But I did tell it. Penelope, my first love, a young woman of much higher standing. She kissed me, being much more versed in such things, but her brother saw us. It was some time before her reputation recovered.

'And what would you have done, Alexsander? Refused her kiss?' Rebecca said lightly.

'Refused her invitation to the greenhouse entirely!'

'Come now, we don't have time for *every* one of your misdemeanours.'

But the first set the mould for all the rest.

As we wandered further I told her of my other significant dalliances. Marta, an older woman who ran her own tailors. Katarina, a scullery maid who grew roses that were the envy of the whole city. Simple Jacquelyn, who understood less of love than I, but felt it twice as strong. And lastly Clarissa. A woman I hardly knew, but we shared a number of mutual friends who were keen to see us both settled. She was a widower, and comfortably so, but friends will meddle regardless.

'I enjoyed talking to her when we had the chance,' I said. 'But I think we were both a little bemused by the romance our friends were planning vicariously.'

'We become children again at our age, don't you think?' As if to demonstrate, Rebecca sat on a low wall by the side of the road, her heels knocking against the stone. I joined her and we watched the sporadic comings and goings of the road into Drekenford in a companionable silence.

She looked west towards the sinking sun. 'How long do we have left?' she said.

I had no answer, but I took her hand in mine.

Christophor was feeling pleased with himself. He had a plan, a way forward, and perhaps for the first time in his investigation, a sense of progress. He had been inspired in no small part by the boy, Victor. While I largely found the Eder children unnerving, Christophor had a kind of affinity with them. One which, I believe, was born of respect.

He hurried downstairs and into the largely empty common room. Even in Drekenford most people did not drink on the Sabbath, at least not in public. The one occupied table stopped their conversation and watched him. The woman, the stumpy one I could never remember the name of, was behind the bar busying herself with something.

Christophor ordered a bottle of ale, the smallest she had.

The woman raised an eyebrow at that. He was not one to drink much at any time of night, let alone so early. It was noted, logged in whatever system of gossip she had. And she was smug about it too.

He left the common room as swiftly as he could. Once out in the street, he emptied the ale into a gutter. This now empty bottle he clutched like some hard-won trophy.

He crossed town with little heed of anything or anyone. At the base of the Eder track he stopped and made sure he was alone. Then he lit a shuttered lamp – clouds dominated the night's sky – but he kept the shutters largely closed. He just needed enough light to not break our neck.

All his previous concerns and doubts were gone or, if not gone completely, then superseded. As he walked he looked to the forest and felt no apprehension. The lights of Fort Seeben could be seen from across the valley. He hoped his efforts would soon bring some relief to the remaining soldiers of the King's Dragoon Guards. They deserved that and more.

He stopped short of the Eder house, at an approximation of fifteen child-length paces, and entered the forest. He let the shutters up a little to see his way.

'Victor?' he said with a hushed urgency. 'Julia?' He stopped, held his breath, tried to listen *harder*. He would not be surprised to find the children had slipped out of Father Popov's sabbath service to continue their work. But there was no reply, no sound from the forest at all. Just the all-encompassing smell of pine. The air was so thick with it Christophor could almost see it, like a kind of smoke. He peered through that smell at every tree he passed, searching for the mark he made with his own knife. Searching for the children's observation post. But the trees defied him by looking so similar and by giving him no discernible landmarks. He soon came to know he'd gone too far and decided to turn back; in doing so his foot caught on something and he almost tumbled to the ground.

He looked down, expecting a tree root or exposed rock, but instead a dirt-flecked whiteness pierced the forest floor. He brushed away dead pine needles and the like. A bone. A large one, half-buried. His first dreadful thought was of Victor and Julia, but he swiftly realised that was not possible – he'd seen them just the night before.

I knew immediately, but Christophor needed more time to remember. I could forgive him that; I was there, after all, he had all but dreamed it. A bone that looked similar to a human's, but different in important, noticeable ways: the scale of it, for one. Then it came to him.

He stood and looked about for the rest of her, the rest of

Tabitha. I had seen her bones arranged deliberately, her flesh in a gruesome river of blood and gore, but Christophor didn't truly believe that. Where he found the one bone he expected the rest of the skeleton in a natural mess. He even went so far as to dig with his hands among the needles and soil nearby. He found nothing. Somehow I understood that the remains of our horse stretched out into the forest. A trail or now dry riverbed, whatever comparison made such a heinous thing more palatable.

He returned to his purpose. Unable to find the children or their post, he decided they must be either in church or about some other business. In some respects that made his task easier. He eventually found his way back to the edge of the forest and the Eder house beyond. Still in the cover of the treeline he lowered his lamp's shutters. He found a stone a little larger than his fist and smashed the empty bottle with it.

The cloudy glass shattered inwards, the jagged edges forming a strange kind of nest for what was his real prize. Slivers of glass of various shapes and sizes. He angled the lantern for a better view, and then produced a pair of tweezers from somewhere in his coat. He made his selection carefully and tested the small shard for its sharpness. It drew blood from our fingertip readily enough. He wiped it clean with a handkerchief, then wrapped it up in the very same cloth. Thusly armed, he turned his attention back to the house.

He needed to be sure of all three doors for any hope of success. It stood to reason that the front door would still be occupied by one of Victor's apotropaic markings, but Christophor's own experiment required a degree of certainty. Stealing across the open ground he made for the front of the house. Appropriate hiding places on the Eder's porch for a square of metal were few and far between; it needed to be close enough to the door to have the desired warding effect. He checked the two large plant pots that stood beside the front door, running his fingers through the wet soil. Reaching deeper, he spotted the square nestled among the trellis beyond.

He found two more metal wards wedged in hiding places at the entrance to the greenhouse. Julia had tried her best to hide them from everyone, including him, but the game was not so fair when the seeker knew exactly what they should look for and where. But the side door had no apotropaic. He checked, and checked again.

The side door would suit Christophor's purposes. He made sure he wasn't watched from any of the windows, and that the track up to the house was as clear for as far as he could see. Then he set to work.

With the tip of his knife he worked at the door's brass handle, supporting it from below – if he broke the damn thing off he'd have rethink the entire enterprise. Before long he had punctured a hole in the top of the handle, but then the issue became one of making it large enough without becoming *too* large. He removed the knife often and was gentle in his working. When he was somewhat satisfied with his tiny act of vandalism he withdrew his handkerchief with the utmost of care.

The shard of glass caught the moonlight wickedly. He stared at it, steeling himself against doubt – against what he imagined might happen to an innocent person should he be wrong, or should they simply be unfortunate enough to use the door first. It would be a minor injury at worst, he told himself. Besides, he believed the vision he saw that night in the Eder's dining hall; Mrs Eder did not bleed from the right hand. In the vision that we shared, in which she crushed a glass between her hands, only one hand bled – and did so profusely. He saw that as something worth proving before he made an arrest.

Once more taking up the tweezers, he readied the glass. He had judged his hole well. The shard wedged there solidly, point upwards, hand-crafted for just this purpose. Confident the shard was secure, he retreated to the forest and counted out fifteen paces before turning around. There he found a suitable observation post, though it still lacked the VM he'd carved for the children.

The Eders did not keep him waiting long. The family returned from church in a lacquered and lamped carriage. Each stepped out in fine garb. Mr and Mrs Eder, Louisa, Julia, and lastly Victor. Mrs Eder was carrying a bouquet. As they made their way along the path and up the steps to the front door, Mrs Eder appeared to say something to her husband. He was unmoved, but she left them on the porch.

Christophor tensed. The woman was making her way around to the side of the house. The children were watching too. Victor went so far as to start towards his mother before his father called him back. Thus caught, he and Julia raced inside past a bewildered Mr Eder.

Mrs Eder carried her bouquet to where the forest met their garden, where she tossed it to the ground. She waited there for longer than Christophor anticipated. She had the significant stillness of someone paying their respects. But as far as he knew, there was no funeral that day – that would be the kind of gossip the innkeeper was unable to keep to herself. Finally, she walked back towards the house.

The greenhouse doors were closer. The more convenient entrance to the family home on a cold, moonless autumn night. Glass shard or no, it was a significant moment in his mind. With every step she took he grew in certainty. The set of her shoulders, her pace, how she navigated the garden's slope; she wasn't going to the greenhouse.

As ridiculous as it was, Christophor was leaning forward on his tiptoes. Mrs Eder wasn't going to the greenhouse.

He strangled a sound of triumph. She was five paces from the side door. Perhaps she had business at the front of the house? Perhaps his efforts, his theories, his experiment was all for nought. Perhaps, but no.

In a matter of moments it was over. Mrs Eder opened the side door, entered the house, and closed it behind herself. No cry of pain or surprise. No recognition of she, the lady of the house, using a door typically reserved for staff. She simply gripped the handle, turned, and entered. The clouds did not part. The trees remained silent. The world was not split asunder.

And yet, he had his witch.

He rushed out of the forest and to the door. He no longer cared if he was seen or heard. He trained his lantern fully onto the brass handle. Its dull gleam was topped by the glass sparkle, clean, free of blood. She did not bleed from the right hand. She did not bleed.

Still, there was doubt. Where did it come from? Was it me? Or was there something else at the root of it?

He gripped the handle, pricking himself. He gazed at the drip of blood forming in his palm. He would rouse the magistrate and make a formal arrest, as was dictated by the King's law. It was almost over.

Above, he saw Victor watching him from a window.

30th October 1721

'Hello, Harriet.'

The eldest Eder girl gave a start. She'd been very much focused on the ambling waters of the Dreken river. If my visit to this far away town had revealed one surprising truth above all others, it was the concentration of children.

'I'm sorry, do I know you?' she said, squinting up at me.

'No,' I said plainly. I introduced myself as the Inspector's day-brother, a musician by trade, and new to these southern lands. She accepted this information with mild interest. 'May I sit with you?' I said. 'Share some wine?' I took a bottle from my coat. This she found more interesting.

I positioned myself beside her on the river bank, trying to ignore the damp feeling growing beneath me. For her part she was sitting on a wooden stool of a design I was not familiar. She noticed my attentions.

'My little brother made it,' she said. 'Folds up so it's easy to carry.'

She appeared at ease with accepting the talents of her younger sibling. Appearing at ease was perhaps the defining feature of Harriet as I saw it. Even talking to a confirmed stranger her posture was relaxed. Her dark hair was tied back loosely; a far more practical style than that of her night-sister's fringe. Her clothes fit well enough, but were plain – again, practical and at ease with that fact.

'What are you doing?' I said, gesturing to the rest of her

equipment. I wondered if she had her little brother's interest in experiments.

'Obviously you're not an angler.'

'Obviously,' I said. 'Perhaps you'd be kind enough to enlighten me?'

She shrugged. 'This is a rod, with a line on it. End of the line has a hook. Hook has bait. This time of year I use worms.'

'Worms? As in, the live animal?'

'They start that way,' she said. She took a sip of wine. 'Fish seem to like them.'

'And that's the whole endeavour, is it? To catch fish to eat?'

'I take some home, yes, but if they're too small or I have enough, I throw them back.'

'You throw them *back*?' I stared in horror at the water; just how many fish had survived such an ordeal only to face it once again?

'They don't seem to mind,' she said.

I sputtered, somewhere between laughter and shock. I wasn't sure what to make of such a statement.

'Some people like hunting,' she said, 'and some like sewing. Me? I like angling, that's all.'

Perhaps I could see the appeal. It was quiet this far up the river, peaceful. It gave one a reason to sit and be still, without risking boredom. It wasn't so different, in that respect, from the practising of instruments. The soft gurgling and muttering of the river saved us from silence. Even late in the year there was a sense of life about the place – insects and birds, all manner of winged things. It smelled richly of soil and fresh water and natural comings and goings.

As it happened, I could recall seeing Harriet make her

way out of town and up the river on a number of occasions since arriving in Drekenford. Largely that had been on sunny days, though I had seen her risk the trip when it was overcast. Just what she was carrying had piqued my curiosity, but not enough to follow her. Until today.

'What does Olesca make of your pastime? Does he enjoy the fish?'

'My night-sister's fiancé eats enough for ten men,' she said with a faint smile. 'I believe he favours trout.'

'Do *you* not favour *him*?' I said. I felt confident I understood her more subtle meaning, but also that I could push the matter fairly bluntly with someone of such temperament.

She plucked the line of the rod, as one might a harp string. 'No,' she said. 'I don't. But I don't begrudge her the right to choose.'

'May I ask why?'

'He is a beauty, no mistake. Have you heard him sing?'

I considered mentioning hearing him sing as I emerged from the forest, but thought better of it. Instead, I explained how overwhelmed my night-brother had been at the Eder's dinner party.

'Overwhelmed is right enough,' she said. 'In all aspects. It's easy to misjudge a man so small, so delicate-looking, but he's entirely in control of my night-sister.'

'In what way?'

'Every way. What she eats, and when, what she wears, where she goes. Who she talks to, even. I don't know how she stomachs it.'

'I can't imagine.'

'Are you not married?' Harriet said.

I laughed. 'No. But not all marriages are like that. It's

possible to love someone without marshalling them. Without being so… protective.'

She put the wine bottle down slowly. 'I don't know anything about that.'

She wouldn't look at me. Something I had said brought on quite the change in the young woman.

'Oh?' I said, allowing a silence to grow and grow until, like most people, Harriet felt the need to burst it like a soap bubble.

'Others have been nicer to my night-sister, I know that much.'

'Was Gregory Harsson one of them?'

'Gregory was kind all right,' she said. 'He and Jan didn't deserve to be sent away.'

'Not even because of Jan's theft?'

'He didn't take anything. Least, I didn't believe it.'

'Do you believe Olesca had him sent away?'

She started pulling in her line. 'Between you and I,' she said, 'when he's a mind to, I don't think there's anything that boy *can't* do.'

'But what does he want?'

Harriet stared at the end of her empty line, at her empty hook. 'A fresh start,' she said.

'So I understand. Seems to me he already has that, in your home, marrying your night-sister.'

'No, leaving the southern tribes was just part of it,' she said.

'Of the coming war?'

She shook her head. 'The way he talks sometimes… He wants to wipe the slate clean. It's more than the war.'

'More than war,' I echoed.

'I think he wants to save us from ourselves.'

That pronouncement, like the tolling of a bell, left a silence in its wake that neither of us could dispel. My suspicions of Olesca, and his relationship with Harriet's night-sister confirmed, I left her to her angling.

As I was banished from the common room, I had to smuggle a bottle of wine upstairs. I had no glass so drank straight from the bottle. I made sure the vintage was not 1717. I couldn't find anything older, and there was indeed a slight bitterness to the wine that I couldn't place.

I paced the floor, bottle in hand, unsure what to do, but certain I should be doing *something*. The hour was late, not long until sunset. No use seeking company and I didn't have the appetite for it, regardless. My appetites had been hard to predict recently. I sat on the end of the bed; the place our body would rest for an hour or so before Christophor navigated us through another Drekenford night. The blankets and sheets, all clean, gave a degree of comfort to the simple, homely ritual that started with the chewing of ettiene and ended with a head on a pillow. It was easy to forget that so many people enacted this ritual in the company of another. My night-brother and I had been alone for so long. I didn't believe it bothered him; but I did believe he knew how, at times, it bothered me. I had chances to settle, marry even, but always made excuses.

I hadn't told Rebecca of my endeavours to prove her night-sister's innocence, and it was gnawing at me. I recognised, at a distance, the logic of my decision. The logic of my deception. To have any hope of proving it to Christophor, she had to be oblivious and not involved in any way. I should have ceased to see her entirely but that was too difficult. But what to do? What to do?

In my desperation I did something I hadn't done in a long, long time: I opened a book. The mould-edged tomes that Christophor had sent for from Esteberg were stacked on the desk. Big, thick things that, though voiceless, seemed to judge me unworthy nonetheless. I knew none of the names of the books, nor the people who had written them. Some of those names had worn away so much I could barely read them. The pages inside were no better: full of words that I knew individually, but arranged in a manner I could make no sense of. Why would anyone subject themselves to such trials? There were so many easier ways to enjoy, to learn, to share, in the little time that was allotted to us. I flicked through page after page of indecipherables. Eventually, I found a page in a book that Christophor felt important enough to mark with a piece of paper.

I held this paper up to the fading light, turning it this way and that, but still couldn't understand the symbols drawn there, nor the words that accompanied them. Were they in my night-brother's hand? I thought so. I remembered him first finding this book back in Esteberg. It had been somewhere dark, a cellar perhaps?

The page so marked was dominated by a picture: a five-pointed star that held a circle within its boundary. At each point was a symbol. The lines of the star were of a different ink, almost black but with something else there which made them catch the light. At the centre of the star was a ball of darkness, a mess seemingly scratched onto the surface of the page. I gazed at those jagged, frenzied lines, sure they described some kind of void – I shuddered at the depth they held, greater than any cave or well, they stretched on beyond what was possible.

And leading to that dark circle were three red-inked streams. I knew they were streams of blood. I knew because I could smell it, so harsh it cut right to the back of my throat. Not just an old blood stain, or a small cut on a finger, but the fresh flowing of something final and total. Feeding that horrible darkness, three streams of blood labelled: *Innocent, Learned, Broken.*

I gripped the arms of the chair to steady myself. I managed to look away, but only so far as below the star. There, I found a list. It stood out boldly among the dense, tight lines. The symbols from the points of the star were repeated, and with each came a line as baffling as any in those strange books:

The unfaithful lose sight of themselves
The sword shrivels to flakes of snow
The law devours its history
The stone moves on water
The broken heart bleeds gold

Christophor's notations appeared to largely refer to this list. From what I could tell, he was trying to determine which of these cryptic notations might correspond to events that had taken place already, and which were still to come. I wondered what he expected might happen were they all to occur. Just then I felt compelled to turn the page, and there I found my answer.

Both pages were taken with a work of art the likes of

which I had never seen. There was no colour, and yet the extent and vivid nature of the catastrophe was undeniable. Mountains had crumbled, seas boiled, where men might have stood there were beasts and, worse still, skeletons made to appear as men. The sun and moon collided in a sky that burned. In every shadow was a demonic face that watched on with glee. The more I looked the more horrors I found, but also the more certain I was that this could not come to pass. Nothing so heinous, so all encompassing, could occur in our world. But then I saw her. I saw Cornet Pitzmun.

Despite her being an acquaintance of my night-brother, I recognised her immediately. A young face, a woman's face, small but so different to the skeletal figures she was addressing from her horse. She held aloft her sword, not to strike them down, it appeared to me, but to rally them. Cornet Pitzmun. A woman that, despite conversing with him normally enough, haunted my night-brother in visions of a similarly apocalyptic kind.

Once I knew what I was looking for, it wasn't so difficult to find the other Horsemen.

The foreigner on his white horse. The quartermaster counting his silver. And the hooded figure driving a cart that overflowed with corpses. Their eyes, the eyes of the dead, they were all empty.

I closed the book and stumbled back onto the bed. My mouth was dry and remained so despite my efforts with wine.

'Alexsander.'

My name, whispered, swirling about the walls and the ceiling until it came to rest on the desk. I glanced at the door but knew it was as I'd left it: locked. The window was closed. I was imagining things. Was that so hard to believe, after seeing such a picture? What sane person wouldn't be so affected?

'Alexsander.'

More insistent, urgent, but high pitched and oddly stressed: *ahLEXsanDER*.

'Hello?' I said, glancing to the door, and then back to the desk. I felt a heat at my forehead. In truth, I did not feel myself at all. I should have left such things to my night-brother, should have washed and got into bed.

But I felt compelled to continue, compelled to look at Christophor's notes. Many words were scrawled in a poorer hand than was usual for him. Others were crossed out. Small drawings or illustrations peppered the pages, but I understood these even less. Some words appeared more than once. It was that repetition that made certainty possible.

Ash. Early. Webber. Order. Weaken.

Those words appeared more than any others. Sometimes writ large, with other nonsense cascading about the letters, sometimes writ tiny in a corner and in danger of being lost in a dog-ear fold. I opened the book to the correct page, with the list and its circle within a star. But it was as if I were seeing it anew, for the first time.

The Ritual of Berith. The abomination had a name, right there on the page, though I hadn't seen it before. Between star and list there was a passage with words heavily underlined. Familiar words: early, order, and weaken. While some text was obscured, I did my best to read those parts of the passage, and read them aloud.

'The delicacy of Berith is inherent to the fabric of its provenance; to begin such a ritual requires conditions and considerations rarely found in an epoch. Were Berith to proceed in order...'

The words that followed were impossible to discern, even when I lit one of my night-brother's candles. He had circled 'order' ferociously.

'... eve, when the veil becomes membranous. Early completion causes an implosion through...'

'... among the consequences to weaken the witch or magus.'

The rest of the passage blurred and I rubbed at my eyes, but I kept coming back to those three words. Just as Christophor had. Order, early, weaken.

But what of the ritual remained?

According to Christophor's notations, he had accounted for three of the five conditions of Berith. The remaining two, *The stone moves on water* and *The broken heart bleeds gold*, were presented in just that order – both in the list and clockwise about the ritual's star.

It was so obvious! One manner of thwarting the ritual was to have it occur out of order. Why had Christophor not acted on it already?

He clearly valued these books and their knowledge. Was he afraid? I knew him to be many things, but not a coward. Whatever the reason, if he wouldn't act then I would. I considered what I might need to make a heart bleed gold, and do so before stone might move on water. A heart, and some gold, of course. And some way to cause the gold to run like blood.

I had it all, right there in the room.

I gave a wry laugh. Someone else might think this was unbelievable good fortune, but I saw something else. I saw the diligence and hard work of my night-brother, what the boy Patrik might have meant by his 'chain of events'. He'd gathered these things during his investigation, and now I'd help him see that investigation to its rightful end.

I rifled through the chest of drawers, the wardrobe, and the desk. I found the gold crown the foreigner had given him in his coat pocket. The pinned heart was splayed open in a desk drawer; we both understood it was too unusual, too potent a symbol to dispose of. Lastly, in a small compartment of his travelling bag, I found the fester-root. He had confiscated the root from a simple street-magician in Esteberg, though that felt like a lifetime ago. When I opened the little pouch a heady, musty smell hit me. It burned at the back of my throat. But the roots themselves appeared in good condition. I would have to grind them to powder, and as far as I knew Christophor had no use for a pestle and mortar. I put the pouch on the desk beside my other findings. Seeing everything arrayed just so, I realised: the heart would provide.

It was what had scared Christophor so much when he attempted his dissection. When he cut away the shrivelled flesh he found its insides lined not with similarly withered tissue, but with clay. This he had seen, but couldn't understand.

I placed a little of the fester-root in the bowl of the heart. I cast around for my pestle. The wine bottle was too large. And besides, I couldn't risk wetting the root until I was ready. On the cabinet beside the bed was his pistol, as yet unfired in Drekenford. A hefty thing with a solid wood grip. I removed the round – including clearing the chamber – so there'd be no nasty accidents. Though there was an excitement upon me, this wasn't a time for foolish rushing. Thus armed, I returned to the desk and set to.

The roots gave little resistance and I soon had a powder of sorts. It wouldn't pass in the apothecaries of Esteberg, but I was confident it would serve. Why so confident? I couldn't say – I had never been a scientific man, prone to experiments or the handling of dangerous substances. And yet here I was, making a powder from a root in a grisly crucible, all by candlelight.

The gold crown fit neatly in the centre of the heart. A man, most likely a king, stared back at me. I felt compelled to apologise for what I was about to do. I cleared the wine from my glass and filled it with water from the wash basin. I wouldn't need so much, a few drops perhaps.

Finally ready, I stood in front of the desk, and felt compelled to raise my glass as if giving a toast – a toast to Berith, whoever or whatever that was. No words came. I tipped the glass, then righted it, for a moment worried I had used too much.

The bubbling and hissing began immediately. A greenish, shimmering smoke rose in tendrils from the heart, twisting and turning like no smoke I knew. It was oddly odourless. Between those tendrils I had a clear view of the dissolving king, his crown now slipping from his head. Like most crowns it didn't take long to fall. The whole coin was reduced to a viscous liquid. But my heart was not bleeding.

I dithered, trying to recall where Christophor kept his knives. Would the molten gold harden once the root was finished? I glanced at the open book, as if I'd find instruction there. I reached for it but stumbled and my hand brushed the heart. Or, more precisely, I brushed one of the pins.

The pins.

With the best grip I could manage, I pushed a pin deep

into the heart, piercing the clay, and then yanked it out. For a breath, nothing. Then, a trickle of gold.

I did the same for the remaining pins. I heard laughter. Full and throaty, drunk even, and looked towards the door. Only in turning from the heart did I realise that it was me, my whole frame shaking with a mirth I didn't feel. I couldn't stop. The gold bled out from the heart in thin streams, out onto the desk.

Laughing, my hands shaking in front of me, I gazed down at what I had done.

On the desk: a five-pointed star sketched in molten gold. At its centre, a heart.

The broken heart bleeds gold.

Who was to say if the heart was broken?

In such times as those, I doubted there was any other kind.

'What have you done?' Christophor demanded of me.

His horror was evident as he gazed down at the gold scorched into the desk. He doubted he could prise it out, even if he could bring himself to touch it. He wouldn't touch the heart, either.

Instead, he snatched the book from where I had left it. He held the page up to the mirror.

'Look at it, day-brother.'

It was too late, but Christophor couldn't help himself. As he read the passage, he struggled to keep his voice even.

'To begin such a ritual requires conditions and considerations rarely found in an epoch. However, there is *no requirement* that Berith proceed in order.'

Again, he presented the book to me. Unmarked by his hand, and free of any circling of words.

'Many scholars believe the ritual may be aided by the advent of All Hallows' Eve, when the veil between worlds becomes membranous. Earlier historical catastrophes, plagues, implosions of empires and states are among the consequences *ascribed weakly*, through supposition and speculation, to witches or magi and the Ritual of Berith.'

He slapped the book shut, the sound echoing about the room.

'You were bewitched, enchanted, under the witch's spell,' he said. I realised he was correct: the calling of my name, the compulsion, the confusion of words. The certainty with which I acted – when, in my life, had I been certain of anything?

'We have been used,' he said. He blamed himself as much as he blamed me. 'We have been used. No more.'

Gathering his coat, he collected his badge of office and his pistol. He locked the bedroom door behind him and sought out the landlady. He refused her offer of breakfast.

'Are you sure, Inspector?' the woman said. 'You look awfully pale, and it's set to be a frightful night out there.'

He glanced about the empty common room. 'Do not enter my chambers, Mrs Lehner. Not under any circumstances. Not until I return.'

'Is it… is it not safe?'

'Not until I return.'

'Oh, Inspector,' she all but wailed. 'When will it end?'
He donned his hat and left the inn.

The people of Drekenford were about their nightly business.
Christophor paid them no mind, except for when they stood
in his way or were moving slowly along the same streets.
However, I found them fascinating in their obliviousness.
They appeared to have no knowledge, or even the vaguest
apprehension, of what was happening in their town. A
woman set out her vegetables for sale, grumbling about the
cold – and with winter yet to come! A father scolded his
daughter for not looking where she was going. Carts rolled
by, their drivers and animals weary but not panicked. On one
street, two neighbours were working together to string festive
decorations from one side to the other.

The town was preparing itself for a festival, not for what
was coming.

The house he stopped at had a wall and iron gate at its
front. He employed the door's knocker liberally.

'Good evening, sir,' a butler said from a half-open door.
'Can I help you?'

'Magistrate Channock. I must speak with him.'

'Is he expecting you, sir?'

'*Inspector*. And no, he is not. But he *will* see me.'

The butler graciously acquiesced to Christophor waiting
in the hallway. My night-brother was rankled. Perhaps out
of the two of us, I was more used to the special disdain of
butlers. After some time – long enough for his coat to stop
dripping on the tiles – Christophor was shown into a drawing
room.

Magistrate Channock was sitting behind a polished dark wood desk, flanked by drawn curtains and standing oil lamps. The thin man's stillness was striking, and gave the whole room the appearance of a painting. His mouth barely moved as he welcomed my night-brother.

'Is it done then, Inspector? Your investigation is over?'

The magistrate's bluntness surprised Christophor, until he realised it was born of ignorance.

'Yes, sir, I have the evidence I require for an arrest.'

'I see,' Channock said, as it became apparent my night-brother wasn't going to say more. Channock gestured towards a seat, but Christophor remained standing. 'I must confess that, fortunately, my long tenure as magistrate for Drekenford has not included the arrest of a witch. How many have you brought to trial, Inspector?'

'Thirty-four,' he said without hesitation.

'Well, indeed. What is it you need of me?'

'For you to remember your position. Above all else. At all times.'

'Of course. Of course.'

A silence grew between them, neither comfortable with just how they were being forced to engage the other. For his part, Christophor evidently resented the role of instructor; one of his many flaws was that he assumed everyone else was as competent in their work as he considered himself to be.

'We should be leaving now, sir. It will be a long night.'

Channock visibly digested the implication of that. 'Is my presence really so necessary?'

'Absolutely necessary.'

'Constable Webber—'

'The late Constable Webber.'

'—did not require my presence for an arrest.'

My night-brother struggled against his impatience. 'As you said, Drekenford has never before dealt with its witches.'

'Careful, Inspector. I may be ignorant of witch hunts, but you have met my wife – I am well versed in veiled insults.' Channock rose slowly from his desk. 'Will you at least tell me who stands accused?'

'It is a name best said as little as possible. You must trust me on this.'

'And a great many things, it would seem.' The magistrate rang for his coat and boots.

The wind had gained some bite. Both of them clutched their coats as if they were in danger of being stripped away, just as the leaves from their trees. Magistrate Channock moved awkwardly, stiffly, even in the brief periods of calm. He was a man made of metal rods but without the grease that allowed a waterwheel – or a simple iron gate – to function. It gave a certain kind of authority to his bearing, until he had to move. Somehow he managed to keep step with Christophor, but it appeared taxing to say the least.

If Channock had any idea where he was being led by this northern man, this stranger to his home, this *Special Inspector* who carried the King's seal, he gave no indication until there could be no possible doubt. Perhaps he preferred simply to refuse his suspicions until the reality of the situation became undeniable. It seemed an appropriate habit for a magistrate.

The bottom of the track was that reality. Channock

stopped. Though Christophor continued for a few paces, he was forced to walk back.

'Are you sure?' the magistrate shouted over the wind, though they were mere inches apart.

Christophor nodded.

'Where it began. The serving boy?'

He nodded once more.

'Another?'

'No,' he shouted back.

'You're sure?'

He turned to the track, but the magistrate caught his arm.

'Hard for the town. Discretion, Inspector.'

Bent against the gale, they pushed on towards the Eder house.

Christophor found that house in no way diminished, no less imposing. What he was about to do would have an impact – the magistrate's nervousness attested to that – but it would not change the nature of that unhappy place. The stones would remember. The wooden window frames and the glass they held would remember. And the house wouldn't let the people that came and went forget.

In the relative shelter of the covered porch, they caught their breath. Christophor had glanced only the once towards the town below, and once then to Fort Seeben beyond, on their way up the track. He did not look again. Was he afraid he might see something that would challenge his certainty, his faith in himself? Would he see a town whose landscape had been so deliberately altered in a year of such significance? Best not to look at all.

Channock made to speak, but my night-brother cut him off.

'Do not ask if I am sure.'

'You trust your evidence.'

'As will you,' Christophor said. Beside the door, he drew aside the leaves of the creeper that clung to the trellis. 'Mark this apotropaic, sir. The witch will shudder, writhe even, when passing this threshold. May even try to dissuade us from this way at all.'

He knocked on the door using the brass stag head. The Eder butler took in the situation immediately, admitting inspector and magistrate with no challenge. If anything, Christophor thought he could detect a hint of relief about the man.

'If it pleases you gentlemen to wait here,' the butler said. 'I will bring the master of the house.'

'And Mrs Eder,' Christophor said.

This time Magistrate Channock kept his tongue, but the effort was obvious to all. Suspicions, Magistrate. You have managed to deny them for so long – years, in fact. As events unfolded, you – like most – found other explanations more palatable, more rational. Commendably, you clung to that rationality for as long as the world about you aided it. But there were times you felt a wobble, did you not? In church. Walks in the forest. Late night whiskey by the fire. Whenever there was a quiet moment to think, to really *think*. Another serving boy? you asked him. Was that rationality now ready to topple completely? I thought so, and so did my night-brother. That was why his hand was so quick to steady you as the full implication of events buffeted you more than any wind could.

'I...'

'Your position, sir. Your duty.'

'I must have known,' Channock whispered. And perhaps he did. Or was that, in some strange manner, the easier dereliction of duty to swallow? Rather than admit you were entirely ignorant. How easy it is to deceive ourselves, either way.

'Good evening, gentlemen,' Mayor Eder said. He was removing a napkin from his shirt collar as he entered the hall. 'How fortunate you caught me before I left for my office.'

Mrs Eder was a few paces behind, in shadow. But the mayor could clearly sense his guests' attentions were directed at her. A flash of concern crossed his face, or so I thought, as he turned.

'Margarete?'

'Don't worry yourself, dear,' she said. 'And whatever happens, don't make a fuss.'

'What—'

Mrs Eder stepped forward. She looked beautiful, that night, in a modest dark-green dress with a silver locket about her neck. Though favouring her hair pinned up, rather than the loose locks of her day-sister, gave a severe edge to her. I found it uncomfortable to see her so, but Christophor considered this the truth of the sisters. Hard. Calculating. Intelligent, in a cruel manner.

'Inspector?' she said. Did she raise her wrists ever so slightly?

'Mrs Eder, with Magistrate Channock as witness, with God as witness, and with the power vested in me by the King of Reikova, I am placing you under arrest for the charge of witchcraft.'

'Witchcraft,' she said, calmly, as if she had expected nothing else. For Christophor, this was confirmation. For the mayor, it was too much.

'Just— Now, hold on— You just wait one minute,' Mayor Eder stammered.

Margarete passed him, arms extended, ready for her manacles.

'No!' Eder said. 'I demand to know on what grounds this charge is made.' He threw his napkin to the floor, as a gentleman might a glove by way of a challenge.

'The inspector assures me he has a weight of evidence,' Channock said.

'Show me.'

'This is not the place, sir.' Christophor produced the handcuffs from his coat. They were loud in their workings, locking with clinks and clanks that tolled there in the hallway.

'*Show* me.'

'I said no fuss, Edward,' she said without looking at her husband. Her gaze was fixed on my night-brother, but not defiantly. She wasn't angry, either. He couldn't read her expression. 'It was clear this day would come, clear from the beginning.'

'I demand—'

Christophor silenced the mayor by drawing his small knife. With some care he took Mrs Eder's right hand and pressed the tip of the knife to her finger. Everyone but she leaned closer in a morbid kind of fascination, caught by the moment – by its audacity as much as its strangeness.

'No blood,' Christophor said.

'Inspector, really!' Mayor Eder said, but he didn't stop looking at his wife's finger.

The knife was withdrawn, leaving behind a dry cut

no longer than a quarter inch. Of all the things my night-brother and I had seen – the horrors of St Leonars prison, the apocalyptic visions, what befell Constable Webber – this cut-without-blood was, in some ways, the most disturbing of them all. Small, simple, yet utterly unnerving. So, I had some sympathy with Magistrate Channock, who was unmanned by the sight. He fled the Eder's hall and house. His parting words were jumbled, half-muttered, but to the effect that he should be sent for if there were a trial.

'Will there be a trial?' Mrs Eder said. 'Will you prick another of my fingers for all the town to see?'

'Not necessarily,' Christophor said, as if explaining a common matter. 'It is preferable, but on occasion the King's Justice must be administered swiftly, with just cause.'

'Justice?' Mayor Eder said.

'For Gregory and Jan Harsson. For Constable Webber.'

'You believe I killed them?'

'No, Mrs Eder. Not killed, not the Harsson boy.' From his coat of many tricks, he took out a sturdy length of black silk. 'If you please, Mrs Eder?'

She gave the slightest of nods. 'But not the front door, if *you* please, Inspector. For propriety's sake.'

Christophor half turned to share a knowing look with the magistrate, before remembering the man had gone. 'I could remove the apotropaic.'

'The side door,' she said firmly. He considered arguing but found no value in it; her insistence only reinforced his theories. Behind her, he raised the gag and tied the silk tight. Her cheeks blanched, though she stood still and stoic.

'This is an outrage,' Mayor Eder said, but his earlier bluster was all but gone. He stared at his wife's un-bleeding finger.

'Does your wife have a hooded coat, sir?'

'A coat?'

Christophor should have waited before gagging Mrs Eder. 'A *hooded* coat.'

After more explanation and effort than should've been necessary, a servant was sent to fetch a suitable coat. It was a small mercy, little more than a gesture to forestall the gossip of the town. But the story of Mrs Eder, gagged and bound in her own hallway, would spread faster than the pox – starting with the wide-eyed young girl who was now clutching a fur-lined coat. My night-brother draped it over Mrs Eder's shoulders and lifted the hood. He led her through her own house, down her corridors lined with portraits and the Eder stag, and to the side door. They saw no more servants or staff or family. The children's absence was a blessing, or so he thought. But a blessing for whom? Victor and Julia had played some part in this, and would those children have wept for their mother? Perhaps their parents were saved the embarrassment of their dry eyes and knowing looks.

The three of them stepped out into a still night. I had wondered, silly as it was, just how Mrs Eder's coat and hood would fare in the howling gales. But there was not even a breeze to stir a leaf. There was no sound but their own as they walked around the house and onto the track. Christophor glanced towards the trees. Fifteen paces, Victor had said. If the children were in there, Christophor couldn't see them.

Mayor Eder started to speak more than once as they walked but stopped himself each time. In all the talk of coats, he hadn't thought to find himself one.

And so they made quite a sight for anyone on certain

streets that night. Two men well-known to the town, and between them a hooded woman. Later it was said her hands were bound in front of her. Some said she was being carried. Others said she wore a mask. What kind of mask? A goat, a demon, a season's reveller. A woman gagged.

Two well-known men. One of them a mayor, the other a witchfinder, and with a hooded woman between them.

Where were they going?

The river to drown her. The hanging tree. No, you fools, they went to the old constable's office.

But, what use in locking up a witch?

A witch, not *the* witch.

What use indeed.

Christophor put her in the larger of the two cells. There was bedding, not fresh but clean enough. The whole large space smelled of stale air and long-settled dust. Mrs Eder stood motionless in the middle of the cell as he lifted off her coat and loosened her gag.

'You know you have the wrong person,' she said.

'I disagree. As does the evidence.'

'But not your day-brother. He knows too.'

This, Christophor ignored. As he had been doing for a long time now.

He lit candles from the lantern he'd picked up at the office's entrance. He made sure none of them were placed inside the cell – she was a woman who could do things with candles.

'You keep talking of evidence,' Mayor Eder said. 'I demand to see it!'

'Very well, sir.' Christophor entered the cell. Mrs Eder made no move to stop him. I could not understand why she did not rage against her accuser, against this false accusation, against these two men who spoke as if she was not even there. I could not understand because I had never experienced the like, and most likely never would. 'You have seen,' he said, 'your wife's bloodless, unfeeling hand. That is what we refer to as "The hand that shakes the Devil's".'

It sounded ludicrous. Madness. The kind of nonsense that a man uttered if he himself hoped to be thrown into a cell for the night. But no one laughed at him. Mrs Eder looked plainly on as my night-brother lifted her hand again, as if to remind the mayor.

'When an individual makes a pact with the Devil, it is sealed with the shaking of his hand. But his is no normal hand. This is the mark it leaves.'

'You're mistaken, Inspector,' she said. 'It was a boy that marked me so.'

The mayor gasped.

Christophor searched her face for signs of falsehood. 'There are reports,' he said eventually, 'of the Devil appearing in many forms, even that of a boy.'

'You do not deny it, Margarete?' Mayor Eder sounded pained, wounded, whereas I was angry with her. Perhaps he was thinking of his own role in her deception, and how over the years he had been gulled.

'Deny I have met the Devil?' she said. 'Hasn't each and every one of us? But to actually shake the Devil's hand... If you are fool enough to believe that, there's nothing I can say.'

'More, Inspector. Show me more.'

'He has marked your wife more than once,' my

night-brother said. He turned Mrs Eder so her back faced her husband. Deliberately and dispassionately, he began to unlace the back of her dress. We both knew what he would find there, beneath the midnight-green folds of silk. Truth was, everyone in that room knew. And still they insisted on the deplorable pantomime. Keeping the other side of the dress modestly in place, he lifted the panel to reveal her left lower back.

There, just above the kidney, was the mark.

A three-pronged scar, like a poorly balanced trident. Or a bird's claw.

'Another reminder of the infernal pact,' Christophor said. 'Lest she forget.'

She laughed at this, causing the mark to pull and stretch. 'Forget? As if it were laundry still on the line? Or bread about to turn?'

The mayor held his head in his hands. 'She has been marked so since we were married. But how, Inspector, did you know of it?'

He cleared his throat. 'My day-brother and Rebecca. They have grown close.'

Oh, I've played my part. That was no dagger to me, no unwelcome revelation. But my part was not over, not yet.

Christophor re-laced the dress as best he could manage. Then, he guided her to the bed and made her sit.

'Why, Margarete?' Mayor Eder asked. 'Why bring this upon us all?'

She looked at her husband. 'What is still to come, despite this,' she said, holding up her shackled wrists, 'it will be an undoing. Of everything. But our family will have a place in the world that follows. Because of my choices.'

'You... you speak madness.' He would not look at her again.

'I speak of things beyond your small understanding, both of you. Even now you cannot see that all this is happening by his design. As he wills—'

'The gag again, Mrs Eder,' Christophor said. After so many years, my brother was numb to the words of the condemned. But I was not.

'Is it really necessary?' she said.

'In my experience, yes.'

Christophor locked the cell behind him. The mayor was keen to be away. He had experienced quite the range of feelings already that night, but evidently Eder was a man quick to turn to pragmaticism. He was considering, weighing, wondering how events might be handled – massaged even.

'What *exactly* has Margarete done?' the mayor asked, at the entrance to the constable's office. 'What are the charges?'

'Foremost, the murder of Constable Webber by witchcraft.'

The mayor visibly paled, but nodded for Christophor to continue.

'The inflicting of pox on a regiment of King's Dragoon Guards. In other circumstances this could be a martial matter. It may well become such if she is found not guilty.'

'Might she?'

'It *will* be a trial, sir. And, lest *we* forget – the evil that began my involvement: the harming of Gregory and Jan Harsson through sorcery.'

'That poor boy. I should never have... Well, yes, thank you, Inspector.'

'For what, sir?' he said. That gave the mayor pause.

'Doing your duty, I suppose.'

Christophor sat with her all night, there in the old constable's office. Soon there would need to be a new constable, either chosen from the local populace by Magistrate Channock or a man sent at the King's discretion from further afield. It was unlikely that man, whoever he was, would share Webber's interest in history. Neither did my night-brother – except when it was relevant to his work. He left Webber's shelves of ledgers and scrolls undisturbed. He didn't open any drawers. He simply sat there as the candles burned lower. He was too dull a man to be bored.

Mrs Eder did little, though that was hardly surprising. She lay on the bed. Took food and water when it was offered, but declined conversation in those moments she was free of the gag. In many ways I admired the strength she showed in those hours. So did Christophor. In his years he had seen numerous men and women in similar situations. He had seen the kind of rage and anguish I had expected, and hardened himself against insult and plea alike. Rarely had there been displays of dignity. Dignity, which was different to resignation – that he *had* known. It came to all of them eventually.

When it was time, he entered the cell and gave her some dried ettiene to chew. More broken souls had spat it back at him in the past.

'No need to undress,' he said.

She shook her head in agreement.

'Blanket?'

'Please.'

He helped her back onto the bed, pulling the threadbare blanket over her.

'Maybe,' he said, 'you know of a way, hands bound and

without the use of your tongue, of freeing yourself. Maybe you can explode the lock. Melt the bars. Crack earth and sky and fly out of this meagre prison.' He gestured about the place. 'But I never met a witch that can outdo a pistol aimed at their heart.' He showed her the gun.

She didn't look scared. She met this with the same knowing calm she had shown that entire night. He felt it, then, a twinge of what I had felt for some time: she knew more than he. She knew that her being there was somehow planned or predestined. But it was only a twinge, and easily brushed aside.

He snuffed all but one candle, and then performed one last duty. He wrote me a short note. Then he pulled a chair close to the bars and, good as his word, loaded his pistol. He held it, aimed at her heart, until he was sure she'd fallen asleep. Finally, he chewed his own ettiene.

31st October 1721

How many times in my life had I woken with a pistol in my hand? Too many, that much was clear. Miraculously, I had never fired one – not deliberately nor by accident. But it said something about a man and his work if he had to sleep with a gun in hand.

This one I nearly dropped before remembering it was loaded. I put it on the floor, pointing away from the cell, then hurried to find the key. He was so arrogant, my night-brother, he didn't even attempt to hide or secure it. I found it right there in his coat pocket.

I fumbled with the lock. My mouth was dry from the ettiene, though my palms were damp.

Before I could open the cell door, her hand came through the bars to still mine.

'No, Alexsander.'

I couldn't bring myself to look at her. Instead, I looked at her fingers. Long, thin, but not delicate. There was a strength in them, like a pianist's. I had never thought to ask if she played. With a hand that didn't bleed.

'We both know what happens if you open this door,' she said.

'We go away. Far away,' I said.

'And then? When we need to sleep?'

'I'd leave.'

'He would find me,' she said.

I glanced at the pistol. 'I'd do it,' I said. 'End us, so you could live.'

She recoiled. 'Don't say things like that! Prove it wasn't us; my night-sister didn't do those things, you know that.'

'How? How am I supposed to do that, Rebecca?'

'You have to try,' she said softly. 'The other way... that's *no* way.'

I took the key from the lock. Then I took her hand in mine, and drew her close to the bars. I felt the cold burn of iron against my cheeks as I kissed her. A kiss, not of passion, but of desperation, of goodbye.

I picked up his pistol. Half-cocked, the sear in the safety notch, I tucked it into the coat. I was about to leave, when

I remembered the note. It was there, on the desk, not even folded.

Let her go and she hangs

I wouldn't let her go.

I opened the door and was met by chaos. Figures of unspeakable sizes and shapes lurched along the street. Carts and wagons made slow progress in parade, and in their beds were gaggles of small demons. They cavorted and jostled and thrust pokers at all and sundry. One was bounced from its perch and came to ruin on the cobbles, where it wailed an unearthly sound. A hellish hawker, proclaiming the sale of body parts – salted and sweetened – narrowly missed the little beast. I gagged at the smell of the hawker's wares. Sulphur and sweat were heavy in the air. Finally, the demon's mother swooped down on poorly made wings to comfort her child.

All Hallows' Eve was truly underway.

It was a bright, if cold, day for the festivities. Perhaps that was the reason for the vigour of the celebrations. It invariably rained in Esteberg at that time of year, more often than not. All Hallows' was a more subdued, private affair of parlour room seances and storytelling. Not so in Drekenford.

I pressed through the throng as best I could, and soon became aware I was moving against the tide. Men, women, and children in all kinds of costumes were making for the centre of town. I had largely been unaware of the preparations for the festival – both Christophor and I preoccupied with other, more significant matters. Now, I wished for better knowledge of which streets to avoid and such. Grimly, I pushed on. I had to reach the Eder house before it was too late. But I was prevented from doing so freely.

One woman – I could see that much despite the grotesque mask and drapery she wore – caught my arm and swung me round as if in dance. She laughed the whole time and then released me, just another stranger among the merriment.

I was about to curse her for the fool she was, and then stopped. I stopped entirely, there in the middle of the street – a rock in the flow of a river.

I was becoming my night-brother.

Not so long ago I would have joined that revelry. I would have cavorted and danced and played any instrument that was offered. I would have drunk anything offered. I wouldn't have cursed a woman who sought a step or two with me but kissed her hand, and likely more.

Try as I might, I couldn't conjure that feeling. And that was more terrifying than any horned mask or blood-blotched dress.

At the corner of a street I was caught once again. This time a man put himself firmly in my way and wouldn't be moved. He wore a heavy sack over his head, with slits for eyes and a ragged mouth. Jovially he offered me roasted nuts. Despite being hungry, I told him I was not.

'Oh no, sirrah, these are not only for eating,' he said with an odd flourish, given his attire. 'These hazelnuts speak of the future!'

I made the mistake of hesitating.

'Two nuts, a penny a piece, for you and your lady love.'

'No—'

But the man had already cast the hazelnuts onto the coals. 'If they jump, sirrah, it is not meant to be.'

They didn't jump. They burst into flames.

'What does that mean?' I said.

'Never seen them do that,' he said, all gaiety and pomp gone from his voice. He let me go then. I managed to squeeze my way through to a side street, but beyond the going was no easier. The only clear path I could find was to cut across the churchyard. Even that was, admittedly, busier than was normal for a morning. But at least there was a degree of calm and decorum among the gravestones.

Father Popov was there, making his rounds. He wore no costume, other than his usual – and this was free of any extra decoration. I didn't know the man but understood our night-brothers had met. Apparently, that was enough for him.

'Hello, Alexsander.'

'Father.'

'What brings you here on All Hallows'?' he said. There was no accusation in his tone, just curiosity.

I looked back at the gate, which I'd thoughtlessly left open, and considered telling the truth. But something else came, almost unbidden. 'I wanted to pay my respects to the former constable.'

'Ah,' he said. 'I understand his office is once again in use. A sad state of affairs.' Father Popov led the way. We passed knots of men and women, predominantly older, and who wore few markers of the festivities. For them, it appeared, All Hallows' was a sombre, sober time. One of reflection and respect for the dead. Their genuine displays made me regret my lie.

'You're not alone,' Popov said, catching me by surprise.

What did he know of me and mine? He evidently saw my confusion and gestured to the gravestone. 'People still care for the Webbers.'

There was a saucer of milk beside the grave. 'What's it for?' I said.

'Some believe that souls need sustenance on such a day.'

'But why milk?'

The Father shrugged. 'Perhaps because it is cheap?'

'Do you think it's possible, Father?'

'What's that?'

I read part of the inscription on the gravestone: '"*Rightly dividing the word of truth*"?'

'A worthy goal, the truth. The truth of ourselves, of our lives, under God. What can we do but work towards that truth?'

I stared at those words. At one word in particular. I was about to ask again, as the good Father had not really answered my question, when I realised he had left to speak to others of his flock.

'Dividing,' I said. Is that what Christophor and I had been doing? Were we closer to the truth for it? Our lives were divided, but then much of our efforts were to lessen that – to live as harmoniously as possible. Coming to Drekenford had made that more difficult than ever. I felt no closer to any truth.

But I still worked my way towards the Eder house, and the boy I believed to be a witch.

I walked the track that was so familiar to my night-brother. Like the feeling of waking with a pistol in hand, I wondered how often, between us, we had walked it. In some ways it was a dizzying day of the new and the repeated. I felt pulled in both directions.

Christophor's coat was heavy, weighed down by the tools of his trade, but it was warm. As I climbed that side of the valley I was caught between the cold air and my own body heat, parts of me sweating while others were chilled to numbing. As the view came clear to the valley slopes opposite, and the town between, I couldn't help but look. The streets were clearly busy, though it was hard to pick out anything specific from the masses – a flash of colour here, a shape there. The fort, however, was silent, empty even. Perhaps it was too far away to see the movement of sentries or the flicker of a cooking fire. But it *felt* lifeless. The way only empty buildings can.

It wasn't alone in that.

I approached the house as if it were a dangerous animal I didn't want to spook. I skirted the treeline to the garden, to the greenhouse and the back door. In every window, without exception, a candle burned. Even so, I had the strong impression there was no one inside. No sound came from the house. No movement. I tried the back door, but it was locked. In desperation, I tried the side door and even the front. There, I took Christophor's pistol by the barrel and readied myself in front of one of the windows. I had never done anything of that sort. In fact, it wasn't until that moment that I realised how sheltered and simple my life had been. I had witnessed common room brawls, cut purses at work, and the like; and in the same way, I'd witnessed the darker acts of my night-brother. But I was the witness, at a remove, not the perpetrator. Part of me doubted I could do it.

Drawing the pistol butt back, I swung for the window pane.

I felt the impact from my wrist all the way to my shoulder. But there wasn't the sound of shattering glass. Instead, a hollow sound as if the butt had bounced off of wet wood, a log or tree trunk. I opened my eyes – it shamed me to admit I had closed them at that moment – and thought I had missed so poorly as to hit the frame. There was no evidence of that, however, no chipped paint or dent. No evidence of my strike at all, not even on the pistol. I stared from one to the other. The house had repelled me.

'Ho there!'

I turned to see a cart coming down the track. I stowed the pistol, wondering how much the driver had seen. I met him at the end of the Eder's garden path.

'Good morning,' I said.

'Is it still?' he said, eyeing the overhead sun. 'Dare say we've both missed some of the festivities, eh?' He smiled, which transformed his weathered, bulbous features into something genuinely warm. He had a large wart above one eye.

'Are you headed that way?' I said.

'Not plannin' on drinking all this meself, now,' he said, gesturing to the barrels on his cart.

'No, I suppose not.'

'They're gone, you know.'

'I'm sorry?'

'Saw the mayor packing up first thing. In a mighty hurry, he was.'

We both looked to the house. 'But what of the candles?' I said.

'Soul candles, ain't they.'

My face must have made my ignorance clear.

'Bring friendly spirits home, keep evil ones out, so my wife says. One in every window – thank heavens we haven't as many as them lot,' he said, smiling once more.

'Friendly spirits,' I said.

'Tha's right. She swears by 'em. But they don't keep her mother out, more's the pity!' He laughed in such a way that I had no choice but to join him, though I could feel how hollow my mirth was. So did he. 'Well, best be on,' he said.

He left me there, staring at the candles in the windows of the empty Eder house. I felt more adrift than ever, among strange customs and traditions. Was this not still Reikova? Was I really so far from home? I hesitated to return to the town, unsure just what I would find there.

But the mayor was gone, along with the children it seemed. Olesca was gone, and I didn't know where.

I wandered aimlessly, rubbing shoulders with pandemonium. I saw fire swallowed. Bodies of sack and straw hanging from rafters. Bands of roving children, demonic in not just their garb. There were spits turned by cackling devils on most streets, though only one in two held pig or meat of some kind. I had no appetite regardless.

Eventually, I came to the Dreken river. I stared at the murky waters and considered throwing myself in. Rebecca wouldn't hear of it, but what else could I do? I had failed to convince Christophor, and I had no authority of my own. This, our body, was the last thing I had any power over. I clambered over the low wall that ran the length of the bank there. It shouldn't have been such a struggle, but my hands were shaking. I was shaking all over. I started a skittering descent but was stopped.

Someone caught my arm. I looked up to see Marcus, as sober as I'd ever seen him.

'Don't,' he said.

'I—'

'No, Alexsander.' He all but lifted me back over the wall. 'That's no way to help her.'

'How?' I said, and then something cracked in me. I pitched forward. My knees went. But he caught me. I sobbed there, my face buried in his shoulder. I couldn't remember the last time I had cried.

Marcus didn't rush me. We stood there for some time. None of the passers-by bothered us; perhaps such a scene wasn't so unusual that day – a man overcome by grief or drink, or both. When I was done, I stood back and wiped ineffectually at the mark I'd left on my friend.

'Let's get a drink,' he said.

I surprised us both and said no. 'You were right. This isn't something to run from.'

Instead, I took us back to the constable's office. The parade of costumes had long since moved on and the street outside the office was largely empty, though detritus littered the ground: greasy paper that held all manners of food; abandoned bottles of ale and wine; and other, less usual cast-offs. One golden masquerade mask lay in the street, catching the last of the fading light. Marcus and I sat on the steps of the office, in some silent agreement that neither of us were ready to see her, not yet. We spoke of many things that were both inconsequential and important. Marcus told me of his parents, both of whom were born, and then died, in Drekenford. How he never married, but came close once with a tanner – she could never rid herself of the smell of the shop, but that wasn't the reason they broke the engagement. He was thinking of giving up painting. He couldn't say why.

I listened, enjoying a kind of respite that came from someone else's concerns. I had been necessarily caught up in my own, but that hour or so was a relief.

When the time came, I stood, my back and legs aching, and opened the office door. But Marcus shook his head.

'You're her friend,' I said. 'She would want to see you.'

'It's selfish, I know, but I don't want to remember her that way. In there.'

It was hard to argue when, in many ways, I felt the same.

'Thank you, for today,' I said. We embraced and for the second time that day I felt the goodbye of something – a goodbye I didn't want, but couldn't escape.

'Impossible. Simply impossible. It cannot be tonight,' the magistrate said, from the perceived safety of the doorway. He had refused to enter the office and refused to see Mrs Eder again until he absolutely had to. All those years of friendship, all those dinners as a guest at her table, the hunts with her husband. Years that counted little, in the end.

'Why not?' Christophor said.

'*Why not?*' The magistrate almost choked. 'Look about you, Inspector! Most of the town is still drunk, or worse, from the day's revels. And this night won't improve matters. Simply impossible.'

'You wish to leave a witch alive in your town on All Hallows' Eve?'

'I *wish* we didn't have to. If she had been found sooner, if you—'

He slammed the door on the magistrate.

Christophor stood there for a moment, staring at that solid wooden door as he reined in his temper. Deep breaths helped. Then he turned and crossed the office to the bars of the cell. 'What will be your mischief tonight?' he said.

Mrs Eder, gagged, gave a helpless shrug. He provided nothing for her to eat or drink, nothing to break her fast. With only a single candle lit, he settled into a chair to watch her. He cleaned his pistol, primed it, then kept it aimed at her. How long passed that way, he didn't know. But the noise from the streets grew louder, more disturbing, with each hour. Until screams cut through it all.

They rang like church bells all around the office, around the cell. They weren't the screams of revelry. The terror at the core of the sound was tangible.

Mrs Eder stood and looked at the barred windows.

Christophor considered ignoring the screams. He came close to convincing himself that to do so would be for the greater good – that guarding this woman was more important than rescuing another. But that did not sit well with him. 'If I find that is your doing,' he said. 'I will hang you myself. No trial.'

She watched him leave.

What I had seen that day was charade, pantomime, costume – the drama of a carnival. Christophor stepped out into something real.

Gone were the children, and gone were the mothers. The

pack of devils that loitered at the end of the street didn't wear masks. They weren't painted or dressed for anything but the night's chill. And yet malicious intent wafted from them. When another scream came Christophor assumed them to be the cause, but he was wrong. As a group they stiffened, like hounds tracing a new scent. At the other end of the street was an alleyway where the scream came from. Christophor broke the stillness first. He faced the group of men, his pistol in hand, and shook his head lest they thought of following.

When he reached the alley he started to run. It wasn't just a passage between two buildings, but a warren of crisscrossing lanes. He had no idea where he was going. Horribly, he found himself wishing for another scream to guide him, to reassure him whoever it was was still alive. He got his wish and dashed down one alley, then across another. At the end he saw them – a blackness more solid than the shadows. Many-limbed, roiling, hard to make out.

Christophor uttered prayers as he ran.

Grabbing whatever creature was atop, he hurled it against the alley wall. It hit with the dull thud of a wet marching drum. There, caught in the light of the moon, was the huge quartermaster. Or, what the pox had left of him. His uniform was burned and blackened, his skin ashen.

Sprawled at Christophor's feet was Cornet Pitzmun, who wailed once more. But gone was the note of terror, replaced by something close to mockery.

'You tarry,' the cornet said.

'Finish what you started.' The quartermaster pointed to the end of the alley where, in silhouette – as he had been once before, back in Esteberg – was the white horseman. The foreigner. Conquest.

When Christophor looked back, he now saw an unfamiliar young woman lying at his feet. A man was slumped against the wall, much smaller than the quartermaster. That Christophor had seen them as the horsemen in a kind of waking dream, in a vision, did not shock him. Not on All Hallows' Eve.

The white of the woman's eyes rivalled the moon. Her dress was torn. The woman shied away when Christophor held out a hand. She got to her feet by herself and kicked the limp man. Blood ran from his temple and pooled in his ear. She kicked him again and again until she was spent.

Christophor waited silently until she was finished. And he waited again until she'd left the alley before going the same way. It was a kindness, but it cost him: when he emerged from the alley, the white horseman was nowhere to be seen.

There was no one in the street – not even the woman Christophor had followed. It was hard, for both of us, to reconcile Drekenford on the night of All Hallows' with the same town a few hours before. Everything, and everyone, was different. But more than that, they all felt *absent*. The celebrations, the gaiety, the customs – I had been a stranger to them. But he knew these kinds of streets.

He heard the echo of hoofbeats on cobbles and did his best to follow them, to follow Conquest. He passed unlit doorways, which were mostly empty, though some held shadowed shapes that he gave a wide berth. When a drunk stumbled across his path Christophor stood still and silent and waited until they were gone. There were mutters and mumbles, but nothing more. The hoofbeats continued and he thought for a moment of Mrs Eder, who he'd left in the cell. Were the horsemen merely a distraction, a chance for her to continue the Ritual of Berith despite her incarceration? But the woman was gagged, there were no candles within reach for her to use as reagents, and she did appear resigned to her fate. And still the horsemen plagued him. He could not abide the uncertainty, the larger design they represented, the doubt. He had to know their role in this.

He hurried after the foreigner.

Except, he realised when all was quiet and strange, the horseman's coin was gone. I had melted it in a heart-shaped crucible. Christophor had considered it a gift, but was that really true? Was that the spirit in which it was given? I recalled the encounter differently, of course. At the time, all those days ago back in Esteberg, I remembered the coin being heavy with duty, with unwanted purpose, and with the unknown. Perhaps gifts were given in such circumstances. Christophor was regretting accepting it now. He was sure he would struggle to keep my betrayal from his face. And yet, he had no choice but to pursue the white horseman through cold, now familiar streets. If he were honest with himself, he knew where he was going – where he was being led. Did all things start and end there? How could they not? It was the reason there was a town here at all. Though there were other contenders. Other places where he had felt the push and pull of events.

The end would begin at the river.

That was the feeling we shared, but he did not like it. His duty was all but done: he had arrested his witch and, following a simple trial, the King's Justice would be satisfied. A thought gnawed, however, as the smell of smoke and chamber pots grew stronger. He gave that thought, that doubt, a name. Alexsander. He vowed never to let me meddle in a case again. And with that, a weight lifted from Christophor – a boulder that had been chained to his neck to be dragged across this small southern town. He would not do this again. He could not trust himself with another case.

Most of Drekenford had gathered by the river for All Hallows'. The banks on both sides were lined by crowds, and the bridge was busier than any market day he'd seen. No hope of moving a cart along it and, thankfully, no one was trying. Instead, the masses shuffled along from one end to the other and, with no sign of the white horseman, he found himself joining them.

He had never seen the bridge so well-lit. The usual oils lamps were outdone by extra torches and coal braziers that gave off such heat he soon felt his coat unnecessary. There were jugglers and contortionists and hawkers, all managing as best they could with little space. A reasonably talented fiddler played unsettling melodies to match the occasion. But the main attraction was the animal marionettes.

The first, a pair of baboons, cavorted mischievously for the crowds. They tried for people's pockets, ran amok among the discarded papers and bottles of the day, and danced in mockery of man and monkey. The likeness was striking – not of a baboon, but of the *stone statue* of a baboon.

But the statue itself was gone. The plinth was empty.

Christophor looked again at the marionette, wondering if he were mistaken. He saw the puppet masters' string and boards, which itself had an air of the deliberate – people were supposed to see the workings.

'Don't fret, Inspector!' one of the puppeteers called over the crowd's noise. 'Christophor here doesn't bite, and neither does Alexsander. Isn't that right, boys?'

They had named the baboons after us.

Their jaws clacked open and shut, and those nearby laughed. But people were eyeing him warily now. One heartbeat too many had passed since the jest, and still no reaction from him.

'Yes, very good,' Christophor said. Someone patted him on the back and he bore it as best he could.

He was more circumspect at the next marionette – a lion. The puppeteers did their best with the roar – to the delight of the children. They appeared to understand how a large cat moved, quite cunningly making it yawn and stretch. Looking beyond the lion, Christophor realised the stones plinths weren't empty at all, but artfully hidden under black cloths.

'Look, Maria, the bear statue has come to life!' a woman said to a less than enthusiastic little girl. 'Look, it must be the statue – it only has one eye!'

The bear was Rebecca's favourite.

Christophor made his way along the bridge at the pace of the crowd, pausing briefly at each marionette, but all the while looking for the white horseman. When he reached the other side, he saw more horsemen than he required. In the distance, far along the valley, many lights were wending their way along the road and up the track to the fort. The second regiment of the King's Dragoon Guards had arrived. Did they know what waited for them there? Regardless, he had to finish his work before they began their offensive. Nothing disrupted an investigation like war.

He turned back to the bridge and thought he caught a glimpse of white heading towards the town square. He tried to push his way through, against the flow of people, but the going was hard. He made it half way back across the bridge, when he heard it.

A crack, so loud it shook the stars.

The silence that followed was fleeting but total. No one – not child nor adult – knew what to make of such a sound. The only response was to be still, every muscle tense, and wait for what was to come. It was like a warning shot from the sky. Christophor was not the only one to look to the heavens.

He saw clouds gathering on the side of the valley, above the Eder house. Clouds that moved too quickly, that were being pulled down, down, down to the house itself. There, they made a tornado. Flashes of soundless lightning fractured their inky darkness. On the bridge they heard no thunder. But there was another cracking sound, closer, something heard by the few, not the world. Then another, and another, more cracks and creaks. And then a scream – small, not far from him, as much surprise as terror.

One of the black cloths over the statues moved.

Cries and shouts went up, seemingly from all directions, and the crowd rolled and roiled. The air was thick with panic.

Beside Christophor, a woman moved to shield her little girl. He took a step forward to do the same, purely on instinct. Then, a stone seal tossed aside its cloth and, with a lolloping leap, crashed onto the bridge. It slapped its flippers together, sending dust and chipped stone over Christophor and the woman, barked silently, and then charged. He was quicker than her.

He met the stone seal in a kind of crouch. He tried to grab its flank, roll it back over away from the crowd, but it wriggled and squirmed as if made of slick, wet flesh. It bit and snapped at his face, narrowly missing his cheek. They wrestled like schoolchildren – the stone seal and the Special

Inspector. Even on such a night, it was an unusual enough a sight to stop many in their tracks.

If winning were possible, perhaps Christophor was. The seal was nearly back to its plinth. But then it grew frenzied. It swung its flipper like a highwayman swings a cudgel, connecting heavily with our side. Another crack joined that night. He gritted his teeth against the burst of splintering he felt in our ribs, against the pressure of a compressed chest, and against the air there that pushed its way free. His vision clouded. The seal stood on its hind quarters, poised. And then something hit it. A body. Someone. A woman, Christophor thought. A woman he knew – that much came through the pain. He helped her but—

'No, Mrs Lehner!' he said.

Death looked back at him. A face with the thinnest covering of pale skin. A face Christophor recognised, but the voice was not the same as it said, 'They come alive on All Hallows' Eve.' It was Victor Eder's voice, the same he'd heard on that very bridge so long ago. Another of the innocents lost to him.

Death threw the seal.

Christophor reached out uselessly. He could only watch the stone creature arc out over the side of the bridge, eclipsing stars, until it hit the water much as it had hit the road. There was no splash. No spouting of river murk, no change in its flow at all. The seal skated, as if on ice, as bewildered as any onlooker.

Mrs Lehner was also leaning over the side to see it.

'Stone moves on water,' Christophor said. 'The last conditional before the ritual can begin. Helping has only made it worse.'

This, he realised, was why the Dreken river had been

diverted. This moment. It was why the animal bridge had been built and why the river was getting faster. I had seen it in Marcus' paintings, but was too slow to realise the significance. All that work and planning, so stone could move on water, so Berith could be satisfied.

Mrs Lehner looked up at him. She was confused, and it was clear she might break at any moment. He saw the same in many faces on the bridge.

'I saved you,' Mrs Lehner said, her voice her own. 'Inspector, I—'

He pushed his way through the crowd. The other stone statues had stopped their rampage, become inert stone once again, frozen now in various new poses. A man had to be helped from the clutches of the bear. A child retrieved its hat from the beak of an eagle.

Stone had moved on water. And Christophor had played his part in that. Perhaps we all had.

He made for the Eder house. Clouds spiralled there, still the only clouds to mar the night – as clear as any beacon. As he left the bridge, the white horseman appeared before him, an apparition. The handsome foreigner clad in perfect, unstained white. The conqueror. It pained Christophor to look at him.

'We share much, you and I,' the horseman said. 'We have taken much, you and I.'

'I thought I'd put an end to it.'

'End?'

'I thought I had.'

'They wait for you,' the horseman said. He smiled, but there was no warmth there.

And then he was just a man: sallow-cheeked and missing teeth, a bulbous nose between eyes that swam in liquor. A man on a wooden horse that was draped with a once-white sheet. My night-brother made to say something, and the man belched.

They wait. And Christophor would attend.

It both was, and wasn't, the house. Each window still held a single candle, but there was nothing behind those small flames. It wasn't simply that Christophor couldn't see the rooms – there was a void, an absence, a chasm where once there had been furniture and carpets and a family.

He stood where the front door had been. Now, there was just an entrance into a jungle. Wet vines and rubbery leaves curled around the doorframe, the foliage inside *growing* as he watched. A damp heat emanated from everything. He touched the trunk of a plant that twisted and turned – he could follow it only so far in the mess that was once a hallway. His fingers met solid, slick bark. For a heartbeat he stood still and silent; that was how long it took for him to accept what he was seeing was real, and not another of his visions. He pushed his way inside the Eder house, which now held a vast jungle. Though he'd never been to the far south, he felt sure these were plants and trees of that land. Of Olesca's home.

Christophor looked up. Between plate-like leaves and fronds he saw swirling clouds. A crack of thunder urged him on, but the going was slow. The ground beneath him was uneven and marshy. Every step had to be made with care and calculation. The jungle fought him. Many plants were inexplicably sharp, with edges honed like cutthroat razors. He quickly learned to spot how they caught the scant light; though not quickly enough to save his coat sleeves, which were slashed all over. Ducking under a vine, he almost impaled himself on a plant that resembled a nest of sabres.

But it was the flashes of the house that unsettled Christophor most.

Wrapped in creepers that tightened as he watched, as if constricting prey, were fragments of the reality he recognised. A carved, polished banister floated in the greenery – bereft of its staircase – until it buckled under the pressure. A gilt picture frame hung high above him. Nothing remained of the canvas, instead the frame was filled, edge to edge, with violently questing branches. As he continued further into the jungle, he found the broken remains of the Eder's piano. The keys rolled and tumbled, free from their previous constraint. He could not fight the urge to press one. Somewhere, far in the distance, he heard the chime. He shivered despite the heat.

It was then he realised the jungle itself was silent. No bird calls, no rustle of animals, not even the creak of wood or the noise of restless leaves. No sounds but his own.

Until he heard the breathing.

It was irregular and quiet, just on the edge of his hearing. But he was getting closer. With each step he took the breathing grew louder, deeper. So loud, each exhale was like the wind buffeting his face.

Then it stopped.

He was in a brief clearing in the jungle. The slick trees stretched higher and higher towards the spiral of storm clouds, and created a kind of atrium.

In the centre was Louisa Eder, night-sister to Harriet, hanging upside down.

Christophor staggered. There was no way to understand it,

even after all his years. I would have fled the sight, forever, but Christophor held his ground.

She was crucified through her feet and wrists with large square-headed nails. Her body sagged with its own weight. Beneath her was the word *Innocent*, scorched in scratchy letters into a wooden board.

Christophor started towards her, and the jungle around him shook. The vines and their leaves parted briefly. He saw a shadow there, a shadow without edges, a deepening of the darkness that pulled at him before it was gone. He was closer to the crucifix now. Louisa wasn't breathing. He hoped there was some mercy in that, but he was under no illusion that the girl had been spared any suffering. The urge to help her was strong, regardless, and he raised a hand.

A snarl came from the jungle, and black claws lashed out at Christophor; claws the size of scythes. He fell back, hitting the marshy ground hard, knocking the wind from him. The giant scaled arm struggled and thrashed against the jungle – its clawed hand somehow wickedly sharp and yet not entirely substantial. A shadow with a keen edge, but one that frayed as it met the world. Its frustration filled the air, until it began to withdraw back into the jungle.

Christophor raised himself on his elbows, breathing hard, in time to see a claw flick out at the last – but not towards him. It nicked Louisa's throat. A small, quick movement for such a huge blade, like the flicker of a serpent's tongue. When nothing happened at first, Christophor wondered if he'd imagined the whole thing, arm and claw and all.

But then the blood came.

It burst forth like a broken dam, running over the cliff of Louisa's jaw, down past her ears, through her hair and onto the waiting ground beneath. There, it struck like thunder and the whole jungle shuddered once more.

'Welcome, brothers Morden,' Olesca said, his voice coming from everywhere.

I found myself standing there, in that impossible jungle, gazing at my night-brother as he got to his feet. He did not see me. Instead, his attention was on the blood of the *innocent*, of Louisa, and what it meant: the final stage of the Ritual of Berith had begun. This was the first of three bloodlettings. Three streams of blood, all leading to a last site where the beast would break free into our world. All this I knew, because he knew.

Perhaps there was still time to stop it. He believed there was. I wasn't sure what to believe anymore. I wasn't even supposed to be there; I lived in the day, under the light of the sun, not in this hellish night.

Despite what he had just witnessed, Christophor left the clearing and entered the jungle again. With no other option, I did the same.

'Neither of you can save the *learned*,' Olesca boomed from somewhere in the jungle, 'as you cannot save yourselves.' The clouds responded in kind, but we both kept our silence. We knew better than that.

I pushed my way through wet, cloying leaves and stepped over thick, exposed roots. The air was so heavy with moisture I was soaked in moments, as if I'd been caught in a hot summer downpour. I gave up wiping my forehead after the third or fourth time, and just blinked through the sweat. I managed to catch the occasional glimpse of Christophor, fifty or so feet away, who was similarly struggling to make any real progress... though progress to where, or what, I didn't know.

I thought about calling out to him, but doubted he would believe his own ears. He would assume I was another of Olesca's conjurations sent to trick him. Perhaps I was.

'You were always needed. From the beginning of days, until the end of nights, needed,' Olesca said. 'Even before St Leonars prison, where an unfaithful boy lost sight of themselves. You were chosen because of your visions. Visions *we* sent you, and chosen by a weak and feeble king bent to *our* will.'

'Lies of a forked tongue,' Christophor whispered, though I heard him as clear as if he were right at my ear.

'The Esteberg horizon ablaze, the four horsemen in all their guises, the Eder's banquet hall...'

That stopped my brother in his tracks. I recognised the truth of Olesca's claims, from my memories of Christophor's visions. And I had had my own visions, had I not? The pages of certain books rearranged themselves, and voices called me to action. Nothing so significant as my brother's, but I understood how we'd been manipulated and manoeuvred.

Christophor stood, head hanging low under the burden of what he had done, what he'd been a part of. My heart ached for him then, despite our differences.

Ahead of him, two yellow eyes appeared high in the canopy. They glanced at me, before gazing down at my brother. Around those eyes the shadow formed again. The impression of huge wings, mostly lost behind the foliage, clawed hands reaching down...

'Christophor!'

He looked around, as if trying to find me, but instead saw the beast. He ran deeper, ever deeper, into the jungle. I did my best to follow. But still we were hounded by the shadowy demon, and the voice of the fallen angel.

'The sword shrivels to flakes of snow. A pox sent by me, but guided by you, Christophor.'

'Lies.'

'The law devours its history, but only did so once you had spoken to him.'

'Lies,' my brother said, though he sounded less sure of himself now.

'The stone moves on water, thrown there by your own hand.'

'L—'

'The broken heart bleeds gold. Whose heart? You have both wondered. But *he* knows. You weren't the only ones sent for.'

I cried out. I didn't mean to, but the understanding hit me like a blow to the stomach. The withered heart I made into a crucible was that of Second Lieutenant Matherson, Rebecca's former lover.

'Alexsander?' my brother said. He ducked through the hanging vines, trying to see me properly.

'I didn't know,' I said.

'Lies,' Olesca thundered.

Christophor tried to come closer, but the jungle defied him, turned him around, sent him on its own path. Until he came to another clearing. In a grotesque mirroring, I found myself stepping into my own clearing.

Stepping towards another inverted crucifix.

I knew him as Patrik, Christophor knew him as Victor. The little scientist from a wealthy family, who shared so much with his brother. The boy Christophor wished he had been. Wished *we* had been.

They were the *learned*. Their blood was already flowing freely – we were at least spared the horror of the cutting, although that thought itself was a kind of horror. The blood from the two boys channelled unnaturally into the jungle to join the ritual.

At the base of Patrik's crucifix was one of his notebooks, splayed but otherwise untouched. In an inexplicable moment I picked it up and tucked it back into the boy's pocket. This simple, foolish act brought forth deep, wracking sobs from my night-brother and me. We wept for the little boy from whom we had learned so much.

Christophor roared at the jungle. He threw his arms wide and offered himself to the beast Berith. There was no will left in him, not after seeing Victor like that. But the claws didn't come for him. The eyes just watched on.

'It can taste your failure,' Olesca. 'It tastes a broken man, at war with himself.'

'That's not true,' I said under my breath, though the words were as thunderous as any in that strange place. We weren't at war with each other. If anything, my night-brother and I had never been so close; in purpose, in experience, in feeling.

'It's not true!' I said again. This time, *I* plunged further into the jungle and it was Christophor who struggled to keep up.

He called my name, sometimes sounding close behind me, sometimes miles distant. I ran as best I could, hurdling roots and ducking branches and ignoring anything that grasped or swatted at me. I didn't take the obvious path or the easy route. That was something I'd done too often, before coming to Drekenford. I thought of all the things I'd seen and done, and all the people I'd spoken to in the small southern town. Marcus, Mr Hennig, Patrik, and of course Rebecca. The woman I'd come to love, wrongly charged with witchcraft.

'The woman you – and you alone – love,' Olesca said, as if he were hearing my thoughts.

Then suddenly we were out of the jungle. Ahead, a desert. An arid, dusty wasteland bereft of life or hope. The fate that awaited the world, north and south, Reikova and the tribes. The only break from that desolate nothing was a huge five-pointed star of Berith, burned and blackened on the ground. At its centre was a dome of brittle, dead thorns.

I felt a moment of vertigo as, once I'd seen that dome, no matter where I turned it was there. Olesca was inside.

I saw the white of his eyes first. They glittered between the lattice of lifeless brambles. But they didn't stop moving. Frantic, juddering movements. A songbird caught in a cage. I hoped Olesca wouldn't sing. Even at such a time, I remembered the effect the boy's voice had on Christophor. Instead, I heard Olesca's fingers raking the wall of the dome. I tried to look away again, back to the jungle, but it was now far behind us.

My brother stood, a mirror of me, staring at the star, the dome of thorns, and the final stage of the ritual.

'One brother understands. In his despair, he accepts.' Olesca's voice broke into a snarl. The whites flickered to yellow, the eyes behind the thorns becoming bestial. Black claws stretched through, and then were gone. 'The other brother refuses the truth. His hope is simply denial,' Olesca said. 'In this, they are *broken*.'

As if summoned by the word, a figure appeared at the furthest point of the star. A hooded figure with their hands shackled in front of them. A woman we each recognised. Though I couldn't see whether it was Rebecca or Margarete beneath the coat, I knew this was the woman I loved.

My brother knew it too. He started towards her, drawing his knife.

'Christophor, no!'

The dome of thorns blocked my path to my brother. I couldn't stop him, so I had to reach Rebecca first.

'He starts to see what must be done,' Olesca said, his face pressed against the inside of the dome.

'Don't listen, Christophor,' I shouted as I ran towards the hooded figure.

'But he already knows. Her power. That *woman's* power,' Olesca said, 'over you all. He knows what to do.'

My brother made it to the hooded figure a moment ahead of me, just long enough to pull back the hood. It was Rebecca. I could tell from the way she held herself, how much softer she was than her night-sister, that much happier. Her hair was loose, as she wore it during the day. But she wouldn't look up, not at me nor my brother.

On seeing her, I felt what I had always felt: the sharp double-edge of love, and the knowledge it could not last. That edge cut so very deep then.

I grabbed Christophor's arm, before he could bring his knife to bear. He looked at me, startled, his eyes wild; he'd clearly thought I was an illusion or a phantom, conjured by the boy Olesca.

'I'm here, brother,' I said. He tried to pull away, but I held him firm.

'She... This *woman*,' he said, unable to even speak her name, 'has to die.' The wildness was gone now, replaced by a kind of zeal. He had believed, really *believed* – as a priest believes in their god – that this woman was a witch.

For my part, I had believed that was the reason he burned with bile when I was with her. I should have known better; Christophor had sent countless men and women to the gallows and the stake. He didn't rage that way with them. I didn't even think my cold, selfish night-brother – who spent most of his life denying me – could feel so strongly. But Rebecca was different.

I loved her. And Christophor hated that.

Enough to destroy everything.

'Yes,' Olesca purred. 'Yes. First her blood is spilled, then each other's, then a world's.'

This had been the boy's intention all along. He wanted to use Rebecca to fracture us, like so many lost souls in Reikova are broken. But in this impossible night he made it possible for us to destroy ourselves directly. That was to be our unique fate.

Christophor struggled to free himself from me and keep hold of the knife. But there was no way to overpower yourself. We wrestled there ineffectually, neither able to move the other.

'She *must* die!' he said.

Blood from the *innocent* and the *learned* flooded the deep lines of the star, summoned by some dark sorcery. The smell was so strong I almost gagged. But still more was needed to complete whatever was happening to Olesca, to bring Berith into this world. I understood that. Christophor just saw Rebecca. A woman he could never meet, but one he could loathe.

'You can't see past your jealousy,' I said, 'even here? Even now?'

'Jealousy?' In his shock, he softened momentarily. Enough for me to pull his hand away, to put myself between Rebecca and the knife.

'Yes, brother. It's how the boy hopes to break us.'

'But we are not broken,' he said.

'No. We're simply different men. And that's fine. You don't have to love her, as I do, Christophor.'

He glanced at Rebecca.

'But you do have to accept *our* love,' I said.

'It's the great comedy of it all, isn't it?' Rebecca said softly, still not looking at either of us. 'To think we could change things if we'd just made different choices.'

'Brother, please,' I said.

Olesca, his face still pressed against his cage of thorns, called, 'There is no acceptance!'

'You love her?' Christophor asked.

'I do.' I said it without hesitation, without guile. No deception or illusion, no bending of reality, just sincere feeling. The witchfinder in him could recognise that much, at least.

He looked to each of us then, seeing us properly for the first time without the distance of night and day. Two people in the later stages of their lives; scarred in their own ways, not naive in their union, but finding some kind of solace in each other.

'I'm sorry,' Christophor said.

As brothers, we both accepted his apology.

He dropped the knife. 'I am not *broken*.'

'I am not *broken*,' I echoed, letting go of him.

The ground shook in response, sending dust and dirt into the air. A great shadow fell across us, and suddenly Rebecca was gone, her coat and shackles falling to the ground beside the knife. My night-brother pulled his plain wooden cross from beneath his shirt.

'I am my brother. My brother is me.' He called it steadily. 'I am my brother. My brother is me.'

The dome of thorns bulged and buckled. Guttural cries came from the beast as its claws broke through the cage, reaching for the air, for existence in this world.

Christophor stepped forward, and I followed. As we closed in on the dome, the thorns began to untangle. More, they began to fracture and split into shards. I joined him in his chant, his prayer, as it buffeted against the beast's howl. The shards of thorn scattered from us like ripples in a pond. For a single heartbeat I saw the beast Berith fully. Its huge leathery wings. Cloven feet. Yellow eyes. It stood over Olesca. It reached one last time towards Christophor, either trying to find purchase in our plane or perhaps to take one final, vengeful strike.

As brothers we stood our ground and said again, 'I am my brother. My brother is me.' And then the beast was gone.

All that remained was the body of a boy from the southern tribes.

We stared at him, the only sound the catching of our breath. So small in stature, but colossal in so many other ways, this boy who almost brought forth the end of all things.

'I should have listened to you earlier,' Christophor said. 'You saw what he was, in the Eder banquet hall.'

'I didn't see everything,' I said. 'I've made my share of mistakes since we arrived in Drekenford.'

'My apology was not just because of Rebecca. I owe you that, and much more. I have taken you for granted, brother, and worse. I ruined what hope you had of living your own life.'

I put a hand on his shoulder. 'I wouldn't say that. You packed my favourite fiddle, remember?'

He smiled, though it was strained.

'What should we do with him?' I asked. 'We could leave him here.' I answered my own question, already anticipating – perhaps dreading – Christophor's response.

'No. The town needs to see.'

Christophor carried the boy out of the desert, and back through the jungle. I went with him, as far as I could go, but as soon as I stepped out of that nightmare house I returned to my day. The moon was his.

The streets of Drekenford were quiet, subdued, in the wake of that night. The clouds that had gathered above the Eder house and spiralled downwards, so that earth might meet the heavens, were gone. Who's to say whether it was the terror of the bridge, the strange thunder, or the excesses of All Hallows' that made people return to their homes. But either way, Christophor cut a lonely figure as he carried Olesca through the deserted town. He briefly entertained the idea of calling for Magistrate Channock, but the man didn't have the stomach for what was to come. There would be the report and recommendations of a Special Inspector on his return to Esteberg. The King would decide the rest.

The town square was entirely empty. The cobbles were by degrees slick or tacky with the remnants of spilled ale and the like. Single candles shone in most windows. Were all the friendly souls now safely inside? Or did a few still roam the night? He was relieved to see the candles' glow against drawn curtains and, in some cases, against the drawing room or parlour beyond; no voids that hid jungles conjured by dark arts. No five-pointed stars that promised the end times.

Christophor eased the body of a boy down by the fountain of a girl. Though Olesca was no great weight, he was glad to be rid of the burden. Typically, Christophor would be more prepared, but this wasn't the first time he'd had to work in less than ideal circumstances. He dragged one of the square's wooden benches to the fountain. Tipping it on one end, he rocked in back and forth, testing it. The cobbles were little help but it would stand. He cast around for more wood.

'Inspector?' Mrs Lehner said, emerging from the doorway of her inn. Her patrons watched from the windows. She held a hatchet, offering it to him. Her hands were cracked and red-raw.

'You deserve better from your day-sister,' he said. 'Make the best of what you share.'

She nodded, and he took the hatchet. He set to on another bench, hacking at the joins until he had a good number of planks. She dragged over some old crates from an alley, and watched as he split these into kindling. Mrs Lehner looked tired, and far from the same worrying gossip he had first met. I suspected that was largely a façade, and so did he, now. But he was all too willing to believe it at first.

'I s'pose we should have known,' she said, nodding to the boy.

'Not all southerners are demons, Mrs Lehner.'

'And not all northerners are saints.'

'No,' Christophor said. He cut some rope from a house's festive decoration. More people watched now from their windows, drawn by the noise, or perhaps the sense that something of significance was happening in their town. He lifted the limp Olesca against the upturned bench and tied him there, looping the rope under his arms, over his shoulders, and back around at his waist. Despite all this he still sagged under his own weight, and Christophor had to look away, recalling other bodies that did just that.

'Do we have to… Isn't the business finished?' Mrs Lehner asked.

'For what he has done.' He began hauling the kindling and larger pieces of wood to the boy's feet. He set the tinder. 'For what he would do again.'

When Christophor struck the flint and steel, he and Mrs Lehner were alone in the square. But there were the onlookers, and their number only grew. He felt the heat growing, felt it pressing at him, but he didn't move. The skin on his face and hands tightened. Beside him, Mrs Lehner shrank away. His mouth was dry and his eyes were beginning to feel like poorly sanded wood. Still he wouldn't move. This, and so much more, was his doing.

Olesca didn't wake. Perhaps he had already followed the beast to his depths, back in the Eder house. The people of Drekenford were spared his screams.

I wondered if they were grateful.

1st November 1721

When I woke, her cell door was open. Rebecca was still asleep, and for one painful moment I watched her. She was just as Christophor had seen her, in that house-turned-jungle: peaceful. Then I could take no more and put a hand on her shoulder. She opened her eyes and smiled, and I sank to my knees.

'Alexsander, what's—' She lifted my face so I could not hide the tears. They streamed silently down my cheeks, like rivers of...

I choked back a sob.

'It's all right,' she said, embracing me. 'Olesca is gone.'

I looked at her, and managed to say, 'Gone?'

'He'll never hurt anyone again.'

'But— how do you know?'

She took me in her arms again. I shuddered at the heat of her, but did not pull away.

'I want to see it,' she said. 'For myself.'

Though the thought brought bile to the back of my throat, I could not deny that I shared it. I had determined, where possible, not to be one more onlooker to my night-brother's investigation. That had to include its finale.

Rebecca refused any notion of washing herself, or changing her clothes. She did at least put on her night-sister's coat against the cold morning, though she wore the hood down. I only had Christophor's tattered coat with its many pockets now empty. I felt similarly spent. I opened the door for Rebecca. Another small gesture, which was all I had been able to contribute, in the end, to the efforts of keeping her alive, keeping her free. But I had tried. We all knew how I tried.

A gloom hung over Drekenford. Hunched shapes made their way along the opposite side of the street. The usual clatter and clang of a morning was softened by some general consensus. Or perhaps it was the fog, dampening our noise as it did our hair. Our steps barely registered on the cobbles. I did not offer my arm to Rebecca, to walk as we so often had whether we were occupied with an errand or simply for the pleasure of it. That morning was neither.

The town square made for a haunting tableau. I had no doubt it would stay with me for whatever years I had left. At its edges, people did their best to go about their daily lives. They dared not venture closer to the fountain. If I was a man prone to a wager, and I once was, I would have placed no small fortune on the fountain's removal by the end of the year. No one looked directly at it, though it was obvious they all stole glances between bouts of pointedly staring elsewhere. Even the children knew better than to satisfy their curiosity. Rebecca strode right up to it.

Some remains of the makeshift stake were still evident – a scattering of half-burned pieces of wood, the corner of a crate that somehow escaped unscathed. But otherwise, everything was ash. It covered the fountain like snowfall.

Christophor had seen such a thing before, at the fort. Ash that defied the stirring wind, that stuck like glue and glistened the same. It covered much of the girl and her book. So much so, I had the impression she could be mistaken for a boy. A little boy who valued books of science, not Romances.

'I wish it had been different,' I said, feeling the shallowness of words. Christophor had hated her because of me. And I was too blinded by my feelings to see how dangerous that was. I could have stopped so much suffering.

'Olesca was so young, just a boy, weak and frail in the end. A poor sacrifice,' Rebecca said.

'But what he did? What he almost did? The… demon.' The

word was strange to say aloud. 'It would have been the end of everything.'

'Would that be so bad?' she said, gesturing to the people drifting towards the town square. Our being there had broken some of the scene's spell.

'So bad?' I said, recalling the horrifying images of Christophor's book. 'Most people are not saints, we're no saints, but I would not wish such a future as Berith on anyone, anywhere.'

'Much worse will come, and of our own making. We may not have another chance.'

'Rebecca, you don't mean—'

'Do you have a penny?' she said.

I didn't think she had such black humour in her – I saw she was serious. I didn't have any money, but my night-brother did.

I offered her the penny, but she shook her head. 'It's your wish.'

I tossed the coin towards the soupy water. I made a different wish, one I would never tell her. As the penny arced through the air, the polished bronze caught the first rays of sunlight.

The men and women of Drekenford squinted against that light and, for a moment, they appeared eyeless.

Except for Rebecca. Her eyes burned with all the fires of the sun, and all the fires of our poor choices.

Acknowledgements

I would like to thank the team at Head of Zeus, in particular my editor Clare Gordon, who saw exactly what this book needed to be, and how to get there. My thanks also to my agent, Sam Copeland at Rogers, Coleridge & White, for always pushing me to do better.

Thanks to Bev, Jamie, Jo, Jonathan, Liz, Lyndall, and Tricia for reading chapter after chapter of draft work and asking all the best questions of this story.

Thanks, too, to my colleagues at the University of South Wales for all their support.

And thanks to Kath, for everything.

About the Author

David Towsey is a graduate of the Creative Writing programmes at Bath Spa University and Aberystwyth University. Born in Dorset, he now lives in Cardiff with his girlfriend and their growing board-game collection. Together, they write under the pseudonym of D.K. Fields whose Tales of Fenest trilogy is also published by Head of Zeus.

David's first novel, *Your Brother's Blood*, was published by Quercus, and was the first in the Walkin' Trilogy. He is also one half of the indie games company Pill Bug Interactive, who have released three titles across PC and Nintendo Switch™.